DARK
DECISIONS

CAM JOHNSON

PAGE PUBLISHING, INC.
Conneaut Lake, PA

First originally published by Page Publishing 2020

ISBN 978-1-68456-947-2 (pbk)
ISBN 978-1-68456-948-9 (digital)

Printed in the United States of America

CHAPTER ONE

The Quiet Before the Storm

At six fifteen in the morning, the alarm clock awakened Brianna out of her deep sleep. She begrudgingly sat up in her plush and comfy California king-size bed, automatically feeling for her hair wrap. Her mind and hearing went back to the annoying sound of her sleep killer that was sitting on her mahogany nightstand; swatting at it twice, she got her aim perfect to put it out of its misery. Brianna's moves were always quite mechanical in the morning; she reached for the remote to her forty-six-inch high-definition television that was mounted to the wall, surfed the channels until it finally landed her on the local morning news. The news was important to her for two reasons: one, to hear of any large Fortune 500 companies coming to Richmond and, two, if anyone she knew had committed any crimes. Richmond was by no means a New York City, but no one could be fooled by that either. For some people, the streets came alive after midnight.

Being that Brianna could never be considered a morning person, it always took her a minute, or two, to seriously get motivated; this morning would be no different, if not worse. This morning's extra fatigue could not be easily shaken; her morning's coffee run would require two shots of espresso and, just possibly, an energy drink. In retrospect, the grogginess and headache that she was experiencing was due to her wonderful job of orchestrating a flawless event being held at the Omni Hotel for two hundred fifty people. In all her planning, what was not planned was her out-of-the-blue ending. Not being able to exit after the conclusion of her event had its surprising perks…

After receiving multiple praises from various potential clients, Brianna could enjoy the feeling of satisfaction. Noticing the time on her Cartier Tank Solo watch, she took the last sip of her vodka tonic that was given to her. Once she placed her empty glass on the serving tray, she began moving ever so quickly to personally thank the hotel staff for their night of excellent service. For once tonight, she began to acknowledge the subtle hints her body was sending, that it had enough of being on the clock. As a result, Brianna began to make her goodbyes shorter. However, when waving at one more guest, from afar, she noticed a prominent and distinguished-looking fifty-five-year-old Caucasian gentleman. This gentleman, who just happened to be dripping with money and class was eyeing her exiting the ballroom; he raised his glass toward her, nodding while mouthing the words *good night*. This man owned one of the largest grocery store chains known up and down the East Coast, growing his father's business and making it into an empire of banks, boutique hotels, and dry cleaners. This well-respected man was her client who had employed her agency's services for the night. Before his endeavors to visit disadvantage children in other countries, he was throwing this grand affair to say his goodbyes.

As she was entering the elevator, she heard a deep voice over her shoulder. "What level, Ms. Godfrey?"

When she turned around, she was relieved to see the very familiar face. "Thank you, Mr. Nelson. I am parked on level P5." Searching for her keys, which had managed to fall to the bottom of her authentic Fendi purse, it appeared that Mr. Nelson also managed to get within her personal space; he gently pulled her to him and began kissing her softy. After making herself come out of an intoxicating trance, she looked at him with intrigue. "Why, Mr. Nelson, I believe that I have provided you with the best customer service that your money could buy. Unfortunately, kissing and anything else beyond that is frowned upon," she said, trying to sound professional as possible.

Giving Brianna a half smile, he softly ran his hand up her dress. Her body began to quiver from his touch; her reaction served as a green light to continue. He was seducing her, and he was winning. His deep-blue eyes were melting her. While he was kissing on her neck, she effortlessly released heavy breaths. She wanted him. Brianna was not only surprised but turned on by his confidence. In her career, she had never crossed this line, but she justified this night by telling herself that she would not see him for at least two years. She had to also admit that for those eight months of planning, there was always a little chemistry between them, and now there she was, in his suite, having her mind blown. The myth about white men was simply that, a myth. It was not small, and neither was the VVS diamond tennis bracelet he gave her. The eight-karat diamonds set in platinum were beyond stunning! The note with the gift read:

> *Your eye for detail and your execution of "every" thing you do is nothing less than perfection! I must admit this is what I have been secretly and patiently waiting for! (JNelson)*

Brianna wanted to ask him if he had been a little overly presumptuous; the note practically eluded to them sleeping together that night. All she could do was chuckle, applauding this man's swagger! *Who cares!* she instantly thought. *This man gave me VVS stones. I ain't mad!* Brianna mounted him with her baby-making hips and rode him until he forgot his name. When Brianna got home at three in the morning, she was exhausted but promised that she would never sleep with a client ever again; she kept her word…

During her shower, she said a quick silent prayer that would get her through her day. She oiled down, slicked back a few pieces of her hair that had gotten a little damp around the edges, and brushed her teeth. Not giving her wardrobe much thought, she threw on a conservative black pencil skirt and a crisp white collared blouse. She dolled up a bit by putting on her three-karat diamond-studded earrings and, of course, keeping on her exquisite gift that Mr. Nelson had given her. Brianna's makeup was kept to a bare minimum—a light application of foundation, mascara with a neutral lip color by Chanel. Her Prada pumps and oversized handbag gave her attire a classy look. While driving into work, she was listening to the *Rickey*

Smiley Morning Show. She found herself laughing at the radio hosts and turning up the volume to hear "Gary with the Tea." She went through the drive through at Starbucks to get a venti coffee and a croissant, which was her morning medicine. When she arrived at her job, she pulled into her usual but unassigned parking space; she managed to pull that exhausted twenty-nine-year-old frame of her White Cayenne SUV. Once inside the building, she switched to automatic pilot by plastering a smile on her face and speaking to various coworkers on the way into her office. Arriving at her desk, Brianna immediately glanced and noted that the message light on her desk phone was blinking. She plopped in her chair and started to organize her leftover work from the day before. Once listening and jotting down her messages, the third one had a warm and soothing tone.

"Hey, Ms. Godfrey, this is Allan—Allan Jones. I hope you are doing well. If possible, I would like to get a chance to speak with you. Not to mention, I would also like to see you. We have a lot of catching up to do. Give me a call. Take care, baby…"

Mmmm…his voice sounds so good. Why have I been distancing myself from him? Then Brianna's pondering came to a screeching halt. *Oh, I know why!* She shook her head and continued to get herself organized. Without looking at the clock on her desk, she knew exactly what the current time was by who was entering the office; it was nine thirty sharp because her boss, Natalie, walked past her door. During Brianna's workday, her amusement came from watching Natalie.

Natalie was an educated, bilingual, tall slim dark sister who was very confident. Though she possessed a beautiful smile and sported a fashion style that mostly went unnoticed, Brianna could never figure out where her grandness came from. Watching her from afar, she had a killer model walk that could be mistaken for the likes of a supermodel, but up close, you would notice the dry, brittle, damaged hair and the unmanicured nails. Her trying to pin up her hair or put a curl or two in it could be applauded but it wasn't working. Her BMW could be found parked at Walmart and the Dollar Tree most of the time, which was totally fine, but it was the way that she carried her cocky confidence getting out of it that made Brianna chuckle quite frequently.

"Good morning, Brianna," Natalie said with a smile.

Brianna responded with a bigger smile, hoping that she looked sincere, "Good morning, Natalie!"

"Brianna, let's take a little time to go over the upcoming gala."

"Okay. What time would you like to meet?"

"I was thinking that we could meet around three o'clock this evening. I would like to go over the details for the gala, as well as, all the events we have on the books for the next two months. Since we do not have any events for this weekend, do you have any exciting plans for tonight and tomorrow?" Natalie asked as if they were good friends.

"I sure do, Natalie, and it is long overdue! I am joining a couple of my girlfriends for dinner tonight. After which, we will probably hit the spot over on Main Street for a little dancing," Brianna said, sounding extra excited. Suddenly, she was hit with a little guilt and wanted to end the conversation. She didn't know if Natalie was fishing for an invite. She had no intentions on inviting her. "What about yourself, Natalie? Will you and your husband do something fun as well?"

"Unfortunately, no. Harold cannot make it home this weekend. However, lucky for me, I have an associate that has relocated to this area. I am planning to have her and her family over for dinner."

"That sounds like a nice plan." Brianna did not exactly understand what she meant when she referred to her company as an *associate* but was happy to hear that she had her own plans. At that moment, she seized the opportunity to end the conversation by changing the subject back to work. "Natalie, I'll catch up with you later. I'm going to return a few phone calls and get things ready for our three o'clock meeting." She did not dislike Natalie but found it hard to connect with her. Natalie had been at the agency for six years, but oddly enough, no one had ever met her husband. The most that anyone knew about her husband was that he was a man who was ten years her senior and, from what she had admitted, kept a very serious demeanor. She also had shared that he was ambitious, which led to him accepting a job in Boston. He would only casually commute home once or twice a month for only a day or two days. The red flag in this estranged marriage was there was no mentioning of her ever relocating.

Focusing on wrapping everything up and preparing for the late meeting only help the day fly by. All was done, and she was in the car homebound, which was typically a twenty-five–minute commute, but the accident on 64 left her sitting, searching for good music for her listening pleasure. She selected music by Jasmine Sullivan. Now singing along and slipping into a relaxed mood, she decided to give Allan a return call. After dialing his number, she was hoping that he wasn't in his office. He answered on the third freaking ring.

She met Allan a few years back at a college Greek party that was being held at the convention center. This "Mardi Gras"–themed event turned out to be a well-attended party. Everyone was dressed in black on black with festive masks. The women found the sexiest dresses that money could buy. The men weren't half stepping either. All the attendees were on point. Instead of Brianna bringing her entourage of girlfriends, she decided to go accompanied by one of her male cousins that just so happened to be in town for the weekend. Bringing her girlfriends would have led to doing the predictable—the girls would have stood in a group, scoping out brothers, commenting on the girls' outfits, and turning down random men who were bold enough to ask for a dance. Brianna—who was at that time twenty-six years old, five feet and five inches, one hundred forty pounds—was what some men considered pleasingly thick. She was thick in all the right places, and her looks were seductive. She possessed a beautiful mocha complexion, warm smile with high cheekbones that were kissed by angels; there were dimples on each side. Her naturally long black hair framed her effortlessly beautiful face; it was on rare occasions that she would let her hair, which was about eight inches past her shoulders, hang down. During the hours of nine to five, she would often keep her hair a bun or a ponytail. However, that evening, her hair was down, flowing with her every move. For some reason, Brianna never thought she had the pleasure of just relying on her looks, nor did she really play up her curvaceous assets.

Instead, she relied on her education and charisma to win people over. Once in her presence, anyone and everyone noticed that she oozed with class and sex appeal. The women either admired her for those traits or hated her for it, but of course, the men melted. She did not have to try hard at all. Many were automatically drawn to her. That night, Brianna was on the dance floor with a friend named Terrance, when he yelled out the word "switch." Next thing she knew, she was dancing with a sexy deep-chocolate brother. He had a smooth nicely shaped baldhead, and his complexion was like silky chocolate. His even, straight white teeth produced a mesmerizing smile. Not to mention, this man was throwing down; before she knew it, he was up close behind her dancing. He gently moved her hair to one side, leaned down, and planted a soft kiss on the back of her neck. *Where the hell did he come from? If he does that again, I am going to lose my freaking rhythm!* She found herself getting nervous and a little excited. Right at that moment, Terrance yelled out "switch" again, and she was back with Terrence. From that night, she had not seen him again until she went to Terrence's wedding eight months later. At the reception, he remembered her, and they stayed in contact.

"Allan Jones's office."

"Hi, Mr. Jones, this is Ms. Brianna Godfrey."

"Well, hello, Ms. Godfrey! It is so nice of you to finally return one of my phone calls," Allan said in a very sarcastic but playful way. Brianna was slightly annoyed but kept a cute and excited tone.

"What do you mean, Mr. Jones? You know I stay just as busy as you. How have you been?"

"Girl, I've been good. I cannot complain at all. I've been working hard and traveling a lot for work. Brie, you know I miss you, right?"

Brianna was good at this redundant game with Allan, so automatically she responded, "Allan, I miss you too."

"Brie, if that is the truth, then why haven't you made time for me? Have I said something to you that could have pissed you off?"

Upon hearing his naive question, she rolled her eyes and went into deep thought. *Is this Negro trippin'? Did he bump his freaking Almond Joy head? How about, yes, you did, my brotha'! Like you forgot* *to tell me after eight months of dating me that you were married! Then much later, you let it slip that because she was having trust issue, you decided to buy her a designer purse to get yourself out of the doghouse! And to add salt in the wound, that if I was your main girl, I could get gifts like that too. Dude, please! It was a $300 Coach bag. Child, please!*

Brianna finally snapped out of her deep thoughts of annoyance and went back to the conversation at hand. "No, Allan, everything is cool. I have just been taking time out for me lately. You know, sometimes you have to stroke your own ego instead of everyone else's." For a short spell when they were going at it hot and heavy, she would entertain the thought of what it would be like in a monogamous relationship with Allan, but as time went on, she learned to suffocate those foolish thoughts. Brianna became tired of investing time in a false relationship that would yield absolutely no return.

"Well, I do understand that, Brie. I hope to see you soon. We have a lot of catching up to do. This position is a little more demanding than the last one, but I think it will be worth all my sacrifices. I am so tied up that I can't remember the last fraternity activity that I've participated in? Brianna, I need to speak with you in person," Allan stated in a very serious tone.

"Okay. Call me next week, and we can schedule something." Brianna wanted to sound concern. However, her sounding concerned would be a façade and she would be lying in saying what he wanted was a priority in her life.

"I will, baby. Take care."

By this time, Brianna was in the garage of her condominium; she sat there, puzzled by his plea. *I wonder what this nonsense will be concerning. Well, I don't know, and I don't care. I am going to have fun tonight.*

CHAPTER TWO

The Girls

Once she got inside her home, she immediately kicked off her shoes and opened the fridge to retrieve a bottle of water. While lying back on her cranberry sectional sofa, she called girlfriend number 1. Angel was the sweetheart of the bunch, the type of girlfriend that everyone needed in their circle; she wanted the best for everyone. When Brianna and Tamika, another one of Brianna's girlfriends, found out that she was being abused by her then boyfriend, they were furious. The girls were even more blown away to find out that she had been keeping this a secret. The day she left him, Brianna and Tamika vowed to protect her and handle the matter without discussing this with Angel. The girls could teach homeboy a painful lesson because thugs don't believe in turning down easy money. The girls were even bold enough to show their faces when the ass-whipping was being done. As it stood to this day, before he would walk past those girls on the street, he would just willingly jump in front of an oncoming bus.

Angel was five feet and one inch, weighing about one hundred and twenty pounds. Her light-brown hair was cut into a perfect short bob with bangs. She held a MBA from the University of Richmond and is a very well-paid financial advisor at a Fortune 500 company. This girl had it going on, but you would never know it because she kept it so real and so humble. Right before she thought she had to leave a message, Angel answered.

"Heeeeellllooooo," Angel sang out in a peppy voice.

"Hey, girl, it's Brianna. Are we still on tonight?"

"Yes, ma'am. I just left my hair appointment, so I can be over around seven thirty or so!" Angel said while getting into her black Mini Cooper.

"That will be fine actually. See you then!" Brianna didn't have time to hang up properly because Tamika beeped in. "Hey, Tamika!" Brianna said quickly.

"What's up, B!"

"Tamika, meet us at my house around seven thirty. What are you wearing?"

Tamika sighed. "Girl, I have no idea. I am going to the mall now."

"Okay, Ms. Thang! It does not mean that you leave the mall at nine. So if you are going, *go now!*" Brianna demanded in a motherly tone.

"Girl, stop sweating me. I will see you in a bit, bye!"

Brianna was still laughing as she was calling Phoebe. A young professional voice answered the phone, "Good evening, Social Services. Ms. Steele's office."

Being a seasoned professional as well, Brianna lost the laughter in her voice. "May I speak to Ms. Phoebe Steele. This is Brianna Godfrey."

"One moment, please." In five seconds, someone answered the phone. "This is Ms. Steele. How can I help you, Ms. Godfrey?"

"Hey, Phoebe!"

"Hey, Ms. Event Planner Extraordinaire, I know exactly why you are calling. Well, let me be the first person to tell you that I am ready to shake my Afro puff a loose and get my party on. Can't wait to see what hot men are out there tonight!"

Brianna and Phoebe were childhood friends that met in the first grade; they had been inseparable ever since. Phoebe was a smart girl who was very simple as it related to her necessities in her life. Even her friends, outside the ones that she and Brianna shared, were plain. She was not as socially comfortable as Brianna; she would wait until Brianna would warm up the group with conversation then ease into the conversation. Phoebe's conversation was narrow, so to speak. She stayed in the status quo lane of partying and speaking very bitterly of men, but ironically, she was ready to screw anything with two legs and a penis. Phoebe was the biggest in-the-closet slut ever, and the men she attracted loved her for being just that. She wasn't very fashion forward or curvaceous, but she was pretty. What gave her a little something extra was that she knew how to work a makeup brush. She was twenty-nine years old, five feet two inches, and weighed one hundred forty-five pounds. Her smooth caramel complexion was complimented by her bright, pretty round eyes and a natural Afro; Phoebe was a faithful friend.

"Phoebe, I agree with you, girl! Well, meet us at my house around seven thirty. I will have a special bottle of something chilling for you!"

"Okay, Brie, see you then. Oh, is that ghetto Ta—"

Brianna knew what she was about to ask, so she abruptly disconnected the call.

CHAPTER THREE

Ladies' Night

It was now six thirty. Brianna knew that if she did not start to get herself together, she would be the late one. She hopped in the shower, followed her usual routine, and sprinkled on some Coco Chanel Parfum. After covering up with a robe, she walked into her closet, taking inventory of her wardrobe choices for the night. *What the heck am I going to where? I should have gone to the mall with Tamika. Nah! No telling what that girl would try to persuade me to wear.* She chuckled at the thought. An outfit picked out by Tamika would absolutely contain next to no fabric. However, she could rock an outfit as if she stepped right off an urban runway. She would have the latest and greatest but did not pay an arm and a leg for it. If Brianna bought a high-end designer bag, she would have paid a lot of money for it. If Tamika had the same high-end designer handbag, she would have called in a favor with no friendly salesperson providing a receipt. She was all about business; she would rather flip the extra cash and save it. Tamika was twenty-seven years old, five feet, seven inches, and weighed about one hundred thirty-five pounds. Her body frame was medium up top, perky B-cup breasts that did not need a bra and a small waist that led to beautiful round hips and a perfectly shaped bottom. Her walk with her shapely, sexy, long legs would cause a man to drool, even with a significant other on his side. Tamika has hair of her own, but no one, as today's date, could vouch for her hair color or length; she spiced up her look by wearing various wigs. Sometimes a short blonde spiked wig or a long black one that stopped at her waist. Whatever variety of hair it was, it always looked good with her dark even skin. Her almond-shaped eyes and God-given hazel-colored eyes gave her a look of an African princess. When she would roll up in her fully loaded, tricked-out Lexus LS460, you would have thought that royalty had just pulled up. Brianna became a Tamika fan when she came to her aid in a nightclub located in DC.

Brianna and her friend Melissa decided to go a throwback GO-GO concert in Washington, DC. That night, Brianna was getting a lot of attention; she received lots and lots of hugs, a lot of warm greetings, and a lot of stares of approval. She was working a black knit top that left her shoulders exposed, fitted jeans with her four-inch high-heeled boots. Brianna's hair was cornrowed back with long, thick braids hanging down her back. The brushed gold door knocker earrings with her nude lip gloss gave her an updated 1980's look. Her girlfriend, Melissa, looked good herself, but did not have the same sort of shape and swag to pull her black-on-black rendition of Brianna's outfit off. That evening, Brianna noticed that Melissa was on a whole other vibe. She was on some sort of mission, and the mission almost had her acting like a competitor rather than a friend. The after-party was off the hook; both girls were standing there, swaying to the music, when a fine-looking gentleman approached them.

"You girls come here often?" he asked.

"We come here occasionally," Melissa quickly answered, trying to beat out Brianna.

"Is that right? Hi, my name is Maxwell, and I am from Miami. Are you ladies from here?"

Again, Melissa jumped in to answer, "My name is Melissa, and I am from here. This is my friend Brianna, and she is from Richmond." Brianna smiled at him while bobbing her head to the music. She was really feeling the old song that they were playing, an LL Cool J song, but mixed with a little go-go.

"So you like that song, baby girl? Well, let's head out to the dance floor," Maxwell said to Brianna. She knew that Melissa was feeling him. She was more than willing to let this opportunity slip away.

"No, you should go out there with Melissa," Brianna answered, trying to be a thoughtful friend.

"I tell you what! Brianna, let me see what you can do, and Melissa, if you are still available, I would enjoy the chance to dance with you too. Damn, let all the men in here think that I have it going on." He was pulling on Brianna's hand, taking her out onto the dance floor. They danced three songs straight. After breaking a little sweat, they both decided to take a break. Not seeing Melissa where she left her standing, she began to look for her while walking through the crowd; Melissa was nowhere to be found. Once inside of the restroom, she dialed Melissa's cell at least three or four times; it went straight to her voice mail each time.

"Where the hell is this girl?" Brianna mumbled under her breath. That was when the girl next to her answered.

"Not to get in your business, Ma, but if you are talking about the chick you came in here with, she left."

Who is this broad? Brianna asked in her mind. A cute dark-skinned girl, sporting a tight-weave job and dressed to the nines.

"Really, how do you know that?" Brianna suspiciously asked.

"When I went outside to get some air, she was outside on her cell phone. She was saying that some *trick* got in the way. That the *trick* was all up in her man's face and was all over him when *they* were dancing." The knowledgeable stranger glanced at Brianna in the mirror all while applying her lipstick. "That girl, I noticed, would not stop talking. She was going on and on. I couldn't tell who she was whining to on her damn cell. The person on the other line probably did not get one freaking word in at all."

"What, man? She was acting weird all night! And you heard all of this?" Brianna asked in amazement, looking for clarity.

"True story, Mami! I am sure I heard exactly what I am telling you. She had keys in hand, jumped in a car, and pulled off. Girl, please! If I were you, I would go back in there and finish talking to that guy I saw you dancing with! That's what's up! If she ain't got what it takes to get a man, that ain't your fault." The informative stranger started blotting her face. "Oh, my name is Tamika. No need in telling me your name. I think she kept calling you by the name

Trick. Nice to meet you, and if you need a ride home, I will be glad to give you one."

From that point on, they became and remained close friends.

By now it was closer to the time for the girls to arrive. Brianna was putting on the finishing touches when she heard her doorbell ring. Still looking in the mirror, she gave herself a small compliment, *Brie, you are looking good, girl.* Letting her hair fall past her shoulders, she decided to let her hair swoop across one eye with a slight bend at the ends. There was a no ponytail or lavish hair bun tonight. She heard the doorbell again and quickly started to descend her spiral staircase. When she opened her door, two of her entourage were present.

"Hey, ladies!" Brianna said with a big welcoming smile while next giving them both a "don't mess up my makeup" kiss. "Girls, go ahead in the living room. I'll bring out some goodies." Angel went directly over to Brianna's extravagant Boise speakers and synced up her phone to play a little Anthony Hamilton and Jill Scott. Phoebe immediately flopped down and kicked off her semifashionable high heels for the night and gets comfortable.

"I am ready to let my hair down tonight. I have worked on too many depressing cases at work that it has sucked up all my positive energy. Brie, can you bring out the beverages a little faster? Angel is over here doing her little dance moves, and I can't get where she is until I knock back a strong one."

"Phoebe, you are crazy. Well, forget the wine and shots tonight. Here, let's sip on this bottle of Dom," Brianna cheerfully brought out the bottle and glasses. In grabbing, the glasses and saying a toast, the phone rang.

"Hello?" Brianna answered while noticing it was Tamika.

"Hey, girl, I am running late. I will have to meet you guys at the club."

"I knew it, Tamika, I knew you would be—"

"B, I don't wanna hear it. What time will y'all get there?" Tamika interjected with sheer annoyance in her voice. Brianna couldn't help but notice; it was on rare occasion that she would get it like that, but when it could be detected, it usually meant she was trying to figure something or someone out.

"We'll be there around 10:45 p.m. or so," Brianna quickly answered.

"Okay, girlie, I'll see you then," Tamika said quickly, but before she was about to hang up, she had a quick question, "Hey, is *everybody* going tonight?"

"Huh?" Brianna said while making a face. "I guess you can say that. Are you talking about—"

"Never mine," Tamika said abruptly. "I'll see y'all there." She quickly ended the call and Brianna was standing there with a strange look on her face. She was trying to figure out the conversation and the question that Tamika asked her. Suddenly, Brianna's thoughts were interrupted.

"Brianna, what's with the look on your face?" Angel asked. "Is everything all right?"

"Do you have to ask, Angel? She just got off the phone with that crazy Tamika," Phoebe chuckled out sarcastically before she knocked back the rest of her drink.

"Angel, I'm cool. Tamika sounded like she was a little angry or something?"

"I hope no drama is following her secretive ass tonight." Phoebe started taking on a sterner sarcastic tone. "Ms. Mystery Woman herself."

"Dang, Phoebe, where is that song by Mary J. Blige when you need it, 'No More Drama'!" Angel laughed. However, she was hoping that this would be a fun night if Phoebe would do away with that negativity. Unbeknownst to Angel, Brianna noticed and was secretly hoping for the same thing.

"Phoebe, be nice and have another drink." Brianna commenced to pouring immediately.

On the way to the club from PF Changs, the girls were exhausted from all the laughing they had done during dinner. Once they were parked, they reapplied their makeup and observed the crowd going inside; it was totally predictable. When this club goes away, which it will, due to too many shootings or a high lease, the same crowd will migrate to another location. Until then, every face was accounted for and present. The fashion was basically made up of the Macy's or Dillard crowd versus the Rainbow and Forever 21 group. Either way, the women were working it. For the most part, the clubs were fun if you brought your own clique. The music was off the chain when they got inside. It was crowded. Unfortunately, they couldn't find a table but found an okay spot in which to stand and look over the dance floor.

"Girl, look at the men in here tonight—nothing but man candy." It almost looked like Phoebe was going to lose her mind.

"Okay, Phoebe, behave yourself!" Angel playfully scolded.

"Ms. Angel, you can live up to your name if you want, but I am raising hell tonight." Next thing you knew, Phoebe was on the floor with a guy that she had made eye contact with when she walked in. Angel looked over at Brie. "What are we going to do with her?"

"Angel, I don't know, just pray for her!"

"Girl, I hear that. Hey, here comes Tamika." They both waved to her; when she spied them both, she immediately came over. "Hey, Tamika!" the girls said simultaneously.

"Hey, how long have y'all been here?" Tamika asked while winking at one of her male suitors.

"Oh, no more than twenty minutes," Angel responded while looking at her cell phone.

"Okay, cool!" Tamika was somewhat relieved that her friends had not been there too long waiting on her to arrive.

"Okay…wait a minute! This is my song!" Angel started swaying with a hand up in the air. It was one of Kendrick Lamar's latest hit. A cute chocolate fellow, who was one inch taller than Angel, came over and whispered something in her ear. He was nicely dressed; he had on an excellent-quality shirt, tasteful dress pants, and Italian leather cognac brown shoes. His haircut was freshly done, and his Versace glasses were just the right touch, not over the top like everyone else's. Angel looked over at the girls and winked at them while she was being led to the dance floor. Tamika winked back.

"Girl, don't hurt him!" Angel turned back around and smiled to acknowledge she heard Tamika. "Brie, a table is waiting for me over there. Let's grab it."

Tamika was very well put together in a fabulous hooch kind of way. She had on a short jet-black wig that was cut into a bob with a flawless application of makeup. She adorned the look with a large pair of thin silver hooped earrings and a short red body-con dress. The dress had an opening that went down to the small of her back that would not allow for a pair of panties, nor a thong. All this was completed with a pair of four-inch gladiator heels. As they were walking to the table, the men looked like they were going to fall to their knees. Once seated, Tamika ordered two vodkas with a splash of cranberry juice.

"Tamika, what's going on?" Brianna asked her with great concern. "When you called earlier tonight, it sounded as if you were a little frustrated."

"Girl, it's hard to explain. I was at the mall earlier. While in the in the fitting room, I thought I recognized a lady's voice."

"Okay?" Brianna said, being now even more puzzled. Tamika nodded to thank the waitress for her prompt service; after taking a few sips, she proceeded with her explanation. "I could clearly tell that the person on the other end of the phone was also a woman. I don't know if it was a combination of her conversation and me thinking that I knew that voice, but when she asked the other person on the phone, 'Does she know that I will be working with her?' it sounded like something was being plotted. Then the person in the fitting room lets out a big laugh, then stops immediately to say that she cannot wait to see the look on *her* face."

"Okay?" Brianna interjected while interrupting. "Tamika, why is that making you so inquisitive?"

"Because she said, 'I have not seen her since we were at the club, where she almost blew everything!' Then she said to please enjoy her night out but don't spoil her surprise. At that point, I really wanted to see who that person was. I couldn't throw on my jeans fast enough! I finally got myself together, ran out to see if I could check out the chick. I did a quick scan and didn't see anyone that I knew."

"Oh, you ladies found a table!" Phoebe sat down all out of breath. Angel found them as well. She had small beads of sweat on her forehead and was relieved to take a seat. A waitress came over to ask Phoebe and Angel for their drink orders. "Ma'am, can you bring these chicks another of whatever they are having? They are both looking crazy for some reason."

"Well, hello to you too, Ms. Phoebe Steele," Tamika said with an insincere smile.

"What's up, Ms. Tamika Grant?" Phoebe said dryly, not honestly interested in a response.

These two never were truly close and probably never would be. However, they were cordial and always managed to share a laugh or two. Brianna never addressed this awkwardness with Tamika or vice versa. Phoebe, on occasion, would have something sarcastic to say about Tamika but was intelligent enough not to say anything reckless in listening distance. Or better yet, she was not crazy enough to even say anything off the wall to Tamika's face; Phoebe knew exactly what time it was. Tamika got down with the best of the worst. She knew to take on Tamika could be like taking on a whole block and then some.

"You two look like you were having an intense conversation. Please share," Phoebe said, being nosy as usual.

Before Brianna could answer, Tamika did. "We were talking about one of my male friends. You know how it is, Phoebe, when a man just wants to use you for one thing? I don't want to be one of those girls who will only allow their selves to be used as a sperm collector."

Brianna quickly knocked back her drink. She did not want to appear available to join in the exchange of shade that was about to go down. However, the response given did send up a red flag. Tamika dodge the truth, firing a warning shot. *Why did Tamika feel a need to lie about the conversation that we were having?* Suddenly, Angel began moving her head around like a snake.,

"Brianna, isn't that Natalie on the floor? Is she…it looks like she is dancing with a sexy guy with dreads? Is that her husband?" Angel couldn't get a good view; all the girls began looking over. Without being able to see through the crowd, Brianna answered, "No, that couldn't be Harold. Don't tell me that Natalie is creeping? I wish I could see the guy. Don't let me find out!" Brianna said while laughing.

Now with a better view, Angel caught Natalie's attention. "Ladies, we have been spotted and it looks as though she is coming over."

"Well, do you, ladies. I am going to the restroom. When I come back out here, hopefully I can find my buddy and get back on the dance floor." Phoebe jotted off to the restroom, almost as if she was going to pee herself up.

"Hi, ladies, are you all having a good time?" Natalie asked while yelling over the music.

Brianna, like earlier that day, again decided to go with a forced cordial flow. "Yes, we are having a good time! We saw you teaching everyone a thing or two out there on the floor! I didn't know that Harold was the clubbing type?" From the few things that Natalie would willingly mention about her husband, she knew that he would not be caught in a place like this.

"Oh, that guy isn't Harold. Remember I told you that Harold couldn't make it into town this weekend? Here, let me get my friend over here so I can introduce you." Natalie turned to summon for the gentleman. "Ladies, let me introduce you to Maxwell King."

CHAPTER FOUR

Sunday Morning Recap

When Tamika walked in the restaurant, she spied Brianna and walked over. "Hey, Brie."

"Hello, how are you doing today?" Brianna responded.

"I'm good. I went to church and got my praise on!"

"What, Tamika? You go, girl! Well, you did better than me. I slept in this morning, answered your text, and then I tried to reach Phoebe. I couldn't get an answer on her phone."

"Really, Brie? Knowing Ms. Phoebe, she is at somebody's house looking for her bra, shoes, and keys." A beautiful dreadlock-haired sister came over to take their order; they both realized that they were both starving. Brianna was ready to place her order without looking at the menu. "I'll take the two-piece fish boat with a sweet iced tea."

"And you, ma'am?"

"I will have the same thing."

"Easy enough, I will be right back with your beverages."

With great curiosity, Tamika was ready to pick up where they left off. "So you were saying that you tried her on her home phone too?"

"I sure did, but no Phoebe. I hope she is okay."

"Again, B, you know how she is. This is what she does. I know you have known each other for a long time, but have you noticed anything lately?"

Brianna was trying to figure out where this conversation was leading. "Like what?" She couldn't change the subject because Tamika always kept it real. She wasn't a girl that sat around and would stir up crap. If Tamika was onto something it's because she wanted you to hear what she had to say.

"I don't know, but I keep getting vibes with her lately? I'll leave it alone for a minute, but trust and believe, I'm usually right about stuff like that."

Brianna didn't know what to say, so she politely shifted the topic and placed it on Maxwell. "Okay, more importantly, why was Maxwell with my boss last night?"

"Brianna, I was trying to figure that out too. I thought we would never see him again!" Tamika began shaking her head in disbelief as she started sipping her tea.

"Yep, that's what I thought too. He's got some damn nerve to stroll back in Richmond like everything is cool, arrogant pimp! Who knew that meeting him that night would be the beginning of a nightmare! Just think, I really thought I was in love with him!"

"Girl, he spoiled you like crazy. He gave you the best of the best. I'm not gonna lie. I was glad that he included me. But homeboy didn't have to play us like that! We would do quick trips down to Miami to enjoy the beach and then jump on a plane and hit New York up for a couple of parties. But—"

Brianna's attentive listening to Tamika's truth was interrupted by the waitress's placement of the food on the table. "Thank you, it looks good. Can you bring us a little more tea and napkins, and then we should be all set?" The waitress pleasantly smiled and nodded. After she departed, Brianna immediately returned to the conversation. "Girl, don't even say it. That one trip was the scariest thing I have ever gone through," Brianna said in light daze.

"I can't say it was the scariest for me, but it did freaking catch me off guard."

They both began to recall that trip.

Get up! Get up now, Brianna!
Brianna thought that Maxwell was playing one of his silly games. "Maxwell! Stop playing."

"Girl, I am not playing with you. I threw your stuff in the suit-case and Tamika is already dressed, waiting for you in the other room." Maxwell was not making eye contact with her at that moment.

"Max, I thought we were having a good time?" Brianna was hit with an enormous amount of confusion as she was trying her best not to cry. However, when she noticed that he did harbor any remorse, her emotional gears had shifted to anger. Maxwell did not have the decency to look at her; she went over to confront his fool-ishness but was shocked when he grabbed her arm.

"Look, I don't have time for this, Brianna—get dress! You have to go now!" Maxwell yelled at her as though she was some sort of random female. Brianna threw on a pair of jeans and a T-shirt with a pair of simple stated Gucci sneakers with the chic large hobo Gucci bag that Maxwell had bought her from Saks the day before. She couldn't believe her eyes; everything that she had brought with her was packed, even down to her eyeliner. She walked into the living room of their suite to find Tamika standing by the door with two thugs. When turning around to question Maxwell one more time, a man that must have been posted up by the bedroom door delivered such a blow to Maxwell's midsection that it sent him down to the floor.

"Max!" Brianna screamed.

"Ma'am, if you know what's best, you'd leave with the nice gen-tlemen by the door." This stern-sounding man, with a thick accent, was now standing directly in front of Maxwell. He was holding his hand up as though he was trying to block her from approaching him.

Maxwell, now making direct eye contact, tried to get Brianna to move with haste. Maxwell whispered his last spoken plea to her, "Leave now, Brianna, please."

Tamika pulled Brianna by her hand to lead her out. The ride to the airport was excruciatingly quiet. Once there, the men hopped out of the black Denali, giving their bags to the skycap along with their tickets. "Ladies, you need to forget this little inconvenience. Please enjoy your trip home," the driver said as he managed to give them a half smile.

"Oh, it's like that with you people? You're not going to explain?" Brianna asked while fighting back tears. The man that she questioned turned around to respond, "Sweetheart, handle this like your friend. Please move on and don't ask any more questions."

"Ladies, this way." The skycap was trying to make small talk, but the girls weren't feeling it. Brianna honestly didn't hear one word. They had an hour to kill, so Tamika practically ordered Brianna to have a seat until she got back. In ten minutes, she returned with a venti coffee from Starbucks and beverage from Tropical Smoothie.

As Brianna began to immediately sip her coffee, she noticed Tamika pouring a travel-size bottle of Patron into her smoothie. In being a little thrown that she got that past the TA, she looked at her watch, noting that it was only nine thirty in morning. Tamika proceeded to take the longest pull off her straw, finally noticing Brianna's fixed stare. "Brie, are you all right?"

"Tamika, what the hell just happened? We have been here for three days. I found myself really falling for him, but what the hell just happened?"

"Brie, I don't know. I really don't know. Maxwell came in my room and told his boy to help me get packed. When I began to ask questions, he told me to shut up. Well, you know I wasn't going to let that go. I jumped up, naked ass and all to cuss him out. However, Rico grabbed me by my waist and told me to play my position. He really needed me to do this. Maxwell looked at Rico and said that he had packed your things and for him to go ahead and leave now because they were on their way. Rico kissed me, gave me a wad of cash, and said it again, 'Do what you do best and play your position.' Saying that, I knew immediately it's a lifestyle where you just don't ask any questions, just go with the flow. As I finished throwing on some clothes, by the door is where I found our two escorts. The third guy was quiet and didn't even notice me. He just kept looking through some papers. Ten minutes later, after listening to you guys screaming, you both came out the room, Maxwell hits the floor, and we are now here at the airport."

Brianna looking more confused than ever, she began to cry. "I'm going to call him." She dialed his number and there was no answer. "Tamika, call Rico. Maybe he can tell us what's going on."

"I can't," Tamika said dryly.

"What do you mean you can't? CALL HIM NOW!" she loudly demanded.

"First, Brie, what you not gonna do is yell at me. Damn, what's this *yell at Tamika day?* Secondly, Rico asked me not to call him because he wasn't going to answer."

"What?" Brianna said, but this time monitoring her volume. "What do you do mean you are not going to call him because he asked you not to!"

"Brianna! Look, when things are going down and it looks shady, the less you know is for your protection. In this case, we are just going to have to roll with it. Rico, for some reason, said not to call, so guess what? I am not going to call."

Knowing that Tamika probably knew what she was talking about, she reluctantly decided to listen to her. She finally tuned into her surroundings and noticed they were boarding for DC. To her and Tamika's surprise, the tickets were for first class. "Damn, he kicked us to the curb but at least by way of first freaking class!"

"You got that right," Tamika said, cosigning.

Both Tamika and Brianna's reminiscing about the crazy trip that almost happened seven years ago was interrupted by Brianna's cell phone.

"Well, now you call, Ms. Phoebe. I will be home in an hour or so—what? I'll call you when I get home."

Tamika rolled her eyes at Brianna after she disconnected the call. "Oh, so now she wants to call you, huh? It's almost three o'clock in the afternoon. Where did she wake up?" Tamika asked in sheer disgust.

Unlike Tamika who still appeared to be very annoyed, Brianna was giggling. "I know! Her little trifling butt just got home!"

Tamika quickly changed the conversation. "Well, anyway, do you think that Maxwell will try to contact you since he's seen you last night?"

"I don't know, girl. I don't know what to expect from that man anymore."

"I really think that he was really feeling some sort of way about you. As it related to money, it was never an issue when it came to spending it on you. Even to this day, he always manages to somehow find out what you need. Not to mention there was the fully loaded Cayenne SUV waiting for you at the airport when we got back," Tamika said, trying to be comforting.

"I know, T, but it doesn't excuse what happened or why it happened for that matter!"

Leaving the restaurant on the drive home, Brianna realized that she missed Maxwell but hated him at the same time. When she arrived home, she ran up her stairs to the bedroom and rushed inside of her large walk-in closet.

"Where is it! Where is it!" she mumbled. There it was, in an envelope that she kept in the inner compartment of her Gucci travel bag that she took on board with her the day of departure. Maxwell had placed it in her bag when he abruptly pushed her out while in Miami.

Butterfly,

I know you are trying to figure this shit out, and as of right now, I can't offer you an explanation. When I saw you for the first time, I instantly fell in love with you. Brianna, you were dripping with sex appeal; I knew I had to have you in my life. Within the year of getting to know you better, I wanted to take care of you. I wanted to provide you with any and everything that you needed.

Right now, I must leave you to take care of a few things. Don't wait for me and don't look for me. What I must take care of will require my permanent attention. I left you a little something in your account to keep you stable and will see over your needs discreetly. But remember, you must complete school. I got my education and you must get yours. I hope that you enjoy your graduation gift early. You don't graduate, it disappears (smile). Look for a guy holding a sign for you in baggage claim. He will take you to your gift.

Even if you are with someone else, I will still have my eye on you.

Love you, baby.
Maxwell

Brianna threw the letter down on her closet floor. *I should throw this away. I should get rid of that damn truck! I will never forgive him!* Brianna fought back tears, but she could not leave the letter on the floor. She placed the letter back in the suitcase. Her heart would never allow her to toss it and she knew that. Brianna got up from the closet floor and glanced at the clock. It was five o'clock. She wept until six o'clock, but why?

CHAPTER FIVE

Natalie's E-mail

Since the night at the club, two weeks had flown by and Brianna had not run into Maxwell; to her amazement, he did not try to reach out to her. Brianna wanted to see if she could strike up a conversation about the whole introducing of Maxwell with Natalie; she thought by steering a conversation in that direction, she could explain how Natalie became his friend. However, Natalie had decided to take an impromptu vacation. The questioning would have to be placed on ice. Oddly enough, it was a vacation where she was finding time to send multiple e-mails asking about all of Brianna's accounts. As it related to the big gala that was happening in a week, she kept reiterating to Brianna to be on top of it by trading e-mails often. If her event planning agency pulled this off flawlessly, they would be the most-coveted agency in Richmond. This was a benefit that would raise a significant amount of money for Richmond's largest hospital. The governor, as well as the mayor, will be in attendance. There would also be in attendance philanthropists from not only just Richmond but from Washington, DC. Brianna's networking at many events in the area made her an asset to the company. She could befriend many key people in the Richmond area, such as topnotch vendors who absolutely enjoyed working for and with her. She worked endlessly, making sure they were contacted; she was meeting with them and meticulously going over plans of execution. If Brianna brought down the house, so to speak as the planner of this event, she would put her name in the book of who's who of planning. Before going home on Friday, Brianna received an e-mail from Natalie, requesting that she leave the file out for the Cancer Society Gala, as well as all her notes and details that were written. She again asked her to run a report showing all the events that were on the books for the next two weeks. *Why does she keep asking me to do that? Why is she starting to micro-manage now?* She began getting everything together when yet another e-mail from Natalie popped up.

Brianna,

I know you have been putting in a lot of hard work. I have given you all next week off with pay as your reward; you have also been excused from attending the gala. Due to all your excellent notes, I'm sure we can pick up the ball from here. I will call you if I have any additional questions.

Sincerely
Natalie

Okay, this is crazy! Why would I do all this work and not want to see this through to the end? Natalie is out of her rabbit-ass mind! Brianna was shaking her head with disbelief. *Let me call her right now!* On several attempts in trying to reach Natalie, Brianna was greeted with her voice mail.

Friday night, Brianna just kept thinking about Natalie and the e-mails. She was still bothered by Natalie's random "acts of kindness." She knew well enough that all this was questionable but couldn't figure out what motivated it all. Brianna continued with another puzzling thought but not relating to her job this time. *What is going on with Phoebe?* Brianna decided to give Phoebe a call.

"Hello," Phoebe answered while speaking over the noise in the background.

"Hey, girl, it's Brianna!" She was trying to yell loud enough so Phoebe could hear her.

"What's up, Brianna?"

"I was calling to see what you were up to, Ms. Steele."

31

"Nothing," Phoebe dryly replied.

"Well, Phoebe, your nothing sounds like fun," Brianna chuckled.

"Oh, that? Uuummm, me and a few friends got together to celebrate a friend starting a new job. I would have invited you, but I know you would have been bored out of your mind, but I'll give you a call later. Maybe we can get a bite tomorrow. I'll call you."

"Okay, that sounds great!"

"Good! I'll talk to you later, girl," Phoebe quickly ended the call.

It was about eight thirty in the evening, and there was nothing on the television. Brianna grabbed a glass of wine and started thumbing through her *Vogue* magazine. Her first love was truly fashion; she could go into a trance when looking at different outfits. Suddenly, the phone started ringing; when she looked, it was Allan. Brianna rolled her eyes back in her head and plastered a fake smile on her face. Hopefully, he could not hear the fakeness through the smile in her voice. "Hello, Allan!"

Allan was so delighted that she picked up her phone. "Hi, beautiful! How are you doing?"

"I'm good, Allan, and yourself?"

"I would be better if you said that you wanted to meet me for a drink."

"For a drink? Allan, where are you?" she asked in a serious tone.

"I just pulled into Richmond and thought I would head to Shockoe bottom to check out the social scene."

Brianna knew she needed something to distract her from obsessing over Natalie's e-mails. However, she couldn't honestly say that she wanted Allan to be the distraction. "Allan, I don't know if I want to be around a large crowd tonight. So—"

Allan instantly reverted to thinking how he could entice Brianna. He interjected with a plan B, "Brianna, if this is okay with you, I have a room at the Marriott. Why don't you meet me there?"

"Allan, are you trying to—"

Again, he was ready with a quick interruption, "Am I trying to spend time with you? Yes! I need to talk to you? Yes! So, Brianna, please say yes?"

"Okay, Allan," she said reluctantly.

"Thanks, baby, I'll see you in a few? I will text you the room number after I check in."

Twenty minutes later, Allan sent her the room number; forty-five minutes later, Brianna was at his hotel. When Allan opened his door, she could have melted; she forgot how sexy this Negro was. He wasted no time in grabbing and planting a warm, sensuous kiss on her; she couldn't help but kiss him back. "Brianna, you look so good." She had on an off-the-shoulder red blouse with a fitted black midi skirt accompanied with a four-inch Jimmy Choo sandal. Her hair was up like the models in the magazines with falling pieces in the right spots. Her Prada fragrance, not over powering, was dabbed in the spots that mattered. She and the whole ensemble was sweetly breathtaking. Allan gently pulled her through the door. "Brianna, it's really good to see you. I guess you can tell that, huh?"

"Yeah, baby, I can tell," she said while giving him a playful look.

"Brie, you are looking sexy as hell!"

"Allan, I can say the same about you too."

"Brie, here get comfortable. What would like to drink?"

"What do you have?" She smirked because his drink has been predictable as his conversations.

"As always, I roll with my Grey Goose, but I have Patrón too."

"Dang, Allan, nothing a little gentler?" She laughed.

"Brie, are you changing on me? Back in the day, you could hold a few rounds," Allan playful reminded her.

"Oh, I am not scared. I'll take the Goose, neat, please."

"No ice, okay, Ms. Thang, I got you."

So after about an hour and a half, they managed to knock back two drinks a piece. Allan wanted to have the serious talk. He pulled his chair close to hers and gently touched her face.

"Do you realize, Brianna, we've known each other for a few years? At this point and time in my life, I must acknowledge the deep feelings and the love I hold just for you. You do realize that I have deep-rooted feelings for you?"

Brianna, who must have been feeling good from the two drinks, had no problem answering him; she purposely took another sip from her now-third drink and blurted her heartfelt answer without blinking, "No, Allan, I *don't* realize that at all."

"What? You are joking right, or are you just feeling the drink?" he asked in complete amazement.

"Nope, I'm not joking, and yes, I am feeling the drink," Brianna said with a half of a smirk.

"Brianna, why would you say something like that? I have always called you, and not to mention, I would drive almost two hours to come and see you."

"With all that being said, you also have to realize that I have never placed any demands on you. I had no justifiable cause to do that because you always made me feel disposable. I was not your focus. I, my dear, was disposable."

Allan looked completely blown because he honestly did not know that she felt that way. "Brianna, you were always so laid-back, and because of that, I always thought we were fine. Baby, let me make it right."

Before Brianna could say anything, Allan removed her glass from her hand, pulled her, and began kissing her very gently. He kissed her forehead in such an enduring way that any woman would revert to being a young girl. He kissed the corner of her mouth and then bit her bottom lip softly. They did something that they had never had done before—they made love.

When they awaken the next morning, Brianna jumped in the shower and Allan ordered room service. When she came out of the shower, wrapped in a towel, she found Allan sipping on coffee waiting for her.

"Here, baby, I didn't want to uncover your food. This one was specially made for you." With great curiosity, Brianna lifted the nicely polished silver dome that covered the plate.

"What is this, Allan?" Her expectancy of finding food was immediately replaced by looking at an envelope.

"Open it and see," Allan said with his big handsome smile. Brianna opened the letter and began reading it. It was documentation showing that Allan had filed for legal separation from his wife of eight years. Brianna could not believe what she was reading.

"What does this mean? I mean, why you are showing me this?"

"Brianna, it means that you are not disposable. I want you. I need you. I love you. Again, Brie, let me make things right."

CHAPTER SIX

Surprise Phone Call

As she was getting on I-95 to go home, her cell phone rang with a private number.

"Hello?"

"Hey, butterfly," the person warmly responded.

"Excuse me?" Brianna voiced quickly filled with confusion.

"It's me, Maxwell."

At that moment, Brianna had been going seventy-five miles per hour but dropped back to fifty-five, with her foot lightly touching the brake. In doing this, a driver of a Ford 150 almost rear-ended her. He quickly went around her, cursing, trying to get her attention. His agitation was fueled as she was not paying any attention to him. However, she did notice that her heart was pounding almost out of her chest and her mouth was getting extremely dry.

"You don't have anything to say to me, do you?" Maxwell asked gently.

"Maxwell, are you freaking serious? What do you want me to say?" She was hoping that she would not start crying. The last thing she wanted was for Maxwell to think, or know, that she still has feelings for him.

"Brianna, I guess that's a fair and honest response. At the club, you looked so stunning. I can't stop thinking about you."

"Maxwell, why are you calling me now? I have no intentions of falling for your shenanigans again!"

"I'm not calling you to make you upset. I just…I just wanted to hear your voice. Please know I have never stopped loving you."

"Oh, really, is that all?" she responded sarcastically. However, the truth was that she never stopped loving him either, and that was a freaking problem.

"No, that is not all, Brianna. I wanted to tell you that it is time for you to move on, branch out. It's inevitable. You will be spreading your wings shortly."

"What? What are you talking about, Max?"

"I have to go now, but you will see. Love you," Maxwell ended he call.

Brianna was so confused that she had gotten off on the wrong exit. She decided to make good on her mistake by making an impromptu detour to Phoebe's house. When she approached her driveway, there was a car parked there with out-of-town license plates. *Damn, Phoebe! What man is in your bed this time? Let me just take my behind home.* When Brianna arrived home, she automatically felt relieved and comforted. *Wow, my world is spinning, but there is no place like home.* Brianna changed into one of her comfortable yet stylish sweat suits, turned on her television, laid back, and obviously thought about the obvious. She was trying to make sense of Natalie's e-mails, Allan's change, and now, Maxwell's special appearance.

Sunday morning was a quiet day. Brianna talked to Angel that morning before going to church. She talked to Tamika for a little bit that Sunday evening. However, as for Ms. Phoebe, she wasn't at church and couldn't be contacted. Brianna wanted to speak to Phoebe about the girl's night out, the job, Allan, and Maxwell. Could Tamika be right about Phoebe changing? Lately, Phoebe had been hit-or-miss. *Maybe I should give her a call. Hell no, she can call me whenever she's finish doing whatever or whomever she is doing.*

CHAPTER SEVEN

All Eyes on You

It's Monday morning around eleven thirty, the first day of Brianna's impromptu vacation. While reaching for her remote, she noticed the notification on her iPhone; she had missed calls and the messages that came with them. All the girls had called her. Angel called while she was at work and Phoebe called on her drive into work. Tamika called during her routine morning tasks. Of course, no one knew exactly what they were, but she was faithful in doing them that's for sure. However, the fourth call was from Allan, which immediately took her back in her thoughts of the wonderful evening she had with him. However, the sweet reminiscing halted when she opened her inbox to find yet another crazy e-mail from Natalie.

> *Good morning.*
>
> *In reviewing all your notes for the gala this week-end, I have noticed, as usual, that you have dotted every "I" and have crossed every "t," thank you. Due to all your hard work, this event will be wonderful. Thursday, we are having a staff meeting and I am asking that all employees be at the office no later than twelve noon. I will see you then. Again thank you for all your hard work.*
>
> *Sincerely,*
> *Natalie*

While rolling her eyes, she tossed her phone on the bed and proceeded to the shower. Brianna had decided to use this day for absolute relaxation and to also figure what was up with Natalie. Not to mention, she was still wondering why Natalie and Maxwell were together at the club. Once Brianna had gotten dressed and ate a light lunch, there was a knock at the door. To her surprise, it was a flower delivery.

"Hi, ma'am. Are you Brianna Godfrey?" the smiling delivery-man asked.

"I sure am. Are those for me?" she asked while blushing.

"Not only these, but you have about three more. Where should I put this one?"

"Oh, wow! You can place it on the table."

Brianna stood there, watching him bring in the other flowers. They were beautiful, white roses, lilies, red roses. The arrangements were stunning. Absolutely exquisite! Brianna went to tip the delivery-man, but he rejected the tip, stating that he was well compensated for this already; he got her signature and immediately left. She went to the first three arrangements and admired them all, but she also was looking for a card. So far, no card was seen. Finally, upon reaching the last flower arrangement, there was the card. She hesitated slightly before reading it.

Love,

This is for the woman that I should have kept in my life. Here is to a new beginning. You mean every-thing to me. I will never let you go again.

Love you, baby.
Your second-chance lover

She noticed that the card was not signed, but she knew the flowers had to have been from Maxwell. This was just like his "out of the blue, over the top" surprises that he was so capable of doing. For the rest of the day, Brianna felt at peace for some odd reason. Instead of calling the Maid Service, she decided to clean her condo from top to bottom. She even found the time and energy to prepare fettuccini with shrimp, not to mention a cheesecake too. *What was I thinking? There is no way that I will be able to eat all of this by myself, and I hate leftovers.* She placed the pasta on the back burner and decided to invite the girls over. Brianna got the green light from all the girls but not Phoebe because she totally did not think to invite her.

Phoebe and Brianna had practically grown up together—same elementary school, then onto junior high and the same high school. They were practically each other's shadows. Going to separate colleges was a little hard for them, but it was due to finances. However, when they were on a holiday break, they became inseparable for that time. The year Brianna met Maxwell, it did cause a little separation anxiety for Phoebe, but they remained friends. As for this dinner, she found herself agreeing with Tamika: Phoebe had been a little different lately—very distant. But in trying to do the right thing, Brianna decided to call her.

A perky little administrator answered, "Ms. Steele's office."

"May I speak to Ms. Steele please?" Brianna asked, trying to sound pleasantly upbeat.

"May I ask who is speaking?"

"Why yes, you may. This is Brianna Godfrey."

What seemed like two or three minutes had finally passed when a voice came on. "Ms. Godfrey, Ms. Steele is extremely busy and asked if she could call you later this evening?"

At that moment, Brianna noticed that just maybe Ms. Phoebe wanted to be distant. Without giving it any extra thought, Brianna nonchalantly replied, "Sure, that's cool with me. Thank you."

*****

It was now six thirty in the evening; Tamika and Angel were at the condo.

"Okay, who has died or who is in love with you now? Where the heck did all these flowers come from?" Angel asked while looking around the room."

"Girls, so much have been happening that it was too much to try and tell you guys over the phone. Friday night and Saturday morning, I spent it with Allan." Brianna was all smiles when looking over at the girls for their approval.

Angel was amazed at the news. "What! Was it good?"

Tamika, finishing off her mouthful of food, began to laugh. "I thought you were done with him since Mr. Man couldn't make up his mind."

"I thought I was through with him too, and to answer your question Ms. Angel, *yes*, girl! It was different this time. And, ladies, to top it off, he showed me his legal separation papers that he filed eleven months ago."

Tamika couldn't believe it. After Maxwell, she thought that Allan would be the good distraction for her, but Allan was turning out to be like the rest of the men they knew. He was a man with some sort of complex, a complex in which he needed many women around to make him feel wanted. Allan always needed to talk about his job and his titles every five seconds to prove his self-worth; he was another egomaniac looking for a jump-off when getting bored with his wife.

"What now, B, he showed you his *what* papers?" Tamika was shaking her head with disbelief.

"Oh, you heard me correctly. Mr. Jones proudly showed me his separation papers. But, ladies, here is the kicker. When leaving the hotel, I got a call from Maxwell."

Angel covered her mouth. She was at a total loss of words, and Tamika started choking on her wine. However, once Tamika regained her composure, she was ready to start the interrogation. "What he has to say?"

"Not much. He only said that he wanted to hear my voice and that I looked nice at the club the other night," Brianna said with a sound of slight disgust.

Angel was a little confused as well. "Brianna, that can't be all that he said. Are you holding back on us?"

"Well, he did say that he still loves me and to get ready to branch out. I am about to spread my wings." Brianna was almost slipping in deep thought while talking and pouring another glass of wine; Tamika and Angel started laughing.

"What? What's so funny?" Brianna asked, being completely clueless.

"Girl, to us, he sounds like he going to push your ass off a cliff." All the girls began to laugh together.

"But on a serious note, has anyone heard from Phoebe lately?" Angel asked with a very sincere tone.

Tamika smirked, "Mmmm...Brianna, I haven't. Have you?

"Well, no, I haven't seen her in almost three weeks. However, she did call me this morning on her way to work, but I missed it. Come to think of it, she didn't leave me a message. Anyway, I called her to invite her to dinner, but she was too busy to come to the phone."

"B, you still don't think she hasn't been acting a little suspect lately?" Tamika asked. "I mean, she hasn't been around lately, and not to mention, she exited the club without telling any of us."

"Tamika, you have made your point. Not to mention that there was a car in her driveway with out-of-town plates on it. I don't know, maybe she's just really busy?" Brianna was really trying to give her childhood friend the benefit of a doubt.

"Okay, Ms. I-always-need-to-find-the-best-in-everybody, keep thinking what you want," Tamika playfully replied.

"What are you trying to say, Tamika?" Angel sincerely questioned. She was clearing the table and keeping her eyes on Tamika.

"Angel, all I am saying and what I have told your girl over there is that Phoebe has been different for a couple of months now." Tamika was widening her eyes and tilting her head while staring at Brianna.

"Okay, Tamika, I hear you loud and clear. So let's all agree that, moving forward, we will pay closer attention to her from here on out." Brianna knew at this point, she needed to take heed to Tamika's observation.

"I can do that!" Angel said like a true team player.

"That's what I'm talking about! Fo' sho my nizzels!" Tamika yelled.

Both girls looked at each other and fell out laughing at Tamika's street response. By now, it was ten forty-five at night, and girls grabbed their purses to head out. Angel winked at Tamika, then looked over at Brianna.

"Uuummm, Brie? You never said who sent you the flowers," Angel said with a slick smile.

With a confident smile, Brianna responded, "Maxwell."

CHAPTER EIGHT

Who Do I Thank Now

Tuesday and Wednesday were peaceful days. Two days of complete pampering. One day, a masseuse came and gave her a full-body massage. The next day, someone came to her condo to give her a facial, manicure, and a pedicure. This was all reminiscent of the things that Maxwell used to do back in the day; it was all blowing her mind. Brianna waited patiently to hear something from Maxwell, but not one call.

Allan was still in California on a business trip. He sent Brianna only a few text messages, saying that he missed her dearly, but no extra conversation. Since she already knew that he really could not afford to be distracted, she only replied with warm, short messages. Allan was working on a very large assignment. If the assignment went well, it would impact his career tremendously. Not to mention that since Maxwell was sending all those surprises to her, she felt guilty.

Now it was Thursday, the day of the big meeting. When she arrived at the agency, she went directly to the conference room. All the key planners were there along with one empty seat beside Natalie; she was beginning the meeting.

"Good afternoon, ladies and gentlemen. Let me first start this meeting by thanking everyone for taking the time out of your schedules to attend this meeting. I also would like to thank you for your hard work and dedication. The company is a success because of everyone's effort, so thank you. The owners, as you may already know, deals very heavily in real estate. The agency was just another investment piece in their portfolio. They have presented me with an opportunity to buy the agency. I would like to inform you that I now stand before you as part owner. After going over the books, we still have much room for growth. This can be done by operating with a very strong, if not stronger, partner. Without further ado, please allow me to introduce Mrs. Melissa King of King Investments."

Oh my god! Melissa? What the hell is going on? I-I haven't seen her since the club incident.

Brianna was shocked and was in complete disbelief. However, Melissa's wicked smile snapped Brianna out of the trance of sheer amazement. Natalie was applauding her, along with the weak applause from the others. Then she continued with her introduction.

"Mrs. King has been doing event planning for about five years. She started in Miami and travels to Washington, DC, quite extensively to handle many top-notch clients. I believe that she will give us and the company the push we are needing. Here, let me stop talking and give her a chance to enlighten us. Melissa…"

Okay, can somebody please explain what is happening right now? It's one freaking surprise after another. I really cannot take anymore…

"Hello, everyone! As Natalie has stated, my name is *Mrs.* Melissa *King.* It is a pleasure to meet you. I do believe I see an old college friend here. Hello, Ms. Godfrey," Melissa said with an evil smile.

Oh, so now this trick wants to acknowledge me as a friend? College buddies? I wish I could get up and punch this bit—no, Brianna Monique Godfrey! Rise above…pull it together! Brianna quickly zoned back in, just like she kept continuously zoning out.

"Yeah, longtime, bestie!" Brianna responded while giving back the same painful smile.

"Well, back to my introducing myself. I graduated from the University of Miami, by way of Howard University in Washington, DC, where I am from originally. I married right after college and have a beautiful little boy, who is now seven years old. His name is Maxwell King Jr." When she said this, she had a fixed stare on Brianna. Brianna, trying to hold a poker face, thought she was going to pass out; she was stricken with the most hurt that any jilted lover could feel. She wanted to lash out at Melissa, but most of all, she wanted to confront Maxwell. Melissa was enjoying every minute of torturing her.

"Now that Maxwell Jr. is a little older, I am now able to pour more of my heart and soul into my career. Before becoming part owner, Natalie allowed me to observe the quality of work from everyone here. In doing so, I could review your accounts and closely examine even the personalities of who was performing what tasks. As you can see, Natalie is now walking around, passing out envelopes with your names on them. We're asking that you take this information home and review it. Hopefully, you will be pleasantly surprised with the bonus checks that are being given. After your review, should you have any questions, please let our secretary know by nine thirty in the morning. He will schedule your appointment within the week to discuss your concerns. Please know that I am looking forward to working with each one of you. There are box lunches that's been placed outside of the door for your enjoyment. You are now dismissed. Brianna, do you mind staying back? I would love a moment with you."

"Sure, Melissa." It took everything in Brianna to muster up a smile.

Over hearing Melissa's request, Natalie dismissed herself. "Melissa, I have a few things that I need to take care of. I will be in my office."

"Okay, Natalie. I will be in right after I reminisce with Ms. Godfrey here." Once Natalie shut the door, the gloves were off.

"Ms. Brianna, I haven't seen you since the club in DC. You do remember our fun night out, don't you?" It was clear at this point she wanted to taunt Brianna about the incident, but Brianna would be ready for her nonsense.

"Girl, I do remember that joyous night. It was almost like you weren't there though! I vaguely remember your presence? No… wait, I do remember. You left the club without notice, and I haven't seen you since. I think you were pouting because you couldn't get Maxwell's full attention?"

The smug smile totally left Melissa's face. "Oh, Ms. Godfrey, but I did one better. I got the man. I got the ring and his last name.

Wait…I got his son. You, *other* women, make it so easy. You put in all the work, but we smart women walk away with the grand prize every time. Brianna, I bet you are still lusting after him, huh? I heard that you were absolutely crushed when he sent your naive carcass on the plane from Miami back to DC!"

"What, Melissa!" Brianna could not deny any of what Melissa was saying. She was accurate but just a little too accurate?

"Guess you are wondering how I knew that? Honey, I knew about the large sum of cash that was dropped in your personal account. I knew about the Porsche Cayenne SUV that was given to you as an early graduation gift. Now look at your face, boo. It's on the floor. *Pick it up!*"

Before Brianna knew it, she and Melissa were toe to toe, and her hand was fixing to leave her side to harshly plant it on the left side of Melissa's face. It was the timing of Peter entering the room that saved her from that physical contact.

"Excuse me, ladies. Melissa, there is a Ms. Steele for you on line 2. Would you like to take the call now?" Peter politely asked while quietly wondering what exactly he walked in on.

Melissa, never breaking eye contact with Brianna, managed to answer, "Yes, I'll take the call in my office. Brianna, enjoy the rest of your vacation. You will need it! Oh, after you have gone through your packet, please call me directly with any questions. I hope you will allow us the opportunity to work together. I took extra time to restructure *your* position."

Notably, Melissa was walking like she was on her way to becoming the "Next Top Model." She walked with confidence that was just arrogant, almost as if she had won the grand prize. Melissa turned to say one more thing. "I will be sure to give Maxwell your regards."

CHAPTER NINE

Who Would Like to Explain

Because Brianna drove home in a daze, she found herself questioning how she drove home safely. However, she had severely scraped the side of her SUV while pulling into her garage. Once inside, she flopped down on her sofa.

How could he play me like this? I wish he would call me back! Call me right now, mofo!

Brianna was hurt and very angry. She was yelling, and she threw her stuff on the coffee table. Her cell phone began to ring, causing her to dump everything out of her very large Jimmy Choo bag to find it.

"Hello!" she yelled.

"Damn, girl! Who you yellin' at?" Tamika snapped back her while laughing.

"Hey, Tamika, you ain't going to believe this!" Brianna said with anger and disgust in her voice.

"What are you talkin' about? Believe what?"

"Melissa—she is back! Not only is that bitch back, but she is back with some sort of freaking attitude."

"Wait, Brie, calm down and fix yourself a drink. I'm on my way."

Brianna poured herself a double shot of Grey Goose. After a few sips, ironically, she did manage to calm down. *Think, Brianna, think.* She couldn't believe that she did not see that Maxwell was running some sort of game on her. But that was okay. Brianna—who was a nice, educated, and professional woman—knew how to rumble with the best of them when and if it was needed. She could go months or possibly years before seeking revenge on her prey. Now that she was older, she worked so hard to suffocate that part of her. However, today was the day to resuscitate that personality trait. She sat pondering, thinking about who she could possibly call to aid her in making Melissa's choice of coming there unbearable. Anyone that was in Brianna's circle had a purpose, even the one that she knew had betrayed her. She kept them close. Today was the day that she would be pulling "B" out the back of the closet and calling in all favors when needed. Of course, this would be the side that Tamika loved! The side that paid a couple of thugs to beat a little sense into Angel's long-lost boyfriend when they found out he was beating on her. Brianna gulped down her drink and was about to make herself another one when an envelope fell off the edge of the coffee table onto the floor. Taking the smaller envelop to open first, she opened it to find a bonus check of $2,000. Brianna was not impressed, and when she opened the other envelope containing information informing her that she was now relieved from all her clients, her blood began to boil. These were clients from top corporations in Richmond that she had sought after, schmoozed, and secured on her own. Now Melissa would be handling them, and Brianna would only contact vendors for delivery times and follow up for problems as if she was some sort of customer service representative. Brianna's pay was now hourly instead of salary.

Oh, so now I am an assistant? The company would still be planning birthday parties and retirement parties if it wasn't for me. Natalie, you are so stupid if you think I am going to put up with this.

Brianna's thoughts were interrupted by the doorbell. Upon answering the door, Tamika went straight to the freezer to get ice, then to the bar and poured herself a drink. Brianna immediately began to fill her in on the infamous meeting.

"Natalie purchased the agency and Melissa is a partner!"

"Huh?"

"Oh, you heard me, but it gets better! Melissa is married to Maxwell, and they have a little boy together who is seven years old!"

"Wait! Her last name is King? Are you sure you heard this right?"

"Yes, I heard it loud and clear. Maxwell King is her husband!"

"Shut up, Brie! And get the hell out of here. If the child is seven years old, then that means that she was pregnant when you guys were together!" Tamika could see the hurt in Brianna's eyes. She immediately moved beside her and gave her a hug. "Brie, I am so sorry."

"You know what, Tamika, don't feel sorry for me. Just help me get revenge."

"Brie, you know I got you."

Brianna went on to tell her word for word the things that Melissa said. Tamika was shocked and then interrupted her. "Brie, do me a favor. Do not react to any of that garbage that was thrown at you today. Hold off from telling Angel any of this and do not, under any circumstances, call Phoebe."

"What? Why, Tamika?"

"Just don't for right now, just get some rest. I'll see you tomorrow." Tamika grabbed her purse and left very quickly. Brianna didn't know what to make of her requests, but she was now afraid for Melissa. There was no telling what she was up to.

It was about eight o'clock in the evening, and Brianna had the worst headache ever. She took a Xanax and turned off the television. When Brianna closed her eyes, her cell began to ring. It was Allan.

"Hi, Allan."

"Hey Miss, you sound a little down."

"It's been a really bad day."

"Damn, I thought that with all the surprises that I sent you this week, you would have been relaxed and upbeat?"

When Brianna heard him say that, she sat up immediately. In her mind, she had given Maxwell all the credit; Brianna had never once considered Allan.

"Sweetheart, you are the best! I wondered why you never mentioned or asked me about what was happening this week. Thank you, baby! In spite of what happened to me today, you still made my week." Brianna was secretly trying to make up for what might come across as unappreciative.

"You are more than welcome, Ms. Brianna. Babe, you never said what happened today?"

"Long story and really I do not want to talk about it anymore. But I should be asking you, how did the assignment go?" Brianna was trying to slickly change the subject.

"It went extremely well. I was able to initiate a new project. I had a conference call with the boss today, discussing the advancement of my career. I am so ready to catch a red-eye back and see my baby. On Saturday, I have an event to attend, and I would love to have you as my date. Do you have to work on Saturday?"

"Funny you should ask. Nope, I am still on vacation."

"Good, make plans to be on my arm at six o'clock. Do me a favor. Tomorrow go the Saks and locate a woman by the name of Alice McNeil. I told her to expect you by twelve noon."

"Why, Allan?"

"Baby, I have to go. My car to the airport is here. I will talk to you later."

Before Brianna could say goodbye, he hung up. She was smiling and could not believe that Allan was really dedicated to "showing" her that he can make things right.

It's Friday morning, and Brianna's awakening, as always, could be attributed to her phone. It was Tamika and Angel on the same call.

"Gooooood morning, sunshine!" they sang out simultaneously.

"What?" Brianna was groggy from the previous day that was, to say the least, emotionally draining.

"Wake up, girlie. It's Angel and Tamika!"

"Why are both of you calling me at the same time?"

"Brianna, I told Angel everything that went on yesterday," Tamika interjected.

"Brie, I was completely shocked when Tamika filled me in. I am so sorry."

"Angel, don't worry about it," Brianna warmly responded. She knew that these two girls have her back.

"Tamika also told me not to discuss anything with Phoebe, and I won't. Oddly enough, I am doing lunch with her today."

"You are?" Brianna was confused since she had not seen Phoebe since the night at the club.

"Girl, I told you that Phoebe is being a little shady lately. I want Angel to listen and act completely clueless about anything and everything."

"Okay, but Tamika, you are going to clue me in on what you're doing, right?" Brianna asked her.

"Yeah, just give me until Sunday."

Angel, a willing participant to whatever Tamika was planning, complied. "I will be sure to give you guys a call after my lunch with her. Talk to you both later."

When they all got off the phone, Brianna noted the time; it was 9:30 AM. She remembered that Allan had scheduled her a special visit to Saks; the thought of her favorite store put a small smile on her face. Minus getting ready for work, she paced out her morning's routine to accommodate today's agenda. When hopping into her SUV, she noticed how crazily she had parked in her garage. Having to back out slowly, she could only laugh and shake her head. Finally arriving at Saks, she asked one of the salespeople if they could assist her in connecting her with Alice McNeil.

"Ms. McNeil is in the executive offices. Wait here and I will call her office," the nice lady responded.

"Her office? Is she one of the supervisors here?"

"No, ma'am. She is the general manager of the store, soon to be regional."

Brianna was quite puzzled, but she went along with it.

What is Mr. Jones up to? she questioned in her mind.

"Ma'am, your name please?"

"Oh yes, Brianna Godfrey."

"Yes, it is Ms. Godfrey. Okay. I will let her know that you will be right out."

In matter of a few minute, a very fashion-forward Caucasian woman was walking toward her. She was slim and appeared to be five feet and ten inches, 115 pounds in her late fifties. Her black hair was beautifully highlighted with one chunk of well-kept gray in front, neatly pulled back in a sleek, long ponytail. With a chic black dress, she wore a long Chanel pearl necklace, simple makeup with a notable Russian Red lipstick. Ms. McNeil's look was stunning.

"Would you be the lovely Ms. Godfrey?"

"Yes, I am, and you are Mrs. McNeil?"

"I am. So nice to meet you. Please follow me," she said with a pleasant smile while escorting Brianna into the fitting room. She stared at Brianna's body and took her measurements quickly. "You know, Ms. Godfrey, you are working with more curves than these little runway models we see these days."

Brianna didn't know if she needed to cuss this woman out or just leave. "I beg your pardon?" Brianna tried not to be rude but was not smiling at her slick comment. Mrs. McNeil could detect a little resentment from what she had just said with no malice intended.

"No, sweetheart, the curves are not a bad thing. You have a realistic body. I just wish that designers knew a thing or two about being realistic. Nonetheless, Allan gave me pretty accurate measurements."

"He did? How do you exactly know Allan?" Brianna asked.

"He works for my husband. My husband is quite impressed with him." Mrs. McNeil was now removing a lovely dress from a garment bag.

"But Allan works in Washington, DC? Do your husband commute from Richmond?" Brianna asked, being extremely curious.

"No, I do. I enjoy the quiet time in the car, or sometimes, I stay here in Richmond for a couple nights or weeks. Here, I had some alterations done. I believe this will fit you perfectly. Brianna looked at the dress and let out a mini scream. It was the dress she had seen in the *Vogue* magazine, the pleated Italian silk Oscar de la Renta Doupionoi dress. After slipping it on, she was in love with it.

"Well, judging by the look on your face, you love it?"

"Yes, yes! I really do. Did he pick this out?"

"You can say that, but with my guidance," Mrs. McNeil laughed.

"Well, thank you, Mrs. McNeil! Your guidance was dead-on!"

"You can call me Alice, and you are welcome. Get dress, we have one more departmental stop to make."

Brianna got dressed and met Alice outside the fitting room. She followed Alice's long strides to the jewelry department. Brianna could tell that she was with the woman in charge because everyone was attentive to her every wish and step.

"Franklin, this is Ms. Brianna Godfrey, please get the two packages that has her name on them, one being a jewelry box and the other is a shoe box. Thank you." With a smile and quick steps, he came back with the packages. "Brianna, he asks that you do not open the jewelry package until nine tonight, when he calls you.

"What?" Brianna was asked.

"Just do as he says and I will see you soon," she said while giving Brianna a warm hug.

When Brianna was approaching her vehicle from the left side, there it was, a long scrape. *What have I done?* When she got closer, Brianna could not contain her outburst of laughter. *Am I trippin' or what? Who cares! That explains how I got my car in my garage at that crazy angle!* When she finally got home from all the extra wonderful surprises, she was able to take a long nap until six o'clock. Checking her phone, there were not any missed calls from the girls. She called both of them, but it went straight to both of their voice mails. Later, around 8:59 PM her cell began to ring. It was Allan.

"Hi, baby!" Brianna said with the biggest smile.

"Well, hey, you sound happy!" Allan said, already feeling quite pleased with himself.

"Baby, I wish you could come over, like, right now! I really want to thank you!" Brianna sounded like she was a big kid at Christmas.

"Really! I was going to wait to see you tomorrow because I wanted to put some finishing touches on my report, but it can wait. If I head out now, I can be there in two hours."

"Oh, baby, no. I can't let you do that. I can wait to properly thank you tomorrow. Thank you for the dress and the Louboutins. Now, what's in the smaller box?"

"Well, that's why I am calling you, darling. I wanted to hear you when you opened it up."

"Don't you think that you should be here to give it to me in person?"

Allan started laughing. "Slow down, partner. It's not like that. It's not an engagement ring." The way he said it actually made Brianna laugh as well.

"Okay, knucklehead, I am opening it." There was silence for about twenty seconds. Finally, she let out a loud scream. Allan had to pull the phone away for a quick second to keep his eardrum intact.

"Brie, the ring is for you to wear with your dress tomorrow!" It was a David Yurman eighteen-karat modern cushion ring, with the stone that matched her dress perfectly.

"Okay. I can't wait to see you!"

"Good night, baby. I can't wait to see you too!"

CHAPTER TEN

Gala

Brianna just hung up with Allan; he was informing her that he would be in Richmond by 4:00 PM. She was delighted to hear that because his timing would allow her to run a few errands. She would go check out the Dominican hair salon and meet Angel and Tamika at Starbucks. When she reached Starbucks, the girls were pulling in at the same time.

"What the hell happened to your truck?" Tamika asked, closely examining it.

Angel was concerned as well. "Brianna, did that just happened?"

"That, my darlings, happened the *Great Day of Melissa*. I think I was picturing her face on the side of my garage door," Brianna nonchalantly answered. The girls went in, ordered, and began catching up. "Okay, ladybugs, whatcha know good?" Brie asked.

"Well, as you know, I had lunch with Ms. Phoebe. She was acting really strange. I think she was definitely trying to pick me for information about you, Brie. However, I told her that I haven't been able to spend a lot of time with you either. I told her that I had to reconcile a rather-large financial deal and that the success of it was riding on my shoulders. Due to overseeing it, I could not spend any time with either one of you girls."

"Really? Interesting," they both commented.

"She began to tell me how busy she's been as well. What threw me for a loop was when she said she was tired of being around a lot of phony people. I asked her who she was she referring to. She then said that I should know who she was talking about. I told her that I had no idea. She rolled her eyes and dropped the subject."

"Huh!" Tamika grunted.

"She kept the conversation moving by asking if anyone in the group have been dating anyone new, or better yet, has any old flames been coming around?" Angel said with one raised eyebrow looking at Brianna.

"Oh, this trick is trying to see if you have been hollering at ole' boy, Brie," Tamika said as if she was ready to beat Phoebe down.

"Yeah, that's what she is doing. Girls, you know what? Come to think of it, when Melissa and I were arguing at the office, the secretary interrupted to tell her that there was a Ms. Steele on the phone for her."

"What? What is going on?" Angel was beyond confused.

"But wait one damn minute! Brianna, do you remember when we went to the club and I told you that I heard a voice that I slightly recognized? The person in the fitting room asked the person on the phone if *she* knew that they were going to be their new boss."

"Oh my god, it was Melissa!" Brianna said as if she was blown away and disgusted.

"You mean those heifers have been plotting the whole time?" Angel could not believe it. "Well, looks like we have some catching up to do with that Phoebe!"

"Ladies, I am already ahead of you. Brianna, you have a wonderful evening with Allan tonight. You need to be prepared for any changes they are trying to make with your future employment with them. If need be, start downloading some of your contacts. How about we get together next week to discuss this a little more? I got to run." She gave the girls a kiss and jetted out the door.

"Sounds like her wheels are turning, huh?" Angel said with a smile.

Brianna agreed while shaking her head, "It sure does, Angel. It sure does."

After the coffee shop, Brianna hurried home to beat Allan. Upon her arrival, her phone began to ring, and she answered without looking at the caller ID. She figured that Allan was calling to inform her of his whereabouts.

"Hello," Brianna said cheerfully.

"Hi, butterfly."

There was a fifteen-second pause before Brianna responded, "What the hell do you want, Maxwell!"

"We need to talk. Can we get together and discuss this? I can explain."

Brianna could hear something in his voice that she had never heard before. It was the sound of desperation. "My name is Brianna, not butterfly! You are damn straight. You definitely need to explain yourself. I guess I fell in love with a lie! And now you want me to listen to more of your fabrications? You know what? I don't have anything to say to you right now! SCREW YOU, MAX!" Brianna hung up the phone. Her heart was racing. She was so furious that she began pacing and fussing out loud as if she was still speaking with him. "Negro, you are trip! You think that you can just waltz back into my life and get what you want? Once I figure this out, I am definitely coming after you and your wife!"

The sound of the doorbell interrupted her fuming. Before answering the door, she took a few deep breaths. It was Allan standing there looking cleanly shaven, dressed in a Ralph Lauren Polo shirt, crisp blue jeans with a little sag, and a pair of Kenneth Cole brown leather driving shoes. His perfectly shaped baldhead, silk chocolate complexion with those pearly white teeth almost looked better than a million dollars. She was so relieved to see him that she planted a long, deep kiss on him. Forty-five minutes after greeting him at the door, Brianna was getting out of the bed looking for her robe. Allan, who came up her behind her, assisted her by tying up her robe. He looked up and caught her glimpse in the mirror; they gave each other a big smile.

"Brianna, if that was my thank-you, then baby, you are so welcome."

Brianna turned to face him, gave him a tight hug and warm kiss. "Allan, you never told me what was the end result of your trip to California, and you never told me where we are exactly going tonight."

"Well, honey, I got the promotion. I am lead department chief at Homeland Securities." Allan was smiling ear to ear like a little kid.

"What, baby! Congratulations." After she hugged him again, she gave him a fist bump. Allan was tickled by that. "Yeah, boy!"

"Girl, you are so sexy and so silly! Real talk, Brianna, I want us to hang in there together. Let's work on us. Are you ready to see where this goes?"

Brianna could see the seriousness in his eyes. A part of her was afraid and a part of her wanted to jump right into giving them a chance. "Allan, I will give us a try, but should things start falling apart and I see that you are not trying, I will walk away. No explanation and no drama."

"Brianna, that's fair. The answer to your second question, we are going to the Cancer Society gala tonight."

A sudden nervousness came over Brianna. This was the major assignment that Brianna was released from overseeing. Did she really want to see Natalie and that evil Melissa?

"Brianna, what's that strange look on your face? Do you not want to go?" Allan was really thrown by her reaction. She decided to only tell Allan a portion of the truth concerning her connection to this event.

"Allan, that is the event that the agency oversaw putting together. Needless to say, I did all of the work, but they have now decided that they do not need my assistance. I believe that this decision is due to the shift in the new ownership at our company. One of the owners just happens to be one of my former college friends. This 'ex' friend, in a nutshell, has basically demoted me and will now take all of the glory tonight."

"That's a joke. She will not take anything away from my baby. Now let's whip up something to eat—I am starving." Allan kissed her on the forehead and led her to the kitchen. After preparing a small bite and relaxing, they decided to get ready.

CHAPTER ELEVEN

All Lights on Me

"Are you ready, Brianna?" Allan yelled from downstairs. "We are running thirty minutes late."

"Honey, sometimes to be late is fashionable," Brianna yelled down.

When he turned around to respond, she was at the top of the stairs. "Brianna Monique Godfrey, you look absolutely beautiful. I cannot wait to show you off!"

When they cut through the garage to get in his car, he stopped abruptly. "Brianna, what happened to the side of your SUV?"

"Just bad parking skills," she chuckled. The drive to the science museum was short, and parking was a little crazy but that was a good sign. Once they arrived, you could see that all of the local television stations were there. The evening was in full effect. When they went into the event, they noticed that people were laughing and really enjoying themselves. The decorations were breathtaking; from the pink-colored ribbon ice sculpture, to the magnificent assortment of pink flowers and the fountains spewing pink-colored champagne. Not seeing Natalie or Melissa, Brianna started unconsciously checking things; she wanted to make sure that no one had altered any plans of execution. Some of the vendors came over to greet Brianna, reassuring her that they were all present and accounted for. However, the vendors did express concern. They were under the impression, from Brianna's agency, that she had resigned. Before going over to attend to Allan, she assured them that she would be explaining things a little later.

To dote on Brianna, Allan brought Alice and her husband over to where Brianna was standing. Alice immediately embraced Brianna, and Allan quickly introduced Mr. McNeil to her.

"Brianna, you look stunning. A lot of the women in here have been commenting on your dress," Alice said while giving a smile and a wink. "Brianna, why aren't you over there with the two ladies from your agency?" Allan had already filled her in, but she wanted to see if Brianna would explain it more.

"Well, I was told that I was not needed tonight, so I am going to hug the arm of my man and just stay in the background." Brianna was trying to seem as though she didn't care, but really, she did.

Alice was taken with Brianna's answer because she did not seize the opportunity to trash talk her new boss. "Well, Ms. Godfrey, yes, by all means, hold on to your man's arm, but please do not leave anytime soon," Alice said with a smile as she began to walk toward the front of the room.

The music started to quiet down and so did the three hundred people in attendance. The key speaker from the hospital got up to welcome everyone. He also announced they had raised five hundred thousand dollars, and with the various corporations who were present, they had reached their goal of raising one million dollars. After the loud roar of applause, the speaker introduced Alice as one of the key people on their chair for fund-raising.

"What? How did I not know that Alice was tied to this event?" she whispered to Allan.

"Baby, that woman is well connected in Richmond, as well as, Washington, DC. Don't sleep on her," Allan whispered back. Both of them diverted their attention to Alice as she stepped to the microphone.

"Good evening, ladies and gentlemen. Let me tell you how we, on the committee, are glad that each and every one of you are here. Helping us fight cancer is a great cause! Cancer is a silent but aggressive disease, and we must be just as aggressive to finding a permanent cure. Please do not let this be the only time you contribute to this cause. If it is in purchasing a special mug, T-shirt, or placing your change in a canister, please do not hesitate to do so.

"In our programs, you will see listed the names of the vendors that are present. Please take note, we recommend that you use them in any of your upcoming events. Also, I would like to recognize the event company that executed this wonderful affair on our behalf. The owners of Executive Meeting Solutions are here to the right of me, Mrs. Melissa King and Mrs. Natalie Stevenson." Everyone was clapping. Natalie and Melissa were smiling ear to ear, waving at the crowd.

"Last but certainly not least, I've experienced the pleasure of hearing about this young lady through other chair members. They were all stating how impressed they were with this person's eye for detail and her professionalism. When mentioning this young lady's name to various vendors in this area, they were more than happy to do extra in making this event a success. I would like for this wonderful person to join me on this stage. Please put your hands together for Ms. Brianna Godfrey, the meeting planner extraordinaire!"

The crowd began to applaud while turning around to see who she was speaking of; one of the vendors made way to escort her. Brianna wanted to melt; all eyes were on her. In Brianna's passing, she managed to steal a glimpse of Melissa and Natalie. While Natalie offered a pleasant smile, Melissa looked as if she was going to tackle her. When Brianna arrived on the stage, she was greeted by Alice with flowers and a hug. She whispered in her ear, "See, Brianna, no one is going to take your spotlight." She then turned to the crowd. "Ladies and gentlemen, enjoy the rest of your evening!"

The music resumed, and the people started to eat, drink, and mingle. A few people came over to introduce themselves to Brianna and to give her their business cards. When she proceeded to walk down the rest of the steps from the riser, Melissa managed to cut her off while holding Maxwell's hand.

"It's nice seeing you, Brianna, and good job," Maxwell said. Melissa was agitated, and it was more irritating to hear her husband pay her accolades too! She quickly interrupted, "Maxwell dear, can you get me something to drink? I am feeling a little dizzy."

62

Maxwell, at that moment, looked very annoyed with her request. Brianna decided to look as though she did not detect his slight attitude. "Sure," he said as he glared at her.

"Brianna, I did not know that you were going to be here tonight. Oh well, did you get a chance to look over your new job duties?" Melissa was grinning from ear to ear. She was hoping that she was getting under Brianna's skin.

"I didn't know that I would be attending either, but my presence was requested and, yes, to your second question," Brianna said with a wink. It was important to show Melissa she was not fazed by her obvious pettiness.

"What are your thoughts, Brianna?"

"I have none. Your lovely husband is approaching us with your drink. I hope you feel better soon, Mrs. King."

If Melissa's eyes were dagger, Brianna would have been bleeding all over the place. However, what stopped Maxwell in his tracks was Allan's loving approach from behind Brianna. He wrapped his arms around her, planting a sweet kiss on the back of her neck. Melissa was pissed because she could see that Maxwell was upset by his display of affection.

"Melissa and Maxwell, meet Allan Jones, the love of my life."

Allan shook both of their hands. "Nice to meet you both. Baby, Alice and the hospital's chief surgeon would like to see you."

"Okay, sweetheart. Melissa, again, I hope you can shake your *dizziness*. Maxwell, have a good evening."

As the night progressed, Brianna was networking with the best of Richmond; her bedazzled purse was filling with business cards. Alice also would pull her in from time to time to take photographs. Brianna, who lost Allan, was trying to nudge her way through the crowd when she felt a hand pull her around a wall that was near an exit.

What is Allan doing?

With people kind of still in the way, she never looked up. When she finally made it around to the slightly dark hidden corridor, he pulled her close and kissed her passionately. Upon opening her eyes, she could not believe them—it was Maxwell. Anger surprisingly took a hold of her, and she was about to slap him; he caught her hand and placed a note in it.

"Girl, I know you were not about to bitch slap a bother. Don't believe that stuff you see on television," he chuckled. Brianna was about to laugh herself, but she was successful in keeping a serious face.

"Look, Maxwell, play games with someone else or, better yet, your wife! You two are fucking unbelievable. Why can't you both go back to hell where you both belong?" Brianna pulled away from him, leaving him standing there. At this point, she could not trust Melissa or Maxwell in the same room. She would convince Allan to call it a night. As she was searching through the crowd, there he was staring directly at her. The look on his face was intense, and it made her feel extremely nervous. *Shit, did he see us? This cannot be happening!* When she got close to him, he whispered in her ear, "I saw you."

"What?" Brianna's heart felt as though it had stopped beating.

"I saw you looking for me. Baby, I want to take you now. You look so good."

Brianna's heart must have received a signal that it was okay for it to start beating again. She smiled at him and they both left. When they got in the car, he popped in his CD with EnVogue belting out, "Don't Let Go." Brianna looked over and gave a smile.

"What's with the big smile?" Allan asked while smiling back.

"Just a smile hopefully telling you that I can't wait to get you home!" Little did he know that it was a smile filled with partial guilt and happiness. She was happy that she had not been found with Maxwell around that wall and guilty because, inside, she wanted another kiss from Maxwell.

"I like that, baby. It sounds good when you say you can't wait to get me *home*."

Upon arriving in the condo, Brianna's alter ego came out. Instead of the sweet and professional Brianna, she switched gears. She became a private stripper, Ms. Black Champagne.

She pushed him down on the sofa and hit the remote to CD player. It started to play "Close to You" by Dreezy. She slowly removed her dress, letting it slide onto the floor. Stepping out of the dress, she stood there in her thigh-high hosiery with the sexy lace-top; her thick legs looked stunning in her pumps. Her strapless black bra and full-laced black panties were absolutely gorgeous. Allan sat back, biting on his bottom lip with half of a smile; he was watching with great anticipation for her next move. While the song was playing, she straddled him, gyrating her hips and planting moist kisses on him at the same time. Allan was getting excited; this was the aggressive side of Brianna that he had never seen before. After helping him slip out his jacket, she began undoing his bow tie and removing his dress shirt. When he raised his arms to slip of his T-shirt, she allowed her tongue and teeth to stimulate his nipples. She knew that he was craving her badly. She hopped off him, turned around, and gave him a lap dance holding and guiding his hand up and down her body. He managed to slip his finger in her treasure box, which he discovered was dripping wet.

"Baby, stop teasing. Let me hit that," he moaned in her ear. She removed his fingers and sucked them.

"No, tonight is your night. Let me take care of you. Just sit back and enjoy it, baby." She continued to stimulate him. She went from kissing him to gently biting him on his lips, neck, and chest. Brianna undid his pants, allowing him to wiggle them down so she could savor his manly treat. She gave him a devious smile when his next favorite song called, "Please Me," started playing. He smiled back at her; she began *blowing* his mind. She grabbed his swollen and throbbing manhood. Placing it deeper in her mouth, she began to suck him like a malnourished cub that had been deprived for months. Allan began to moan and groan, "Damn, Brianna, represent, baby!" It got so good that his hands went from the arms on the chair, to pulling back her hair to see her face. This had got to be the best head he had ever received in his life, and he wanted to stare at the face that made this all possible. "Wait, Brianna! Stop! I am about to cum!" he said breathlessly.

"Baby, what's stopping you!" She winked and then went back to servicing him like never before. Allan didn't know what to think, but it was so good that he wasn't going to tell her to stop this time. He began to shake like he was about to have a seizure. When it was all over, he went limp. He couldn't believe what just happened. He would never want to do something to her sexually that she didn't agree with, but when he looked at her, he saw her take the back of her hand and wipe her mouth. Then she smiled.

"Baby, I am tired. If you can make it up the stairs, let's go to bed."

Allan had one eyebrow raised. He was amazed at her swag. "Oh, it's like that? Damn, baby! Whatever you want."

CHAPTER TWELVE

Make It Last Forever

On his drive back home on Sunday, Allan and Brianna spoke on their phones for what seemed like two hours. As she was speaking, she could not help but stare at the photo of the two of them from the gala. She was mesmerized; they absolutely made a stunning couple. After their conversation, she wanted to take a long bubble bath and enjoy a little television. In tossing her clutch that she carried last night onto the bed, the note from Maxwell had fallen out. She opened the note that was written on a napkin.

> *You look so beautiful! Please give me a call at this number, 202-555-3451. Everything you are seeing is not what it truly looks like! Talk to me.*

She didn't throw the note away, but placed it in the nightstand. While lying back in her sunken tub, listening to the song called "The Worst" by Jhene' Aiko, she closed her eyes and began thinking about the kiss that Maxell had planted on her at the gala. Brianna's heart sent a message in the form of an impromptu tear streaming down her face. It saddened her that she still harbored love for the man that stole her heart. *Where did the anger go? He wronged me, so why the fuck am I crying?* She couldn't help but reminisce about her and Max's first date.

Four weeks after meeting Maxwell at the club in DC, she finally decided to go out with him. Brianna had scored wonderfully on her economics exam and was feeling quite proud of herself. Normally, she and Melissa would go out to the Pentagon Mall to do a little celebratory shopping, but this time, she decided to settle for a celebratory nap. Melissa was still missing in action from the whole craziness that went on that one particular night. It was as if Melissa had fallen off the face of the earth. The rumor was that she had moved back to Miami, but Brianna, feeling taken for granted as friend, did not care to investigate. In the meantime, she kept blowing off Maxwell only because it was the girlfriend's unspoken rule. If you knew that your girl had a liking for a certain guy, that meant hands-off. However, since Melissa did not care enough about their friendship, then all bets were off. She decided to give Maxwell a chance.

As promised by Maxwell, a car was sent to pick her up by six thirty. Her hair was hanging down, and she wore a cute short sundress that had a halter top. Since she did not know where this date was taking her, she decided not to wear extremely high heels. The guys coming into the apartment building found Brianna very sexy and did not waste any time today in letting her know. Of course, it was all in fun. The guys knew that they were not ready for a classy act like Brianna. The driver got out the car to greet her and presented her with white roses before opening her door. Once they were both in the car, she asked him where he was taking her.

"Ma'am, I was told to keep that confidential. However, he asked that you give him a call once you were in the car."

"Oh, okay." Brianna dialed his number; he picked up his phone immediately.

"Hi, Brianna, I am glad that you are on your way," Maxwell said, being full of energy.

"Hello, Maxwell. Yes, sir, I am on my way, but where am I going?"

"Can't tell you that, baby girl, but you should be here in about thirty minutes or so. See you then." So he wouldn't have to answer any additional questions, Maxwell disconnected the call abruptly; she thought that was a pretty slick and funny move. When the car finally stopped, she found herself in front of the Marriott Hotel.

What? I know this brother don't think it's like that?

The driver came around to let her out. "Ms. Godfrey, this way please."

Once inside of the hotel, Maxwell appeared. The driver shook Maxwell's hand after an envelope was exchanged; she suspected that Maxwell was paying the driver for his services. The driver looked at Brianna, smiled, and wished her a good evening. Maxwell turned to Brianna to give her a big hug, but she stopped him cold in his tracks.

"Mr. King, I am very delighted to spend an evening with you; however, I am looking at our current environment. I do believe that you may have the wrong idea about me." Brianna kept a very stern look on her face to show him that she wasn't some easy little trick. Maxwell thought that was too funny and started to laugh immediately. This man was not just sexy but appeared to be a mover and a shaker. Not only was he easy on the eyes, but very smart. This former captain of his soccer team graduated with honors from University in Miami, just a year ago. Not being sure of his exact ethnicity, you could tell that he was not 100 percent black, but oddly enough, there was no trace of an accent. His swagger was absolutely incredible, borderline intoxicating. For a woman to basically say that she had no intentions of sleeping with him was new and refreshing.

"Well, laugh all you want, Mr. King, but I hope you know you will find the rest of the night just as entertaining when we are still just talking three hours from now," Brianna said with delightful sarcasm.

"Dang, girl, I hear you loud and clear. Well, we are going to catch the elevator up to the suite. Please know that I have no plans of taking advantage of you. Feel free to keep your cell phone in your hands at all times," he said while still chuckling at her. When they reached the suite, there were white rose petals outside the doors. As soon as they walked in, the sweet aroma of flowers met her. There they were again, beautiful display of white roses lined up around the perimeter of the room. White candles were lit throughout the suite to enhance the ambiance; she blushed with amazement.

"Oh, Maxwell, this is beautiful," she gushed out.

Maxwell pulled her over to the sofa and indicated for her to have a seat. Once she was seated, he handed her a glass of champagne. Next, he made way past a few chairs with what looked like music stands in front of each one. He knocked on what looked like a bedroom door and indicated that he was ready; coming back quickly, he proudly took a seat beside her and gave her another wink. Brianna nervously watched to see who or what was coming from behind the door. It was four people all carrying musical instruments. The next thing was wonderful; the people, who ranged in age and ethnicity, began to play the latest R&B songs in orchestra form. From Trey songs, Ne-Yo to Usher, it was being played by the most outstanding musicians. Once the talent left, they had effortless ongoing conversations.

His mother came from as wealthy family in Cuba, and his father came from a struggling, hardworking family in Haiti. His mother's family did not approve of her relationship with his father. His parents eloped once they found out that she was pregnant. Unfortunately, she became very ill during her pregnancy, and his father knew it to be best to take her back home. However, when his mother's family found out about the pregnancy, shockingly they accepted the pregnancy but not the father. In taking his mother back home, his grandfather had his mother's marriage annulled. After Maxwell was born, his father continued to have many brushes with the law, which, as a result, affected his relationship with him. The father would only see him maybe once or twice every month.

On the other end of the spectrum, Brianna came from an upper middle-class family. Her father worked as an engineer, and her mother was a college professor; her families were devout Christians who only hoped that Brianna would not stray in life. What she and Maxwell only had in common was that neither one of them had no siblings.

They did so much talking that they did not notice that it was now two o'clock in the morning.

"Maxwell, I really need to get going," Brianna said with a little regret in her voice.

"Do you have class tomorrow?" Maxwell asked while looking as if he wanted to shake his head no for her.

"No, but I need to study for my foreign language exam."

"Well, baby, you are in luck! I am fluent in Spanish and French, so take your pick. I can help you study. Look, Brianna, it's late, and this suite is paid for—plus there are two rooms." It totally flew over Brianna's head that this brother could possibly be bilingual.

"Maxwell, didn't I say that I was not going to sleep with—?"

"Slow your roll, ma. I haven't so much as kissed you or put my hands where you *want* them," Max said to her while laughing.

"What? Okay, Mr. King, you have jokes!" Brianna responded while laughing at him. "Look, little man, I'll take the larger room, and you, Mr. King, can take the smaller one." He laughed at her "little man" joke, and both agreed to retire as they both began to notice they were getting equally tired.

"Okay, girl, I guess I'll see you in the morning," he said while looking into her eyes.

"I guess so and thank you. This is the nicest thing that anyone has ever done for me."

Right before he could tell her that she was welcome, she planted a sweet kiss on his lips and gave him a playful wink. The next thing he saw her do was close the door to her room. Thankfully, she had worn a cute little cami-and-panty set under her dress, so she was able to sleep comfortably versus going to bed fully clothed or nude.

About fifteen minutes later, she heard three light taps at her door. She rolled over to look, noticing Maxwell walking into her room. He had only his Lacoste boxers on, exposing his tattooed chest and well-chiseled biceps. His dreads were long and hanging almost down to his waist. He came over to the bed, looking down at her.

"Baby, it's not about sex. I just want to lay with you and hold you. I promise, that is all."

At that moment, she didn't see Maxwell as this suave player, but as this gentle and caring man. "That's fine, Maxwell." She pulled backed the cover to let him get in, laying her head on his chest. Maxwell wrapped his arms around her and gently kissed her on her forehead.

He whispered to her before they both drifted off to sleep, "You are the one. You are my beautiful black butterfly."

Brianna, while still in the tub, began to wash her tears from her face. *Maxwell, when I think I can handle talking to you, trust, oh, I will be calling your treacherous ass! You most definitely owe me an explanation!*

CHAPTER THIRTEEN

Pushed Out of the Nest

On Monday morning, there was absolutely no one smiling in the office, under the new regimen. "Hey, Ms. Godfrey!" Peter said in his usual flamboyant manner. He got up from his desk to slow her down.

"Good morning, Peter. You are looking quite fabulous this morning." He was the only guy that could rock a pair of lavender pants with a white, lavender, and orange argyle sweater accompanied by a bow tie.

"Thank you, girl!" Peter began lightly, pulling at her elbow.

"What's going on, Peter?" She finally noticed that Peter wanted to prepare her for something.

"As you know, Mrs. King is in here and making it known, girl! Let's just say that your office is no longer your office. Your chic office is now being occupied with another body."

"What? Are you kidding me? Am I sharing an office with someone? Please don't tell me I am sharing an office with Melissa."

"No, girl, you are sharing *space.* You will be out here with me. I had to come in yesterday and move all your personal effects out here. I heard Natalie trying to convince her not to do it. Melissa wasn't trying to hear that. She said that with your new job duties, you could be out here with me. I'm so sorry, girl."

"Don't worry about it. Just show me to my desk." Brianna was fuming on the inside, but she was going to play it calm; she was only hoping to get under Melissa's skin. Brianna sat at her desk and began going through her messages and e-mails. Most of her accounts had been either taken over by Melissa or reassigned to other planners.

It was so apparent that Melissa was phasing her out. However, the e-mail that got under Brianna's skin was the one telling her that she needed to leave today in order to meet with vendors in Washington, DC, first thing tomorrow morning. She glanced at the clock and it was already 11:30 AM. *What happened to properly informing people ahead of time!* Brianna was so consumed with irritation that she didn't notice Melissa standing over her.

"Well, good morning, Brianna! I see that you are getting settled into your new location." Melissa was smirking while waiting for Brianna's response.

Brianna was too annoyed to play her little games. "Melissa, I just checked my e-mails, and it seems as though you are having me travel to DC today, to meet with vendors?"

"Seeing that you do not have any children, Brianna, you were the convenient choice. Have Peter make reservations at a hotel for you. Feel absolutely free to leave now."

"Melissa, I have a list of highly recommended vendors that I already work with, and there is no reason to take this trip."

"Look, Brianna, if you are going to have a problem with every assignment that I give you, then we are going to have a talk about your future here!"

"You know what, Melissa? I do not have any problems with this assignment."

"Good, Brianna. I'll see you back on Wednesday." Melissa's smile was one of victory and dominance.

Brianna furiously began to export her to-do list from her desktop into her smartphone. She also took it upon herself to take the information of her top old and new clients—no game plan—but just she knew she just needed to hold onto that information. She gave Allan a call to let him know that she would be up his way for a few days, but he informed her that he was about to catch a flight out to Philadelphia for the week, on business. He assured her that he would spend time with her over the weekend. She continued to work in the office until noon, after which she went back home to pack a duffle bag. Peter made her reservations at the JW Marriott, and she was able to check in by 7:00 PM. She charged her laptop and took a

74

hot shower. On her phone, she had one missed call and immediately hit redial.

"This is Alice McNeil speaking."

Thank God, Brianna thought.

"Hi, Alice, it's Brianna!"

"Hi, sweetheart! I am on my way to a late dinner meeting, and this cell phone of mine has been ringing nonstop, so I apologize for not leaving you a message. I was calling to see if you would be able to help me put together another benefit, but here in DC?"

"Sure, when is the..."

Alice sounded as though she was driving and multitasking; she interjected, not noticing that she was cutting off Brianna's response. "Also, my husband's fifty-fifth birthday is coming up, and I wanted to do something for him on the grand side. That event, I would like to host in Richmond, not here in DC. If your schedule permits, I was hoping that you could possibly take that job too? I tried calling you at work this morning, but Melissa something or another insisted on me leaving a message with her. I didn't want to do that, so I called Allan and he gave me your number. He also informed me that you are actually here. I hope it was okay that he shared this information with me?

"Alice, that is totally fine and I would be more than happy to help you. However, I must tell you that the agency has taken a lot of my planning duties away." Brianna was so embarrassed saying that to a person with such social clout as Alice.

"That's absurd! We will talk. In the meantime, figure out what you are going to call your new company. Brianna, you don't need them—they need you. We'll have lunch tomorrow. Talk to you later, sweetheart."

Brianna hadn't thought about starting her own company with all the unexpected chaos going on. She knew that tomorrow had to be a productive day; Alice had triggered many entrepreneurial thoughts. Tomorrow she would begin working on branding herself. She threw on her sweats and ordered room service, not leaving out a delicious vodka and tonic.

All while enjoying her gourmet burger, she diligently worked on her laptop, brainstorming with the thoughts of her own company. By now, it was 9:00 PM. She decided to kick back, relax a little, and of course, give her girls a quick call to tell them of Melissa's wonderful plays from her book of petty. Once done, she could not fight her body's need for sleep. Finally, she closed her eyes. About forty minutes into her late-night nap, the sound of the hotel phone startled her. Partially out of breath, she answered the phone.

"Hello?"

"Don't be mad. It's me. Can you come down, or can I come up?"

"Max, is that you?"

"Yes. Can you come down to the lobby?"

Glancing at the clock, noticing the time, she became very annoyed, "Maxwell, it is twelve midnight, and I have a big day tomorrow. Your lovely wife thought it would be entertaining to send me up here without any freaking notice!"

"I'm sorry, baby. Will it be okay if I came up to your room?"

Brianna knew that he was not going to accept no for an answer. "Sure, Max, I am in room 747, and trust me, nothing is popping off when you get up here!" Brianna found herself ready to finally hear this so-called explanation.

"Okay, I will be right up."

Brianna ran into the bathroom to brush her teeth and to check her ponytail; thank goodness, she had fallen asleep in a T-shirt and sweats. She applied just a little matte lipstick and waited for him.

Finally, the telling moment, there was a light knock at the door; the nerves began to kick in because her first true love was at the door. Once she let him, her questioning began. "Max, how did you know where to find me? I am more than sure that Mrs. King would be beside herself if she knew that you were here," she said while walking away from the door. She plopped onto the bed and kick at the chair, indicating for him to have a seat.

"When I was speaking to Melissa on the phone earlier today, she told me to hold on. I heard her discussing your whereabouts with Peter. I didn't know exactly what hotel so I had to do some calling around to actually find you. I was in Delaware closing a deal, so she thinks that I am still there tonight. I am not due back in Richmond until Friday." He finally took a seat. "Brianna, I do not know where to start. I had no control in this situation. Melissa was a part of a puzzle that my father needed to continue his wealth. I was instructed to befriend Melissa because my father wanted her father to be his personal lawyer. That night at the club, I was given a picture of Melissa so I could seek her out. All she knew was that her father's friend wanted us to meet, but what wasn't the plan was me meeting and falling in love with you."

"Maxwell, what book did you get this shit out of or, should I ask, what movie?" Her blood was boiling at this point.

"Baby, what? This didn't come from some fucking movie, Brianna! Listen, where do you think I got all of that money to spoil you?"

"Fuck the money, Max! Did you have to play me? Now what, both of you want to come back and rub my face in it?"

"Brianna, don't get it twisted! I did those things because I love you and I could. You thought that what? The loot I was dropping on you wasn't coming from me punching a clock."

Brianna could hear the plea in his voice, hoping that she would understand what he was saying. "Think about it! I really never told you any extra details about my family. Truth be told, my father uses me all the time. He sent me to college not just to learn, but to network. I had to seek out the wealthy kids and work my way into those circles. I would pay attention to their parents, seeing if they had money-hungry parents who were looking to make more money. I kept a high GPA, played soccer and sometimes golf, anything to keep me bonding with certain types of students. My father didn't want to be some sort of common drug lord. He wanted to get his hands in real estate and stocks. Now remember, Brianna, I just told you, what it is that Melissa's father does for a living?"

"Something about him being a lawyer!"

"He is a *prominent* corporate lawyer, Brianna. The feds were on to my father for illegal trading of stocks while forcing people to sell their most-desired pieces of real estate. Now getting to Melissa, you met her at Howard?"

"Of course, I did, so what's your point?"

"I am more than sure that she told you that she graduated from the University of Miami. My father made her father a deal that he could not refuse. Her father was able to start up his own law firm with established, filthy rich clients being handed to him. However, Melissa's father wanted assurance that my father would not send him up the river should this deal not work out. The assurance would be that my father was in it completely by being tied to him. A marriage between Melissa and myself would keep both parties linked and invested. To take down one is to take down the other. One pay, all pays. Mr. Myers keeps the feds away and the IRS off his transactions—all is well. I was instructed to keep her happy and out of her father's hair!"

"Oh my god, you have got to be kidding me. I don't believe you!"

Maxwell got up and went into his wallet. He retrieved a photo, placing it onto the bed directly beside her. Brianna picked up the photo, and tears began to roll down her face. "Why are you showing me a picture of your family?"

"No, Brianna, look closely at the older man in the photo."

"Oh, this can't be! That's the thug that hit you the day we were in Miami together!" Brianna was stunned. "Why the hell is he in the picture?"

"Yeah, that was the morning of my wedding and that 'thug' is my father." Maxwell's eyes were filling with tears. "The night before, I told my father that I did not want to marry that girl. I also told him that I was unable to get him some information for a potential deal. I was tired, Brianna. I just wanted to spend time with you."

"Baby, I am so sorry. You basically left me assuming that you didn't care enough to give me an explanation as to why you walked out of my life." Brianna got up to give him a hug; however, the hug led to a kiss, and nothing at that point and time mattered. They both wanted to express to each other just how sorry they felt. She was sorry because she harbored so much pent-up anger toward him, not to mention she could only imagine how alone and isolated he must have felt. While still kissing, he slowly guided her back onto the bed. They both were sharing a tearful moment, one was letting go of a painful secret while the other embraced the secret. Neither one of them wanted to hurt anymore. He somehow managed to let her hair out of the ponytail and got her out of her T-shirt. Her firm breasts were fully exposed with the nipples being at full attention. It was as if her breasts were waiting to be greeted by his mouth. He sucked them gently, placing tender kisses lightly down to her stomach. The kisses were ever so passionate. She began to moan and cry softly. Maxwell began to undo the drawstring on her sweatpants.

"No, Maxwell, we can't," she whispered.

"Baby, please don't tell me no," he whispered back to her. He continued to kiss her on her neck and lips. "Why do you want me to stop?"

"I'm in a relationship, Maxwell."

Maxwell placed his finger in her lips. "You are in a relationship with Mr. Frat Boy and I am married. Tonight, just for tonight, I need to make love to you. I can have anything I want, but I need you, baby. I never stopped loving you." Maxwell finished removing her pants and went below to her pleasure her. His tongue traced every inch of her clitoris. He began to plunge in and out of her until she began gyrating while holding his head in place, and she trembled. Her body felt as though it was going to explode. She began to shake until her orgasm left her weak. Without any effort, he flipped her over onto her stomach. He held her by her voluptuous hips and placed his hardness inside of her. He could not believe that it was being welcomed in such a tight, warm, and wet way. Within minutes, his body could not take it. He gave her all of his love that he could not possibly give any other woman. He collapsed on top of her.

When Brianna opened her eyes, it was 9:00 AM, and Maxwell was not lying beside her. She got up to go the bathroom but was confused. He was not there either. *What the hell? He disappeared again?* Then there was a knock at the door.

"Good morning, senorita. Shall I wait here at the door, ma'am?"

"Pardon? Don't you want to come and place the tray down? Just come on in." She was puzzled at his hesitation.

"If you would like to grab a robe, I would be happy to wait right here," he said politely. When she looked down, she was relieved to see that, in the middle of the night, she had put her T-shirt back on. However, Brianna wanted to run and hide when she saw that the skimpy shirt barely covered her below her waist.

"My goodness! Wait right here." Brianna let the door slam and ran to her overnight bag to retrieve her robe. "Come in and please forgive me. My mind was truly somewhere else. When I ran to the door, I thought you were my boyfriend coming back because he forgot something." When she realized that she referred to Maxwell as her boyfriend, she knew she was in trouble with her inner emotions.

"That's okay, Ms. Godfrey. You would be amazed at what I saw earlier this morning. To see a three hundred-pound man in his hot pink bikini underwear is not pleasurable by any means." Brianna and the room service attendant both chuckled. "Ma'am, please enjoy your breakfast and take time to smell those pretty white roses. Also, read your letter before you start your day. These are the strict orders left by the gentleman who ordered your breakfast this morning."

"Oh? Okay. Have a good day." Brianna shut the door and ran back to see what the breakfast was all about. There were two lovely white roses and a note. Then she began to read,

Butterfly,

Baby, being with you last night was like a dream coming true. I spent so many days and nights wishing that I could hold you one more time. You have made me alive again. I hope I have made you feel the same. I'm sorry I had to run out this morning, but I had a business deal that I had to take care of. Please don't regret last night. I don't. I will not disrupt your life, but I know you are realizing that we are soul mates forever.

I want to see you again. We have more to talk about.

Love,
Max

80

What have I done? Brianna thought to herself. She ate her breakfast, took a shower, and got ready to start her day.

She met with the six vendors that Melissa wanted her to meet. To Brianna's amazement, all six vendors expressed that they desperately wanted to meet with her because she had built such a name for herself. It was now 1:30 PM, and Brianna was meeting Alice for a late lunch. They met at the quick quaint little restaurant in the DC area. Thank goodness for valet parking. She would not have found anything else. When Brianna walked in, she couldn't help but notice the stunning ambiance of the restaurant. It was so Alice McNeil, very classy and very white.

"Good afternoon, madame. May I have your name?"

"Brianna Godfrey," Brianna happily replied.

"This way, Ms. Godfrey. Your lunch appointment is waiting for you." Brianna smiled and followed the dapper little host to the table. She was sure that whatever the lunch specials were, there wasn't going to be a selection for $7.95. Arriving at the table, Alice was ready to greet her with a warm hug.

"Thanks for meeting with me, Brianna, on such short notice."

Alice was always well put together. She had on a black Oscar de la Renta pantsuit with an Italian crème silk camisole. Her hair was pulled back and placed in a neat bun. Her three-tiered pearl necklace, pearl earrings with her red lipstick should definitely be her signature look.

"Not a problem, I am glad to see you," Brianna said sincerely.

"Now I think this is too cute. We look like twins," Brianna said proudly.

"My goodness, we sure do. Well, I always wanted a daughter, so I can adopt you." Alice giggled.

"Ladies, would you like a few minutes, or are you ready to order?" the waiter asked.

"I take a mojito and the pecan-crusted salmon with the asparagus."

"That's an excellent choice, Mrs. McNeil, and you, madame?"

"Please forgive me. I've never had the pleasure of dining here. What do you recommend?" From when she was a young child, her excellent etiquette always kicked in, especially if she was a fish out of water, so to speak.

"Forgive me, Brianna. I should have given you a few minutes before ordering, huh? Take your time and review the menu."

"No, I am fine. You know what? Let's make this easy. I will have what she is having but with the steamed broccoli and a cosmopolitan."

"Will do," the waiter graciously nodded, then walked away.

"Brianna, I heard that Allan is in Philadelphia. I know you miss him."

"I do. I was hoping to stay with him while I was up here on business, but we will spend time with each other this weekend when he returns," she said, with a glowing smile, while reaching for her cosmopolitan the waiter had just placed in front of her.

"With this new position, do you think that you will be able to handle all of his required traveling?" Alice asked with great concern. "I remember the last person who held that position, their marriage almost fell apart because he was never home."

"I guess it won't be that bad. Did you know that couple very well?"

"I sure did. It was me and Mr. McNeil."

At this point, Brianna had a fixed stare on Alice, hoping that she would say that she was just kidding. Apparently she wasn't, she kept sipping her beverage.

"Really, Alice?"

"Really, Brianna. Unfortunately, he traveled extensively. He cheated, I lost a child, and I followed suit by cheating. It takes great work for us to be a couple. He is trying to make this work, and I am trying a new adult beverage every week."

Brianna could hold back the smirk that she quickly produced by Alice's dry sense of humor. It was too funny. "Wow, Alice. Well, I don't know what to say."

"Dear, no response is needed. You and Allan remind me so much of us, but anyway, let's talk about you starting your new business. I did a little homework on you, and you are well spoken of by different people in Richmond. The company you are working for is really working and surviving because of your great work ethics. Now is the time for you to work up a business plan and get started. Now is the time for you to spread your wings and become a butterfly."

When Brianna heard those words, she began to seriously choke on her drink. Coughing until tears were coming up in her eyes, Alice and the waiter stood over her, ready to assist if needed. Brianna was so embarrassed.

"Are you all right, sweetheart?" Alice said while rubbing her back with great concern.

Brianna took a sip of the water from the glass the waitress handed her. She was finally able to regain her composure. "I'm sorry for the commotion, Alice."

"Sorry? That's silly," Alice said playfully. "There is no need for an apology."

"Well, getting back to what you said, I guess I never poured a lot of thought into doing something like that. How would I get started?"

"Well, start by downloading your files from the agency. Take this folder and read over my ideas for my next two functions. We can meet and discuss this further at a later meeting. Also, there is a list of names and phone numbers in the larger folder. In there are the names of some very important people who are having all types of events. They are looking for a callback from you."

"From me?" Brianna asked.

"Yes, sweetheart, from you. Call me Monday of next week. We'll pick a day that you can come out to my condo for cocktails and go over my events. By then you should be able to tell me what your fees are?" The look on Alice's face was that of a mother—sincere, but she meant business at the same time.

"Okay?" Brianna said as though she was a little kid.

"Well, Brianna, I have to head back to Richmond. When are you leaving?"

"I think I may stay and do a little shopping since you have inspired my resignation." Brianna had the biggest smile ever.

"Sounds like a plan."

"Can I interest you ladies in dessert?" the waiter asked.

"No, thank you for me. Brie, would you like any?"

"No, I'm good, Alice."

"Mrs. McNeil, shall I do the usual with your check?"

"Yes, and thank you for everything. Please add in your 23 percent, please."

"My pleasure and thank you, ma'am. I'll see you next week sometime?"

"Yes, Adam, take care. Okay, Ms. Brianna, give me a hug so I can scoot."

They embraced and their cars were brought around. "That large scrape on your truck, Brianna, did that just happen?" Alice asked.

"Oh. No, I did that at home." Brianna felt again a little ashamed yet again.

"Dear, hold on." She went into her Chanel bag. After much searching, she pulled out a card. "Run over and see this man. He can help you with that, okay? Just tell him that I sent you." Alice jumped into her silver Mercedes S500 and waved goodbye.

When Brianna got in to her SUV, she looked at the card before pulling off. It was to a car dealership. By now it was 4:00 PM, and Brianna felt rejuvenated.

What the hell, I'll go to the dealership.

The dealership was only twenty minutes away. When she walked inside, the dealers were all over her. I guess they were happy and amazed that some was still coming through the doors in this recovering economy.

"Good evening, ma'am. My name is Robert Gooding and yours?"

"Good afternoon, I am Ms. Godfrey and I was told to ask for a Mr. Conti?" she said with a big smile.

"Very well, ma'am. He is a very busy man. Let me get him for you."

After a five-minute wait, another gentleman appeared. He was a sharp dresser. This gentleman was in a well-tailored three-piece pin-striped suit with a pair of impeccable shoes. His olive-colored skin with hair brushed back, made him look like an up-to-date slimmed-out "Godfather."

"Hello, Ms. Godfrey, I am Mr. Conti. I have been expecting you. So you want to get rid of that white Cayenne?"

"Get rid of my SUV?"

"Yes, Mrs. McNeil told me that I should assist you in the selection of another vehicle."

"She did? I am not sure that I want to get rid of my SUV."

"You should. It's more than just a few years old. A beautiful woman such as you should drive in something a little more up-to-date. It would be a nice look for you—the president of your own company, yes?"

Brianna was blown away by what he knew. "Well, what do you want to show me?"

"Are you are wanting another SUV, yes?"

"Yes, I am," Brianna said firmly.

"Okay. Right this way?"

The cars in his showroom were out of Brianna's league. They were cars such as Bentleys, Aston Martins, and Ferraris. *What was Alice thinking by sending me here?* With the money that Maxwell had given her a while back, plus the CDs and the stocks that were set up by him, she never indulged in her gift of wealth. Brianna did not want to overspend her nest egg. Her parents, being financially comfortable, always made sure that Brianna did not want for anything. However, they also wanted her to have a great understanding of money. This translated in Brianna making purchases that reflected quality over quantity. She also had men that would come into her life and spoil her like crazy too, so of course, that helped her staying within a budget. Mr. Conti went right over to the SUVs.

"Ms. Godfrey, what do you think of this Escalade?" he asked proudly.

"It's very nice." Brianna took a the glance at the sticker, and it was moderately priced at $72,970. "It's a little bulky. What else would like to show me?"

Mr. Conti smiled at her. He could tell that he would not be able to throw her just anything for the sake of a sale. "Okay. What do you think of this BMW X5 or even the 7 series?"

"Well, the X5 is very preppy looking." She walked over to the 7 series. "Now this is very sophisticated." She walked around it and opened the door and got in. She was falling in love with it.

"Would you like to take it for a spin? I guarantee you a powerful yet smooth ride."

"No, this is beautiful. Maybe as a second vehicle; however, I see something that I have been admiring from a distance."

"Oh? What's that, Ms. Godfrey?" He was really interested in exactly what she had her eyes on. She walked over to a black fully loaded Range Rover. This SUV was complete with every bell and whistle, which was important to her. In her mind, this vehicle demanded respect. When she looked at the sticker, the price was a little overwhelming. The SUV was listed at $95,000.

"Whoa!"

"This is the one, yes?"

"I guess you can say that, but I would like to stay within a certain budget. To be honest with you, I thought Alice was referring me to someone who could repair my truck," she sweetly stated. If she was going to possibly resign from her job, she needed to hold on to her money.

"No, no, no," he gently said to her. "There is no reason that you should think about repairing your truck—start new. What is it that you would like to spend on this SUV?"

"Well, let's just say that I am addicted to an SUV, but I only wanted to spend 55K. That's crazy, right? Let's talk about something that is gently used?" She knew she was possibly pushing but perhaps that would work out.

"My darling, let's not talk about a used anything. It's done. Let's go in my office and get the paperwork done!"

She was like a little child at Christmas. Brianna wanted to scream. He was giving her a forty thousand discount? That made no sense! "Are you serious? Are you sure?" She couldn't hug him enough and she wondered if Alice had something to do with this large deal.

CHAPTER FOURTEEN

New Beginnings

After completing the paperwork and making sure that she had taken all of her personal things out of her Cayenne, Brianna felt a little sad. She felt that she was giving a piece of her past away that had something to do with Maxwell. Her true love had given that to her, but why hold on to it? She rested her hand on top of the hood as if she was saying goodbye to it. She gave Mr. Conti another big hug, which he enjoyed, then she drove back to the hotel.

She checked her e-mails and found that she had one from Natalie. It was a general e-mail that went out to the entire office. There was also one from Melissa, asking that she stay longer to visit additional vendors. Brianna just laughed; she thought of the gratifying moment that was coming. Who knew that a resignation had the potential of being orgasmic? Pissing off Melissa would cause her to light up a cigar when she was done for sure! Her thoughts were interrupted by a call from Allan.

"Hi, baby."

"Hey, sweetheart! How are you doing?" Allan asked.

Brianna immediately started to feel guilty, but she swore that what happened last night would not happen again. "I'm good. How are you?"

"I'm missing you a lot. I was thinking that if you are still in DC by Friday, you should stay with me for the weekend instead of me having to travel down to Richmond?"

"Okay, I can do that. According to my latest update of my schedule from my boss, my workload will have me here until then anyway. I will be here two more days instead of leaving in the morning. That sucks for them because now I will need to use a sick day so I can bond with my boo!" She thought that was the least she could do for him since she had officially cheated on him.

"Okay, baby. I will be home Thursday night. I'll call you then. Take care, sweetheart."

Brianna went through her usual ritual of relaxing. For Alice's husband, she thought of putting together a Moulin Rouge–themed event. She listed out some of her vendors and possible places to host the affair. Tomorrow, she would call different sites to get proposals together for Alice. Brianna was amazed at the information that Alice had given her to work from. The possible clients listed had dates and their budgets already listed out for her.

Oh my god. These people are not joking.

She drafted a letter that would be sent out to her prospective clients. Tomorrow she would look for her professional stationary. *Wait! What will I call my new company? I will keep it simplistic, "Events by B. Godfrey."*

Brianna didn't realize that it was eleven o' clock until the phone interrupted her planning.

"Hello."

"Hey, butterfly, what are you doing up so late? I thought I would probably be waking you out of a deep sleep. Guess I didn't, huh?"

"Hi, Maxwell. No, I was working." She was not going to tell him about her new adventure; after all, he was sleeping with the enemy. "Where are you?"

"What? Do you want me to come over?"

"No, I was wondering why you are out so late." She really wanted to be in his arms one more night, but she didn't want to hurt Allan. However, spending time with Maxwell now seemed so right based on the explanation of his disappearing act in Miami. Having Maxwell in her life could mean more heartache, as well as added grief from Melissa.

"Business as usual. Brianna, let's go out and have a nightcap." He knew if he asked to come up to the room, she would have said no instantly.

"Okay, where should I meet you?"

"Downstairs, I'm parked out front." You could hear the smile in his voice.

"What, Max?" She started laughing. "You just took for granted that I was going to say yes, huh?"

"Girl, throw on some jeans and come on." He laughed.

Fifteen minutes later, she came out. He was admiring her every stride. She had her hair down, combed straight back with a Rhinestone-tipped baseball cap, a white tee. Partial zipped hoodie and a pair of tight jeans. Her shoes, as usual, were on point, a nude color of four-inch red-bottom pumps. One of the valet attendants bumped into the door looking back at her as she got in his black two-door Bentley. Maxwell leaned over and greeted her with a kiss.

"Damn, baby, you look sexy as hell!"

"Thank you. You look good in that entire black linen outfit yourself. So where are we going for a nightcap?"

"You'll see." They chatted and he asked about Tamika. Before she knew it, they pulled up to the hotel of their first date. He handed his keys to the valet and came around to take Brianna by her hand. Once inside the elevator, he kissed her and pressed the button to the top floor.

"Maxwell, why are you doing this?"

"Shhh… Let's enjoy it, okay? I've been answering questions all day, Ma."

He was still holding her hand. When they stepped off the elevator, again there were white rose petals sprinkled outside the door. She looked over and smiled at him. They went inside; he didn't miss a beat, white roses around the room with candles lit. This time when they entered the suite, the music was already playing. There were four people with instruments serenading them with one of Mary J. Blige's hits. They were continuously playing ballads by Mary J. Blige and then mixed it up a little with a few John Legend's songs. Seeing the group was made up of much-younger players, the fact that they played music until 2:00 AM didn't bother them at all. They stood in the middle of the floor, swaying to the music. When the small orchestra finished playing, Maxwell and Brianna stood there, staring into each other's eyes. When Maxwell heard the door shut. He began to passionately kiss her, and she reciprocated. He started removing her hoodie and shirt passionately; he picked her up and placed her on the chase, which was near the patio windows. Who cared if the curtains were open? He peeled her jeans off slowly, slipping her pumps back on her feet. He kissed her, licked her, and sucked her. Anything else that was possible to do with his mouth, it was done.

"Wait, Papi," she said breathlessly.

"Wait for what? Don't you think that we have been waiting long enough? We are so good for each other!" Maxwell almost sounded a little angry. He continued to give her pleasure while he was being pleased with her every moan and groan. They thrashed around, from the chase to the sofa and even up against the windows. On their last and final round, they found themselves on the balcony. Her brown full breast was dangling over the rails where he was penetrating her from behind. She was too caught up to even think that someone could possibly be watching them, nor did she care. They were not making love tonight; it was just sheer fucking. Maxwell and Brianna were both okay with that.

After a long night, they slept until noon. They fed each other brunch and drove back to her hotel. "Butterfly, have a really good day. I am heading back to Richmond, so I won't be able to see you anymore this week." Maxwell looked very upset. Almost like a mother had taken a child's favorite toy away. Truth be told, Brianna was secretly relieved. She knew that she could not continue to keep crossing the line with him.

"I understand. Maxwell, we can't keep doing this. We have both moved on."

Maxwell leaned over and gave her one more kiss. He did it because he didn't want to hear it. "Here, take this with you," he said with a smile. She looked down and saw a pretty black wrapped box with a silver bow on top.

"Can I open it now?" she asked.

"Look at you—sure, baby." He watched her unwrap it. It was a platinum necklace that had a five-karat diamond butterfly suspended from it.

"This is beautiful, Maxwell, but I can't take this. Every time I would wear this, I would be reminded of how much I want to be with you."

"That's the point, Ms. Godfrey. I won't let you forget me. So please, accept it because it would mean a lot to me. Please?"

"Okay," she said reluctantly. He took it completely out of the box and placed it around her neck. It was beautiful.

CHAPTER FIFTEEN

The Ego That Have Shown Its Head

The rest of the week went by rather quickly. She filled Angel and Tamika in on all the festivities and found herself alternating between calls from Maxwell and Allan. As it related to those two, she was so frustrated with herself.

She was trading e-mails with Melissa as well as Natalie. Natalie seemed to be getting out of the picture little by little. It was as if she had little to no voice in the running of the agency. Whatever she instructed Brianna to do, Melissa would override her; Brianna found that pretty entertaining. She informed the ladies that due to the running around and lack of proper rest that she has been doing, she would be knocking off early because she was feeling under the weather. Brianna could care less if they believed it or not. Allan had called her Friday morning, giving her instructions on how to get to his house. It had never dawn on her that, over the course of a few years of knowing each other, she had never met him at any place other than her house or a hotel. Arriving at his house, she couldn't believe how nice it was. He lived in Chantilly, a very elegant upper middle-class area. He had an all-brick home that was attached to a two-car garage. She knew he was home because she saw his 7 series black BMW and his BMW motorcycle. When she pulled into the driveway, he came out slowly, staring at her Range Rover. When she let down her tinted window and waved at him, he trotted over, smiling from ear to ear.

"What! Baby, this is tight. Is this you?"

"Yep. You like it? I bought it yesterday. Alice referred me over to a particular dealership."

"Really? You and Alice are really getting close, huh?" Allan climbed inside to inspect it; he thought it was a good purchase. He grabbed her bag and they finally went inside his home. Before she could look around, he gave her a warm kiss.

"Damn, girl! I have really missed you. I have a bottle of wine chilling for you, and I have lit the grill out on the deck, but first, let me show you around." The living room was fabulous; his furniture was very contemporary, complemented by his expensive mahogany hardwood floors. The hardwood flooring was throughout the entire house. A lovely staircase could be accessed from the kitchen as well as the living room. When taking the staircase up, it led to the second floor where the four bedrooms and three bathrooms were located. The three bedrooms located at one end were tastefully done. One room was the guestroom, the other one was being used as his office, and the third room was done in pink for his daughter. Oddly enough, he never discussed his daughter at all. Walking to the other end, there were five steps that led up to his bedroom; this was the master suite. The room was gorgeous; there was no need to leave this room. He had a California king-size bed that was set up on a platform. The sky lighting with recessed lighting throughout the room was a wonderful look. He had a forty-six-inch HD television mounted above a fireplace with surround sound in the corners of the room. The plush leather chase and beautiful blanket was positioned in front of his floor-length windows. His bathroom was huge; it could fit six people in there easily. The space allowed room for a separate step-in shower, away from the sunken-down bathtub. The shower has a total of six showerheads position—overhead, with the others aiming at the upper and lower parts of the body. All these luxuries with a towel warmer on the wall. The two sinks looked like clear bowls sitting on top of black marble with the faucet and handles coming out of the wall. The black toilet had no handle but a button on top of the toilet to flush it. The lighting was the same as the bedroom, sky and recessed lighting.

"Baby, this house and this room is fit for a king."

"Thanks, baby. If this is true, then all it is missing is a queen. Do I have any takers?" he asked while smiling.

"There might be one that I know of." She winked and gave him a kiss. "Feed me first, and then I might have a name for you later."

"Your wish is my command." He playfully bowed and then smacked her on her butt.

Once downstairs, she helped him prepare their meal on the grill. Enjoying each other's company, they sat outside until it was completely dark. The only company they had was that of the shining moon, stars, and the fire that they had lit in the fire pit.

"So Alice wants you to go into business for yourself, huh?" he asked while taking a gulp of his Corona.

"Yeah, it kind of threw me, but then she gave me a file with all these incredible leads of who would like to plan events. The names were pretty impressive. So I have placed an order for my stationary, and I have set up appointments with all those people. So for the next couple of weeks, I will be extremely busy." She was smiling like a little kid. It even amazed her how giddy she was being about the whole thing.

"Well, congratulations, but are you going to be too busy for me?" Allan asked with a little disappointment in his voice. Brianna was thrown by the change in his mood. She thought that he would be jumping up and down for her or at least give her a fist pound like Michelle gave Barack.

"I thought you would be happy for me?" Brianna was not only confused but insulted.

"I am, baby, but you asked me if I could make things right. So I am trying. Just don't forget it." He got up to go in the kitchen to get another beer. *What the hell is his problem?* He came back out the kitchen and leaned down and gave her a kiss. "Baby, I'm sorry. I am happy for you. You are a smart, sexy, and an intelligent woman. Not to mention Alice is freaking in love with you. So do your thing, baby. I will always support you."

"Thanks, Allan. You don't know how much that means to me."

"You're right. I don't know how much that means to you. Why don't you show me?" He was smirking. She stood up, so he stood up, thinking that they were about to go in the house.

"What are you doing, Allan? Sit back down in that chair!" He had a puzzled look on his face. However, he did what he was told. She dropped her little mini dress and removed her thong.

"Baby, what are you doing?" he said with a nervous laughter.

"Stop asking questions and lower your pants and boxers." He did it quickly and sat back down. She came over and rode him like a jockey riding a huge stallion. He thought that he was going to scream like a little bitch. Within two minutes, he buried his head in her chest and held on to her tightly; he was too weak and sensitive to move.

The next morning, they took a shower together, and he asked her to whip up breakfast while he returned a few calls in his office. She was happy to do so, but it kind of sent up another red flag for her. She didn't know if he wanted to make her feel at home by giving her free reign of the house or if he was the typical male making her stay in the kitchen. Over breakfast, they continued to talk. She proceeded to talk about Melissa but only to a certain degree. She didn't want Allan to know that her first love was back in town.

Allan handed Brianna a small box that was wrapped.

Am I racking up or what? Another gift? "Allan what's this? After that lovely dress and that David Yurman ring, I am so satisfied."

"Well, I hope this is better and, hopefully, more meaningful—open it."

She opened it slowly and then kissed him. "Is this a key to your house?"

"No, silly, my heart." He started laughing like it was the best joke ever. "Yes, baby, it's to my house. If you are going to be doing a lot of work up here, or in DC, should I say, then there is no need in spending a lot of money on hotel rooms. You are welcome to stay here when I am here."

I'm welcome to stay here when he is here? Why the hell would I need the key? He can just unlock the damn door.

95

"Allan, that is too sweet. I love you." *What the fuck did I just say! Why did I say that? What have I done? I didn't mean to say that. Please do not respond to that!*

"Brianna Monique Godfrey, I can't believe that you said that. I love you too, baby." Allan was happier than he has ever been in a long time. "I've been waiting for you to say that for a while now. I wasn't sure if you were ready to hear something like that." He couldn't kiss her long or hard enough. Saturday and Sunday, they did a little light shopping. They really had a good time together. Brianna almost didn't want to leave Sunday night.

CHAPTER SIXTEEN

So Watch Me Do Me

Monday morning, Brianna called the office to inform them that she would be in around noon. Peter, the assistant, couldn't help but laugh when she told him that she had a hair appointment.

When she arrived at work, the office was too quiet.

"Hello, Mr. Peter Lopez." Brianna was looking quite radiant in her jeans and her RL black T-shirt. Her hair wasn't in her traditional bun that she wore to work constantly; it moved with every step she took.

"Good morning, *Ms. Godfrey*. You're looking quiet urban today? How are you feeling?" he asked while smirking. Brianna had never worn denim to work. He figured that she must be definitely sending some sort of signal. He grabbed his bling-out coffee mug and pursed his lips. Peter was ready for action.

"I am feeling quite rejuvenated this morning. Here, I bought this for you while shopping at Tyson's Corner. You have always been a hardworking employee and have helped me a lot. I just wanted you to know that I appreciate you!" She leaned over the desk and gave him a hug.

"Brianna! Why, thank you. That is really sweet." He started unwrapping it immediately. It was an *YSL* pullover sweater. "What! This is fierce! Thank you." He hugged her again. While they were standing there talking, Melissa and Natalie were walking over to them.

"Good afternoon," Brianna said to them when she noticed them approaching.

"Good afternoon! Brianna, thank you for the report that you sent pertaining to the vendors you met. We'll have Peter place the information in the database," Natalie said with a smile.

"No need for that, Natalie. Brianna can place that information in the system. I need Peter for another project." Melissa was up to being her sarcastic self.

"Is that right?" Brianna instantly replied.

"*Is* that a problem, Brianna?" Melissa was ready to put Brianna in her place. Brianna was ready to respond when Phoebe suddenly appeared out of Melissa's office with a handsome little boy.

"Mom?" The little boy ran over to Melissa and placed his arms around her waist. "Aunt Phoebe wants to take me out for lunch and then over to Toys R Us. Is that okay?" Phoebe stopped dead in her tracks when she saw Brianna standing there.

"Sure, baby. Mind your auntie while you're out, okay?" Melissa stared at Brianna with a smile as she was answering her son. She knew that she was disrupting a friendship and she was loving that.

"Good morning, Phoebe. I haven't seen you in a while. I *guess* you have been busy plotting." Brianna, who was obviously annoyed, was doing a wonderful job keeping her composure.

"I beg your pardon?" Phoebe wanted to fall through the floor but was trying with all her might to look tough. "Melissa, I'll see you this evening. Have a good day, Brianna." She took the little boy by the hand and led him out the door. Brianna wanted to go behind her and hit her upside her Afro puffs, but it wasn't worth a charge.

How dare she cross me! No, this bitch don't think I'm going to let this go. She should know better, but don't worry. She will need me before I need her.

"Melissa and Natalie, as you can see, I'm not really dressed for work today. I came in to collect my things. I am resigning from the agency." She was delighted in telling them the information, but her heart started to beat rather quickly. Brianna knew that she had to brace herself; no telling what was about to come out of Melissa's mouth now or hers for that matter.

"Brianna, can we discuss this?" Natalie was not comfortable with this sudden decision.

"No, Natalie! There is no reason to discuss anything. She's a grown woman. By all means, do what's best." Melissa took this as a victory. "But just know, Brianna, we will not be able to give you a good reference. Most professionals would at least give their two-week notice."

"I'm good. I fortunately do not need a reference as I have started my own company." At this point, Melissa started to walk toward Brianna's desk. Brianna was amazed to find that Peter had begun putting her things in a box for her. She wanted to scream out laughing at Peter's quick thinking. "Thanks, Peter."

"Do you think that you are going to be instantly on top? You have to put in a lot of hard work. No one will be able to buy you success," Melissa said with a stern look.

"Yes, I do believe that I will be on top, and it appears that your former clients believe that I will be on top as well. Unlike you, no one is going to buy or sell their soul to the devil to assure me a comfortable future." Brianna stood there, waiting to see what she was going to come back with.

"*Excuse me?*" At this time, Melissa was beyond upset. She was steaming. Melissa knew that she was trying to insinuate something about her marriage with Maxwell.

"I'm just saying, no one has to make deals on my behalf when I can do it myself. *My* father is not in a back room making any deals on my behalf. Now, if you will *excuse* me, Mrs. King, I will continue to get my things together so I can start working on my new future. I already have some appointments to set up."

"Take care, Brianna. You will be missed and thank you for everything." You could hear the confusion and hurt in Natalie's voice. Natalie didn't know if she was implying any of those comments to her, but at that moment, she felt as though she had sold her soul to the devil.

Peter helped Brianna place everything in her truck and gave her a big hug, followed by a few other coworkers. Brianna pulled off, singing; she was too happy and too relieved. She went downtown to city hall to get her business license and then to the post office to pick up her delivery of office supplies. When she got home, she set up her spare room as her office. Brianna dedicated the rest of her day to setting and confirming appointments. She also got a message from Alice to come over to her apartment around eight thirty that night. It was now 6:00 PM, and the doorbell rang.

Who can that be? When she answered the door, it was her girls, Tamika and Angel. "Hey, ladies!"

Saying hello almost simultaneously, they both came in, giving Brianna hugs. "Girl, you know we came over just to find out what the hell is going on in your world!" Tamika wasted no time in going to the fridge to retrieve two bottles of waters, waiting for her reply. Her bottle of water was going to serve at a chaser for the Patrón shot that she was about to hit. Brianna filled the girls in on Maxwell and, not to mention, Allan.

"Oh my god, Brie! You are in a love triangle," Angel blurted out laughingly.

"Get it, girl!" Tamika said while giving Angel a high five.

"Tamika, that's not funny!" Brianna said while partially smirking. "I should be with Allan, but I want Maxwell."

"Let's not forget that this is almost your second round with Allan. Don't you remember how the last time you thought you and Allan were getting really close? He produced a kid and stayed with his wife. Then to add insult to injury, the man flamboyantly demeans you yet again by arrogantly elaborating on his assorted affairs with other females. What kind of foolery was that?" Tamika had a look of sheer disgust on her face. It was at that moment Tamika looked over at Brianna and Angel. They both were staring at her like she had turned a different color.

"What?" Tamika asked them both while she was taking a seat.

The girls started laughing. "Umm, Tamika Grant, we hear you talking, girl. Angel, did you hear Ms. Thang '*flamboyantly* demeans,' and '*arrogantly* elaborates'?" The girls were playfully using Tamika's passionate word choices. It appeared that her vocabulary was changing from street to nice embellishments.

"Yeah, I heard her. Don't forget that look of disgust after asking, 'What kind of foolery was that?'" Angel said while cracking up.

"Oh, so what y'all trying to say? I'm not educated?" Tamika gave them a "Be careful" look.

"Hold on, Angel, I got this. Let me be Tamika, who we know and love. I don't know who this female is right here, but this is how Tamika would have said it. 'Naw, bitch, what had happen was this nigga knocked his little wifey up. Then he thought that his punk ass was gonna hold on to you while still trying to hold on to all those other tricks, as if you were some sideline-ho! He thought that you were some chicken head that was going to sit around and wait fo' him to stop smokin' crack! What kinda fuckery was that?'"

Brianna and Angel were really impressed with their role reversal. The girls could not help but laugh. Tamika was tickled by the reenactment too.

"Aight, girl, you got me. I see how you two want to treat a sister when she wants to express herself without profanity. Damn, I know how to use the freaking Queen's English," Tamika chuckled.

"Seriously, ladies, we may need to do a little plotting. How about Phoebe was in the office this morning when I resigned," Brianna interjected after her poking fun at Tamika.

"What!" Tamika yelled with amazement.

"Did she see you?" Angel asked, losing her smile.

"Yep, Angel she saw me all right! She couldn't get out of the office fast enough. Melissa's little boy ran out and said that his *aunt Phoebe* was going to spend time with him." Tamika was calm but had a very devious smile. This was the confirmation she had been waiting on. "I knew it! I knew that trick could not be trusted. Didn't I tell you, Brie, that she was acting a little shady lately?" Tamika said full of anger.

"You did, Tamika. Let's give her a few days to see if Ms. Judas will come out again."

"Amen to that, sista'," Angel said. The girls chatted the night away, but they had to end the soiree because Brianna had to meet up with Alice at her condo near Stony Point Mall.

Upon her arrival to Alice's home, she noticed how cozy, yet elegant everything appeared. Brianna couldn't help but notice that not one picture of Mr. McNeil was present. She remembered that Alice had shared that she and Mr. McNeil had experience a difficult spell in their marriage. Perhaps she never put any pictures up because of that reason. Once seated, Brianna told her all the good news about the people that she had arranged appointments with for the next couple of weeks; Alice was sincerely happy for her. Brianna also went through her plans for her husband's birthday party; she absolutely loved them all. She gave Brianna a few blank checks to put down the deposits on the venue and the caterer of her choice. She tried to get Alice to wait and see the venue and sample the food first, but Alice insisted on her taking care of it all. Their dinner was interrupted by a knock at her door; Alice excused herself. Brianna could hear a man at the door so she just assumed that it was Mr. McNeil. The interruption came at a good time since they were done discussing the preliminaries. As Brianna began to put her folders back into her messenger bag, the voice that was coming toward her began to sound very familiar.

"Well, so we meet again, Ms. Godfrey." When she turned around, it was Mr. Conti from the car dealership.

"Why yes, we do. How are you?" She gave him a big smile. She was hit by curiosity. Mr. Conti could not help but chuckle a little. Alice covered her mouth because she too noticed the look on Brianna's face.

"I'm good! Are you enjoying your Range Rover?"

"Yes, I am," Brianna politely responded.

"You know, you got a really good deal on that, thanks to this lady over here. I could have sold that SUV for $95k easily. You are prettier than the person that I was holding it for, yes?" He was quite tickled at his own joke. Mr. Conti was adorable.

"Brianna, thank you for handling this party for me. Let me know if you need anything else to plan this event. I will give the board your recommendations for the other benefit this week. Here, let me walk you to the door," Alice said.

"Mr. Conti. Take care!"

"Ms. Godfrey, you do the same please. I'll see you soon." She couldn't help but notice Mr. Conti walking toward the bedroom. *Whoa!*

"Brianna, we'll talk soon. I know that you have questions going through your pretty little head. We girls need to stick together. Our boys don't need to know everything." She gave Brianna a hug as she always did. Brianna, while hugging, whispered to her, "As long as you are happy, that's all that matters. Your secrets are safe with me."

When Brianna jumped into her rover to go home, she was still processing what she had just seen. *What! Alice didn't tell me she was creeping with Mr. Italy? Well, she definitely has good taste.*

Once at home, she began doing a little work. She checked her office phone and was surprised at the nine calls confirming that they would like to use her for their events; she began thanking God immediately. It was too late to respond. She would tackle the return calls first thing tomorrow morning.

Brianna could not wait to partake in her nightly ritual, relax and process while taking a long hot bubble bath. Unfortunately, five minutes into her relaxation process, her phone rang. *Damn it, I left it in the bedroom!* She jumped out, tracking water and suds through the room.

"Hello."

"Hey, my little butterfly! I heard that you decided to spread your wings."

Now she remembered that was what he said when he gave her that surprise call. "I thought you also said that you didn't know what she was up to? So you knew that I was leaving?" she said in a very inquisitive tone.

"Sweetheart, once this little mission of hers became a little clearer to me, I thought that she would fire you immediately, not to try making your work life miserable."

"Well, I'm here to tell you, she didn't. I can tell you that she was definitely trying to torture me, and yes, she was starting to work a nerve. I am tough, but damn!" Brianna didn't want to get too carried away with talking to Maxwell about his wife. She would feed him information on a need-to basis.

Maxwell started to laugh; he knew that Brianna could definitely handle herself.

Once in her partying life with Maxwell at a club, he remembered watching Brianna handle a confrontation while being in New York. Brianna was dressed in a form-fitting all-white dress. The dress hugged her curves as if it was a matter of life or death. The front of the dress offered a traditional covering, but the back of the dress was an unexpected show stopper. It had just a few thin straps going across her back, stopping nicely at the crack of a new dawn. She had on four-inch heels with a thin strap that wrapped around her ankles. Her hair was loaded with big wavy curls all leading, draping over one shoulder. Her makeup had been done by the leading makeup artist at Barney's of New York. She was absolutely stunning that particular night. There was no sleeping to be done on Maxwell's attire. He was looking sexy as hell in his all-white linen outfit. Rico and Tamika, who accompanied them, all looked as though they walked right off the runway.

The party was top-notch, pure New York flavor. Maxwell and Brianna were getting stares left and right. The guys were trying to find out how they could get down with him because some had vaguely heard about who he was while others were just gritting on him. The girls who wanted to be with him thought that, just maybe, since he had some bama from Virginia, it would be like taking candy from a baby. Those hidden thoughts of others alone would make for an interesting night. Rico and Maxwell thought nothing of the attention they were all getting. Tamika took note of everything; that was simply in her nature. What shocked Maxwell was that Brianna totally ignored the females, but kept her eyes on the guys, not to flirt but more for security reasons. However, that would be placed on the back burner after a young lady decided to step to their table. She tossed her long wavy brown hair out her face and began to address Maxwell.

"So, handsome, stop sitting there and come out on the floor with me. Are you having a good time, Papi?"

"Yes, darling, I am. Please go back to doing you. I am here with my friends and my beautiful woman." Maxwell leaned over and gave Brianna a kiss.

If some guy looked like they were going to approach Max in the wrong manner, Brianna would be quick enough to make sure that both Max and Rico were watching. When she saw this trick coming, initially she was not fazed by her at all; however, Brianna was now becoming annoyed because she would not leave. This female just wouldn't sit down; this was partially due to her entourage that kept egging her on. She danced in front of Maxwell and Rico seductively, by herself and with another female. Now there she stood again, up close and personal, looking Brianna up and down, but then she quickly returned her attention to Maxwell. "You don't know me, but we can change that now. My name is Stacey and yours?"

Before anyone could say anything, Tamika cut in, "Bitch, ain't nobody trying to get to know your skanky ass. Go sit down."

"Excuse me, bitch. I wasn't talking to your country ass," Stacey said to Tamika while still looking straight at Maxwell.

"Stacey, you really need to go back before you get hurt," Rico said after taking it all in. He knew that Tamika wasn't going to let her think that she could just come over and disrespect her. Stacey was too pissed; she was a pretty girl that received her confidence from obviously trying to intimidate and bully people. This night, however, she had hit a brick wall. For the rest of the evening, they managed to ignore Stacey and have a good time. To avoid the mad rush for the door, they decided to leave the club around 2:30 AM. As they were walking to the car, they looked over and saw Stacey posted up as though she was waiting for her friends or maybe them. Stacey spied them as well and kept staring. Brianna let Maxwell's arm go and walked over to her.

"Look like you still have something to get off your chest, Ms. Stacey?" Brianna said to her.

"Bitch, if you don't know what to do with him, leave him with me." Then she winked and waved at Maxwell.

"Bitch, did you just wink at my man? Here let me help your ass out with the other eye!" Before anyone could pull Brianna away from her, Brianna took her fist and punched her dead in the other eye. The girl screamed and grabbed her face. Brianna took that opportunity to clock her right upside her head. Tamika and Rico could not stop laughing. Max picked Brianna up around her waist.

"Okay, Rocky, she got the point." When they looked through the car window, the poor girl was being helped by her three girl-friends. They were a little too late.

"Okay, baby. Well, whatever you are about to get into, just know that I will be there for you. Let me know if you need anything. When can I see you again?"

"Maxwell, you and I have discussed this before. You know that I am trying to move on with Allan. After you explained your situation with Melissa, you and I can never be." Brianna didn't want to seem cold, but *this*, or whatever was happening with her and Maxwell, needed to stop.

"Brianna, tell me that you don't love me and I will stop calling you."

She knew that she couldn't. She craved him. She knew that if this man was a drug, she would be in rehab right now. "Max, I love you and I always will, but we cannot do this. Please stop asking me to spend time with you." She hung up the phone.

CHAPTER SEVENTEEN

Take Him but Love Me Only

Four weeks had gone by and Brianna's business was booming. The weather was beginning to change; it was starting to get a little nippy. It was Thursday around 8:30 PM when her phone rang. It was Phoebe. *Oh, look who is calling.*

"Hello!" Brianna wanted Phoebe to hear the annoyance in her voice before she could even put it into words.

"Hey, Brianna." Phoebe was nervous but she really wanted to talk to her.

"Phoebe, believe it or not, I don't have anything to say to you at the moment, so make this short."

"Brie, I'm sorry."

"Really? Sorry for what? I am so stupid to have believed that you were my best friend. A best friend does not go and side with the freaking enemy. What the fuck did I do to you that would justify you stabbing me in the back?" Brianna wanted to stay calm but found her voice escalating.

"Brie, it's always all about you! It's Brie that gets the men that want to spoil her like crazy. It's Brie that has to outdress everyone. Then you started spending time with that Tamika more than me. We have been friends since elementary school, but I guess that don't mean anything to you!" Phoebe began to start yelling back.

"Phoebe, you sound like a fucking two-year-old! Give your new girl a call with all this bullshit! We are through!"

"Brianna!" Phoebe yelled into the phone. She wanted to talk more but Brianna had hung up on her.

Brianna was fuming. She didn't know what she was going to do to teach her a lesson about friendship, but she promised herself that she would let her wallow in feeling like crap. To set out to destroy her would probably present a challenge because they had been so close, but it could be done. However, things in Brianna's life could not be placed on the back burner to get back at Judas. *She will definitely need me before I need her.*

When Brianna got out of her truck, she checked her mailbox before going in her condo. As she was walking up to her door someone called out to her.

"Ms. Godfrey?"

When she turned around it was Maxwell. "Maxwell, what are you doing here?"

He gives her a kiss. "Let's go in, baby."

Brianna opened the door and he glanced around. "You have a beautiful place, babe."

"Thank you, but seriously, Maxwell, what are you doing here?" She went in the kitchen to pour them a glass of iced tea.

"I'm here because I needed some fresh air. When I looked up, I was here." He took her hand and led her back to the sofa in the living room.

"So how did you know that I lived here?"

"Brianna, I told you that I would always make sure that you are okay. Well, to do that, I had to have known where you live, right? Baby, take a shower and relax. If it's all right with you, I am going to whip something up for us to eat?"

"Max, I am too tired to fuss with you. Give me thirty minutes to freshen up and put on some comfortable clothes."

When Brianna came down from her shower, he had the table set. He whipped up grill cheese sandwiches with a bowl of soup and a bottle of white wine. She started to giggle at his attempt of a gourmet dinner.

"Bon appetite." He laughed. Needless to say, after dinner and cuddling, they ended the evening in bed. She decided she really wanted to know what led him here, to her home.

"Max, what's going on with you tonight?" she gently asked him.

"I don't know, baby. It would be wrong of me to lay here and discuss Melissa with you."

"Baby, she has a problem with me. I don't have a problem with her." *Like hell I don't, but I need any information I can get on this trick,* she thought.

"Yeah, baby, I guess you are right with that one. It's weird, she wanted to argue about every freaking thing she could think of today. I really get tired of kissing her ass. My father shows up and decides that he was going to cosign her foolishness by getting in my face. He told me that she deserves better. Ironically, they left together. Do you believe that? In about thirty minutes, I get a call from her telling me that she and my father was taking a quick flight down to Miami."

"What? Where is Max Jr.? Did she give you a reason as to why she needed to go there?"

"He's with my father. Some shit about needing a break from me and wanting to see her dad."

The phone rang, the automation on the phone announced that Allan Jones was calling. It was like Brianna was frozen. "Go ahead, get the phone," Maxwell ordered.

"No, I'll let it go to voice mail," she said, half smiling.

Maxwell wasn't trying to hear that. He picked up the phone and handed it to her. Brianna was nervous and felt very awkward.

"Hey, Allan…"

"Just lying in the bed…"

"Yes, silly, alone…"

"Okay…sure…"

"Miss you too…"

"Yes, I love you." When she disconnected the call, she was pissed that he picked up the phone but wasn't able to express it because he got out of the bed abruptly.

"Oh! What you're mad now! You shouldn't have picked up the damn phone, Maxwell." She got up and jerked his shirt out of his hands.

"You love him, huh?" he sarcastically asked while removing his shirt from her hands.

"Max, give me a break. What the fuck do you want from me?"

CAM JOHNSON

"What I want from you is all your love. Don't ever say that to him again! You want to spend time with him, fine! Make a decision now, Brianna! Will you tell him that you love him again?" Maxwell had a look that showed her that he meant business. She couldn't believe what he was asking her to do. "Brianna, make a *decision* now!" He began to kiss her. He turned her around, and as a mindful, forceful lover could, he passionately pushed her onto the bed. He began taking her from behind. "Give me my answer. Who do you love?" Not getting an immediate answer, he asked her again. Finally, she uttered out an answer.

"You, Max." She could never deny her body that type of pleasure from him.

"I can't hear you."

"YOU, MAXWELL!" she moaned out loudly and passionately.

"Will you say that to any other man ever again?" He began to pound her faster, harder, and deeper.

"No!"

"What are you saying no to, Brianna?" Maxwell wanted her to answer in a complete sentence.

"No, Maxwell, I won't...I won't say it to anyone else. I only love you!" She began to shake and scream and he followed suit.

CHAPTER EIGHTEEN

Closet Talk

The next morning, she picked up the invitations to Alice's husband's birthday bash and met Alice at Baker's Crust in Carytown for lunch to show her. She was too ecstatic when she viewed them. The invites had cancan girls on the front. When you open them, festive music sounded from the actual invite.

"Brianna, this is wonderful. Well, here is the list of names. I believe that there are about two hundred names on there."

"Wow. Okay, I will get these out by Monday. Would you like to go with me down the street to sample the cake?"

"No, actually, Brianna, I trust you. Here are two more blank checks to handle any other deposits or balances that you may have to take care of today."

Brianna was puzzled as to why Alice had such a hands-off approach to this birthday party. "Okay, is there anything else that you can think of that you wanted to add to this event? Like one of your signature touches?"

She was looking at Alice to see if she would try to come up with something. It took her all of two seconds to respond. "Nope, not a thing. However, let's talk about my guest that was a surprise to you."

"Oh, we don't have to. I totally respect your privacy," she said while sipping on the rest of her beverage.

"Brianna, I want to. I really like you, and for some reason, I know that I can trust you. In trusting you, I know that this will not be pillow talk for you and Allan late at night." Brianna nodded, consenting to her wish. "I told you that Mr. McNeil and I went through a rough patch. During that rocky period, I met Mr. Conti at a function in DC. He was my tall, dark, and handsome lifesaver. This man was sweet, gentle, and a great listener. It wasn't a physical relationship in the beginning at all. He had just lost his wife of thirty-eight years to cancer. Believe it or not, he believes that a couple should stay together no matter what. While he does not encourage me to leave my husband, he refuses to let me go. This can only be just one of the darkest decisions that a woman will have to make in her lifetime, having to choose between two men that loves you."

"Somehow I can understand what you are saying." Brianna did not feel comfortable telling her that she herself was in the same situation.

"Well, I don't want to delay you. I know that you have a lot to take care of with your other clientele. Thank you for letting me spill one of my little secrets." The women walked out to their vehicles with something added to each of their lives. For Alice, it was the daughter she never had. As for Brianna, Alice would be a great mentor, a good friend, and on her way to being like a second mom. When Brianna got in the car, she was checking her iPhone.

Oh my god! I have too much to do. Then a thought hit her that she should hire an assistant, not to mention at least two other employees. She called the agency.

"Executive Meeting Solutions, this is Peter. How can we assist in planning your next meeting?"

Brianna was so happy to hear his voice. "Peter, shhhh, it's Brianna. How are you?" she said laughingly.

"Hey!" Peter was happy to hear from her. He really admired her, not to mention, he loved Brie's clothes. "What's up?"

"Peter, if your schedule permits, can you meet me for dinner tonight?"

"I would absolutely love to. What time and where?" he eagerly asked her.

"About six thirty at Maggianno's?"

"Okay, I'll place the reservations. See you there."

Brianna ran around like a chicken with its head cut off. She met with the caterer to finalize the menu. She met with the entertainment that will be at Mr. McNeil's party also, and she had two conference calls with two clients in DC. On her way to meet Peter, Allan called her. Thank goodness, he could not spend a lot of time on the phone because she would have needed to abruptly interrupt the conversation to place another much-needed call to a potential client. Besides, talking to him after spending time with Maxwell produced such an overwhelming feeling of guilt in her; she had no time to deal with that.

When she promptly walked in the restaurant at six thirty, she heard her name. Peter was walking toward her to escort her to the table. He gave her a big hug. "Come this way. I got here a little early to ensure prompt seating. Your seat awaits you." When they were seated, the waitress walked over and placed a vodka tonic in front of her.

"Oh my goodness, how did you know?" Brianna was blown away because that was exactly what she wanted, and she truly noticed that he was on point with great follow through.

"I remember you screaming that out loud after you met with a difficult client. I believe she was working your last nerve." Peter began chuckling and so did Brianna. "Melissa is getting on your nerves, so this is for you, a vodka tonic."

"Thank you so much! Peter, let me cut through the chase. I have started my own events planning company. I already have clients. As of an hour ago, I have eleven confirmed events with awesome revenue potential. The earliest event is in two weeks."

"Dang, Brianna, you have been really busy since you left us on the plantation." They both started laughing.

"Mr. Lopez, I would like to offer you a job. If you can start right now as my assistant, I can offer you a $1,000 signing bonus check tonight. Not to mention that your pay will increase by 50 percent than what you make now." Peter sat there with his mouth wide open. "Peter, you are going to catch flies. What do you say?"

"What do I say? What time do I report in?" Peter knew if he stuck with Brianna, he would learn a lot.

"Thanks, Peter, you can start Monday morning. Be at my home at 9:00 AM."

They ordered their meals, and Peter proceeded to tell Brianna what has been going on in the office.

"Brianna, since you have left, they really have not been doing that well. We had three calls this week in particular. Once they heard that you were no longer with the agency, they decided not to use the agency. The callers that asked for you, Melissa decided she would take them. Let's just say those calls did not go over well at all. She has pissed off about half of our clients. The worst day was when Melissa and Natalie got into a heated argument."

"They got in argument about what, Peter? I thought they were going to be the fabulous gruesome twosome?" Brianna could not believe what she was hearing, and it was too funny. "It's only been two weeks."

"Yeah, that's what I said. It's seems as though those two have two different ideas on how to run the agency. Natalie also thought it was a bad idea to let you resign. Oh my god, when she said that to Melissa, she turned in the *queen bitch*. She told Natalie that if she ever said something like that again, she would force her out of the company."

"Peter, did she say all this out in the open?"

"No. She said this while yelling at her behind the closed doors of her office. When she opened the door, you should have seen us. We all scattered like roaches when the light came on!" They both started laughing uncontrollably. Brianna could not help but think that this was why Melissa had been picking fights with Maxwell. Melissa was pissed that she was not winning at taunting her.

It was now Saturday morning, and Tamika, Angel, and Brianna had a day planned; they met at the spa. They enjoyed their much-desired massages and facials. After which, they were all in a row when getting their pedicures done. "So, ladies, what are we going to do about Ms. Phoebe Steele?" Tamika asked.

"Well, you can send her on *hike* like you guys sent Brian on," Angel said unexpectedly. That comment made Tamika and Brianna take deep breaths and look at each other. How could she have known that they used great persuasion to get her abusive boyfriend, Brian, to leave Richmond? They never discussed with her that they paid two thugs to kick the shit of him.

"You know?" Tamika asked.

"Girl, I found out a month later. After your thug buddies took care of him, I went into his account and took $5,000. Ladies, that was the deposit on my Mini Cooper. Trust me, he cursed all of us!" They laughed so hard that the women doing the pedicures had to stop for a moment, waiting for the girls to regain their composure. "Ladies, let's stay isolated from her for a hot minute. Trust me when I tell you that would be enough torture for her right there," Angel said.

A week and a half had almost flown by. Brianna and Peter were really busy with her new business. She had driven back and forth to DC about four times, all while dedicating quality time to putting the finishing touches on the birthday extravaganza. She and Allan were able to spend two nights together. Both noticed, without expressing it, that they both had a great desire to make the best out of their careers, which was making their time together very strained. That being the case, they really tried to make every moment count when they were together. Maxwell, however, took advantage of the physical distance between Allan and Brianna. He was too smart to compromise what they now shared being in the same city; he came to her house often. He would send her a card or flowers and sometimes refer business to her. He wanted to reinforce the fact that he would always be there for her in any shape or form.

CHAPTER NINETEEN

Where Is the Support?

The venue was a madhouse. People were everywhere. It was two hours before the birthday event, and believe it not, everyone was accounted for and present. The caterers were placing the chaffing dishes in various spots, as well as, the careful execution of placing what carving stations and action stations in what corners of the room. The birthday cake was beyond beautiful; it was a five-tiered chocolate ganache cake. The decor was very colorful and different. She took a moment to stand back and watch everything fall in place. Peter was too cute with his clipboard and ear radio. Brianna admired the fact that he took his job so seriously—he meant business.

Once she felt like everything was coming together for the party, she headed back to the hotel through the catwalk to check on the guests checking in. When she checked into her room, she found a quick moment to take a shower, rest her feet, and get dressed. Using the mini bar, she savored a small drink before going back to work. Just to say thank you to Peter for all his hard work, she had a small gift bag delivered to his room. She sent a text to Tamika and Angel, telling them both to arrive at the party at 9:00 PM sharp. It was her company's first official event, and she wanted to share the moment with her best friends. Brianna's professional look was done with a simple, yet elegant black Calvin Klein dress. For a splash of color, she wore a pair of tan patent leather Christian Louboutin shoes. She pinned her hair up, letting a few soft ringlets fall freely in different places. She checked her iPhone several times to see if Allan had called. She thought it was quite strange that he did not call to give his estimated time of arrival.

Surely, he is coming to celebrate my first event, not to mention that it is for his freaking boss! How rude! she thought.

It was now 7:45 PM, and she returned to the venue. Peter let her know that everything was going smoothly. Two girls from the other agency told Brianna that they wanted to work with her as well; she called them to work the door. With the extra bodies being in place, this would allow her to move around to check the guests. The festivities were beginning; music was playing and the guests were now arriving. She got a text from Alice, stating that she and the guest of honor were now in the lobby of the convention center. Peter stood near the escalator to call Brie to let them know when they were in sight. The last of the guests hurried inside to get ready for Mr. McNeil's arrival. As Mr. McNeil and Mrs. McNeil were walking up, Mrs. McNeil looked like she was stepping out of *Bazaar* magazine. She had cut her hair—no more bun. Her hair was cut into a cute short pixie cut. Mrs. McNeil looked almost ten years younger. She had a flattering haute couture outfit on by Chanel with yet again her signature red lipstick. Alice grabbed Brianna's hand while holding her husband's. As they were walking in, everyone was applauding and whistling. The festive music started with the cancan dancers dancing onto the stage. Brianna pointed upward. Mr. and Mrs. McNeil looked up at the four aerial fabric silk dancers suspended from the ceiling; they could not believe what they were seeing. Mr. McNeil leaned over and gave his wife a very endearing kiss on the cheek. She, in return, gave Brianna a warm smile while rubbing her back.

"Brianna, this was worth every penny. Thank you, sweetheart."

Brie smiled back at her. Brianna walked around to make sure everyone was happy. When she stood to the side, she felt a hand wrap around her waist. How she wished it was Maxwell, but she thought that it had better be Allan.

"Hi, baby." When she turned around, it was Allan. He kissed her, but he noticed that she did not kiss him back. "You are mad at me?"

"Babe, where have you been? You are late. I wanted you here a little earlier than this." Brianna was really agitated by Allan, and it was showing.

"Brianna, you're not the only one with a job. Everything looks beautiful. Don't mess things up by giving me attitude." He kisses her and walked around her to greet his boss who was still engrossed in watching the cancan dancers like a little kid watching his favorite cartoon. Brianna turned and watched Allan as he eagerly walked away. *He just wants to brush me off. Okay!*

One thing Brianna did not lack was confidence. She collected her thoughts and looked at the crowd of people who were enjoying the live entertainment. She looked at her watch and noticed it was time for the cake to be rolled out. Peter informed the caterer while Brianna got Alice and Mr. McNeil to come onto the raised platform. She looked over at the band, and they began to play "Happy Birthday." Mr. McNeil blew out some of the candles and had Alice help with the rest. The crowd thought that was too funny. He took the microphone.

"I would like to thank each one of you for coming out to my surprise birthday party. Who would have thought that this many people like me?" The crowd roared with laughter.

"I hope that many of you, if you haven't already, find such a loving spouse such as I have. She really surprised me with this one! Thanks, honey. I would also like to thank Ms. Godfrey and her staff. I was informed that she just started her own company, and boy, what an outstanding job! Well, guys, stay as long as you want and enjoy!

The music began and his guests continued to celebrate. Brianna went over to Peter and gave him a glass of champagne. "Thanks, I am so glad to have you on my team. Cheers! This is too a great beginning!" They hugged and started to do a little happy dance.

"Well, aren't you quite the dancer?" She looked over, and it was Mr. Conti. They gave each other a big smile and a hug.

"Hello, Mr. Conti."

"Please call me Edmundo. This is a nice party. Brianna, do me a great favor, yes?"

"Sure, Edmundo, what is it?"

"Dance with me. I can't dance with the love of my life over there. I understand that she is entertaining her husband. Will you distract an old man and take a spin with me on the floor? I will be a complete gentleman with you." Edmundo had such a sweet, innocent look on his face. There was no way she could have said no. She felt kind of sad for him.

"Let's head out on the floor."

They swayed to one of Barry Manilow's songs. Edmundo was a suave man and a smooth dancer. It's no wonder Alice could not let him go. "Brianna, do you have someone special in your life? I never thought to ask Alice if you did or did not."

Brianna hesitated as though she had to think about it before answering. "Yes, I guess you can say that. Why do you ask?"

"Just curious that's all. Love can be a complicated thing. Some forms of love hurt, and if it has you in a way that you cannot function, it will suffocate the life out of you. If that is the case, you must let it go. However, if you have found *true love*, that is a good thing. That is something that will stand the test of time and can never be destroyed. It will force you to make a decision that you do not want to make." At that moment, he looked over at Alice dancing with her husband. "I hope that the love that you have will not allow you to be on the outside looking in. Watching the love of your life loving someone else can be hurtful and a lonely thing. One day, my Brianna, you will have to decide about the type of love you will have in your life. Whatever love you chose, please promise me that you will fight for true love. It will be worth it in the end. I look at Alice. I love her, and even though it pains me to see her with another man, I cannot let go because I love her so much. What I have for her is true love, something that I thought I would never find again."

Brianna had a tear in her eye; he looked at her and smiled. Edmundo gave her an endearing kiss on her cheek and whispered, "Please tell my true love I said to have a good night."

As many guests started to leave, the night was coming to an end. Tamika and Angel told her that they were really impressed with the party. Angel also informed Brianna that Phoebe had been trying to contact her, but as they agreed at the spa, she has been ignoring her for right now.

"Brianna, Angel and I noticed that Mr. Allan came and left. Did he go home, like back to Northern Virginia?" Tamika asked. It hadn't dawned on Brianna that she had not spoken with him since his little brush-off.

"I don't know where he went, and right now, I really don't give a damn."

"Whoa, ladybug," Angel said to her. Tamika chuckled; she thought Brianna's eye-rolling was a little funny.

"B, what happened?" Tamika asked her.

"Sometimes Allan is hard to make out. One minute he is sincere and loving. Then he can switch on you and become evasive, self-absorbed, and distant. I don't know if he wants me for my bedroom talent or to stroke his ego?"

"Oh, damn, well, looks like you are going to get a chance to ask him. He is back and walking toward us," Angel said in a subtle manner.

"Hello, ladies." Allan shook both of their hands. "Brianna, let's go. I'm a little tired."

At that moment, she shot him an annoyed look. He checked his tone then proceeded to clean up what he said. "I'm sorry, ladies. I just want to spend time with this beautifully smart woman, who has graciously allowed me to be her man. If you are ready, I would like to massage your feet and give you a back rub." The smile he was giving her was disingenuous. Everyone could see it.

"Peter, thanks again. If you like, enjoy your room for the rest of the night. There is a gift bag in there for you. I'll see you Monday at 9:00 AM. Tell the girls I will have a check for them then. Good night."

"Thank you, Brianna, and Alice asked that you give her a call after 1:00 PM tomorrow."

She gave Tamika and Angel a "sister girl" look and turned to walk away with Allan following closely behind. As Brianna was walking through the catwalk back to the Marriott, she made no attempt to hold a conversation with Allan. In the elevator, she glanced at her watch. It was going on 1:00 AM. She went into the room, removed her dress and pumps, then threw on a small silk robe. Allan, who was watching her, started to remove his suit and was now standing there in his boxers.

"So you don't feel like talking to me, Brianna?"

"Honestly, no." She went in the bathroom to remove her makeup. When he began speaking, she flushed the toilet, not out of usage but out of the necessity to drown him out. When she came out, he was sitting on the edge of the bed, looking at her like he had a few things on his mind.

"Brianna, what is your problem tonight?" he asked as though he was trying to express that he had enough.

"Allan, I don't know what is going on with you either. Tonight was my night. Tonight, I was living my dream. When I told you that I was going into business for myself, you didn't seem so happy. Tonight was like my first event, and I heard nothing from you all day. Then to top it off, you came in late and brushed me off the whole night. Oh, and let's not forget you got in front of my friends to rush me to leave. What the hell, Allan?"

Allan was angry at this point; he was not going to let any woman talk to him like that. "Who the hell are yelling at, Brianna? I've been working long hours, not to mention, I have to fly out again tomorrow. To add to the stress of it all, I have been arguing with my child's mother for the last two days. The last thing that I have time for is concentrating on you planning some damn party!"

Brianna wasn't making eye contact with him. She was sipping on the rest of the water in her bottle. However, when he completed his argument with those final words, Brianna was fit to be tied. He wanted her to feel insignificant.

Please let this Xanax take a hold quickly! This brother must really think that I need him. Why doesn't he learn how to fuck before he tries to make someone feel small!

"Brianna! Brianna!" Allan was yelling. Brianna didn't realize that she had fallen deep in thought. "Brianna, what the hell is that little smirk on your face? Am I entertaining you?"

"Unfortunately, no, you're not saying anything that is worth my attention. I'm going to bed." Brianna could finally feel the Xanax trying to work. She got into bed knowing that the silence would absolutely kill him and a glimpse of her in her black push-up lace bra and black-laced boy shorts would torture him. Not to mention, she knew that he loved her bedroom talents. He got in the bed, closely behind her, and wrapped his arm around her. He kissed her on the back of her neck and began to fondle her breasts. She could feel his erected penis pressing on the back of her thighs. Allan began to then push back the covers so he could look at her round, firm, voluptuous bottom in her panties. He kissed her on the small of her back and came back up to nibble on her ear.

"Brianna, let's put this silly argument behind us. Why don't you turn around and show big daddy that you are sorry for being mean to him?"

"I'm good. Good night, Allan." When he jerked away, she smirked. She felt for her butterfly diamond necklace and drifted off to sleep. The next morning, she awakened to him kissing her on the forehead. He was fully dressed and on his way out the door.

She got up and saw a note beside her phone.

Brianna,

That was our first real argument. I am more than sure we will have more, but we will be okay. Our next rendezvous will be better.

Love you
Allan

This Negro can't even say that he is sorry. This could be another character flaw.

Two months had gone by and Brianna had at least two more events under her belt that were done in crunch time. She had managed to book ten more events; the company was off to a good start.

Tamika had been busy doing whatever Tamika does, and Angel had been consistently dating the younger gentleman that she met at the club a few months back. Brianna and Maxwell had been stealing moments together when they could. Allan and Brianna had their good days and their bad days. She held on to Max because every time they were together, it was better than excellent, if that was even possible.

122

CHAPTER TWENTY

Surprise!

Brianna was exhausted. She and the staff picked the coldest day to move into their new office. It was convenient to Point Stony Fashion Mall and in the office building next to Stony Health Center. They were arranging desks and setting up office equipment. When she got home, she was tired. While in the midst of her bubble bath, her phone interrupted her.

"Hello."

"Brianna, it's Alice. I will see you tonight for dinner at seven thirty, right?"

"Sure, unless you would like to postpone it to another night." Brianna really wanted Alice to use her motherly instinct to hear that she really wasn't up for it.

"Brianna, I'm sensing that you are little under the weather?"

"No, I'm fine. I guess this hot bubble bath is relaxing me a little too much. I will be there, Alice."

"Good, see you then, dear."

Knowing that Alice was such an elegant woman, she had to find something that was simple, but classy. Brianna threw on a pair of Jones of New York wide-leg black trousers, with a light cashmere cream-colored tunic sweater. Her outfit was accompanied with a black pair of Stuart Weitzman pumps and a very simple clutch. She wasn't in the mood to fuss with her hair; she slicked it back in her favorite ponytail and played up her makeup. She was hoping that this look would be something that Tyra Banks would approve. She jumped in her Range and popped in her John Legend CD. Ten minutes into her drive, Allan gave her a call.

"Hi, baby." Brianna was trying to sound warm as possible.

"How was your day? And what you are up to?" Allan cheerfully asked.

"My day was very busy with settling in our new office. Now I am off to meet Alice for dinner." Brianna grew even more tired just talking about it.

"I wish I could have been there to help you get settled in your office. Well, enjoy your dinner with Alice. Tell her that I am jealous that she gets to stare at my beautiful woman and have dinner with you tonight."

"I will, baby. Alice has been wonderful. Almost like a real mother since my parents relocated to Atlanta. She has, in her own way, filled in for my parents. What timing, huh?"

"Are you almost there?" he caringly asked.

"Yep, I will be there in five minutes exactly."

"Okay, baby, call me when you get home. Love you."

"I will, I miss you!" Brianna found herself unconsciously not saying the words "I love you" back to him. She loved Allan but wasn't in love with him. With all the talking on the phone, she still managed to be on time. When she went in, people were waiting on available tables. "Good evening! How many people in your party?" the smiling little hostess asked.

"I believe my person is already seated. Her name is Mrs. McNeil."

"Yes, she has been expecting you. Right this way."

As they were walking into a private section, not only did she notice Alice waving at her, but a slew of other people. There seated was Mr. McNeil, Tamika, Angel, Peter and the other two associates from the office, and her mom and dad. They all yelled, "Surprise!" Brianna was really surprised; she was not expecting this at all. She hugged and kissed her parents and friends. There was an older attractive couple there whom she didn't know. Alice walked her over to them and introduced them.

"Brianna, I would like for you to meet Mr. and Mrs. Jones, Allan's parents."

"Hello. It's nice to meet you both." Brianna was warm but did not understand why she was meeting them for the first time tonight. This whole thing was not making any sense. Everyone started to take a seat, but there was a chair that was empty. She turned to Alice. "Are we expecting someone else?"

"We sure are, Brianna. He is right behind you," Alice said while nodding her head, indicating for Brianna to look the other way. When Brianna turned around, there was Allan.

"Hi, baby!" He leaned over and gave her a kiss. Brianna could not make heads or tails of what was happening. "Attention, everyone, thank you for coming out this evening. I know that I did this on short notice, so thank you, Alice, Tamika, and Ange, for all of your help. To both sets of parents, I know I should have waited to have a more intimate setting in which both of us could have met together, but I couldn't wait. Mom and Dad, I really wanted you to meet the woman that I am so proud of in her new business venture. To her parents, I hope you will allow me the chance to get to know you as time go on. You have a great daughter." Both parents were smiling from ear to ear. "Brianna, this is just my way to say congratulations. I am, again, really proud of you."

She began to tear up. This is the side of him that she really loved. Everyone was clapping for her. "Okay, but before we begin to order, I have one more thing to say." He moved the chair out of the way and pulled her out of her seat. He held her left hand, reached in his other pocket, and began placing a 3.5-karat engagement ring on her finger. "Brianna Monique Godfrey, will you do me the honor of being my wife?" It was an oval-shaped solitaire with two diamonds on the side, set in platinum. The diamond had amazing clarity.

No, this can't be happening. What will Maxwell say about this? She looked over at Tamika and Angel immediately. Angel was covering her mouth, and Tamika flashed her a nervous smile. When she turned back to Allan, he had a nervous smile as well.

"Yes, Allan, I will marry you." Everyone cheered and clapped. The rest of the dinner went over well. Alice, unknowingly to all the guests, gave Brianna a comforting pat on her leg under the table. After dinner, fortunately, Brianna's parents insisted on staying at the Hyatt near the airport as they had to catch a very early flight in the morning. Allan had to drive his parents back to Maryland that night, because his father was not feeling well and left his medicine behind. Allan felt really guilty that he had to leave, but Brianna insisted that he take care of his parents. Everyone had left except for her entourage, Tamika and Angel, who sat there quietly waiting for the flood. And there it was, a flood of tears. Angel asked the waitress to bring over a glass of white wine for Brianna.

"Girls! What the fuck? I'm not in love with him."

Tamika hugged her around her shoulders. "Brie, go home. We can talk about this tomorrow."

Brianna went home, took a Xanax, and fell straight to sleep. When she woke up the next morning, she looked at her hand.

"No, it wasn't a damn dream," she muttered.

She called Peter to let him know that she would be working from home. She did. She poured herself in her job. Maxwell had called her five times, and she refused to answer his calls. Allan called and she pretended that she was sick so she didn't have to discuss last night. She knew that, at some point, she would have to speak to him. It was now 2:00 PM when her phone interrupted her working. In looking at the phone, it was the hospital.

"Brianna Godfrey speaking."

"Ms. Godfrey, this is Dr. McPherson from ICU. We have a Ms. Phoebe Steele here, and she has you listed as a point of contact for emergencies."

Brianna's heart began to race. She was hurt and pissed with Phoebe, but she didn't want her dead. "What's wrong with her?"

"I would need for you to come down to the hospital. She's not looking too good at the moment. If you can come down, we are authorized to give you more details."

Brianna threw on some clothes and was at the hospital in twenty-five minutes. She was able to find her in intensive care. She had on an oxygen mask with plenty of monitors as well as an IV stuck in her. A nurse was in the room checking her vitals.

126

"Excuse me, I am her friend, Brianna Godfrey. How is she doing?"

"Well, she is very weak right now. I'll get the doctor. He is expecting you." Phoebe looked so pitiful lying there.

"Ms. Godfrey?"

"Yes." Brianna was immediately struck with fear when the doctor had such a stern look on his face.

"Ms. Godfrey, as you probably already know, Ms. Steele was in here to get an abortion. On her form, she indicated that she only had two previous procedures. Once we began, everything seemed to be going rather smoothly until there was a drop in her blood pressure and heart rate. She began to lose almost an exorbitant amount of blood. This crisis lasted for about two hours. We had to call in a special team of doctors who were then able to get the hemorrhaging under control. Her uterus was in an awful condition and needed an emergency hysterectomy performed. It also appeared that she had several abortions before this one. She will never be able to conceive children. Hopefully, she will be okay, but we will have to monitor her closely for the next three days or so. I'll leave you alone with her. She was sedated earlier. She should be coming out of it in a few."

"Thank you, Doctor." Brianna sat by her bedside when, after forty-five minutes or so, Phoebe began to open her eyes. When she noticed, she went and retrieved a nurse. The nurse once again checked her vitals and removed Phoebe's mask.

"You are awake, Ms. Steele. That is awesome! If you need anything, press this button. You are a little weak so continue to rest." The nurse then left the room.

"Hi, Phoebe, it seems as though you put the doctors through the ringer."

Phoebe started to clear her throat before trying to speak. "Thank you for coming, Brianna. I had no one else to call. You are listed on all my medical information."

"I was told. No worries."

"I did all of this to get you in here to talk to me." Being weak, Phoebe was trying to joke with her.

"Well, missy, I will make sure you are okay, but you know, we are not okay. You betrayed me and I don't know why. Let's not talk about it now. Just get better." Brianna meant what she said but slid a sincere smile; she did not want that to be the focus of her being there for her.

"No, I want to talk about it now. I don't feel a thing. They have me on some good shit. So let me take advantage of it." She again began to clear her throat. "I met Melissa about five months ago. She said that she remembered me from that one visit to your college over a weekend. I didn't remember her; however, she appeared at my job and introduced herself. Years later, I would say that I only heard you mention her name vaguely, like once or twice. If you think about it, I really wasn't around all of that chaos. At first, she made it seem like she was back to make amends. Then it went from wanting to make amends to her bashing you. I really let her get in my head. She said that you went to Howard to get away from me and that you thought that you were so much better than me."

"Are you serious, Phoebe?" Brianna could not believe what she was hearing.

"Yeah, I am. So once she found out where you worked, she vowed that she would get back at you for two-facing her and me. That night at the club, when her husband ran into you, that was planned. Her becoming your boss and making you miserable, that was planned. From what I can tell, Natalie and Maxwell, they were just innocent bystanders." Phoebe started making faces. The medicine that she thought was good was actually starting to wear off. Phoebe began to breathe a little faster and harder from the sharp pain.

"Phoebe, are you all right? Stop talking and let me go get the nurse." Even though Brianna was caught up in the story, she didn't want to see her in pain.

"No, Brie. Let me finish. One day I went to visit her and Maxwell Jr. He went to his room and her husband was away on a business trip. She received a call, and I distinctly heard her tell the person on the phone, 'No, your son is out of town on a business trip.' Then she excused herself and went into the next room. What she didn't realize was that she pressed the intercom button on the phone, which placed her call on the speaker. A man with a heavy voice and a thick Haitian accent asked her when she was bringing his son down to spend time with him. Melissa replied that she couldn't keep popping down at a drop of a dime. In return, the man on the phone told Melissa to tell Maxwell that she was going to visit her father. He wanted to *have* her now and that he would not take no for an answer. She was ordered to be in Miami within forty-eight hours. He did say to her that the silly vendetta against you could wait. Brianna, I believe she is having an affair with Maxwell's…"

At this time, the pain must have been too much for Phoebe. Her face was twisted, indicating that she was experiencing great pain. Phoebe was sweating profusely and said that she was freezing. Brianna called the nurse. She ran out the room, trying desperately to get anyone that could possible help. She went back to Phoebe's side to hold her hand.

"Phoebe, hang in there." Brianna began to tear up. She had never seen her in so much pain.

"Brie…Brianna, please forgive me. There is so much more, but I need to know if you can forgive me?"

"I do, I do," Brianna answered while holding her hand tightly. One of the nurses asked Brianna to move to the side. When they pulled back the sheets, they saw that her bed was full of blood.

CHAPTER TWENTY-ONE

I Need You

People started to leave the gravesite. It took everything within Brianna not to walk over and slap Melissa. She took her lover away, and she caused distance between her and her childhood friend. Brianna wanted to run over and expose the dark secret to Maxwell. Tamika, who was never close to Phoebe, could not believe that she was gone, and Angel was blown away as well. Allan never let Brianna's hand go. He stayed with her that night, but of course, he had to get back home to spend time with his daughter and then take a flight out the country shortly thereafter. That night, she really didn't want to be around the girls. She was at home looking at old photos and drinking. There was a knock at the door. When she opened the door, it was Maxwell. She looked at him and broke down in his arms. He picked her up and took her to the bedroom. He removed her clothes and took a warm washcloth and wiped her face.

"I love you so much, Maxwell."

"I love you too."

"Maxwell, make love to me, please."

"That's not what you need. Let me hold you tonight." Like their first date, that's all he did. He held her close. The next morning when she woke up, he was staring at her. She was sure that he would be gone. "How do you feel?" he asked with concern.

"Drained I guess. Thank you for staying with me last night."

"No problem. I guess Mr. College Boy had other things to do?"

"You guess right. He is flying off to Italy." She placed her left hand on his thigh. Unknowingly, the drama was about to begin.

"What the fuck? You are engaged now?" He was holding her hand, looking down at her ring. "Damn, it's like that, baby?" Maxwell got up and put on his pants and shirt.

"Max, don't leave yet. I need you." She jumped in front of him. She wouldn't know what to do if Maxwell decided to leave her again.

"What's going on with the ring, Brianna? Does anyone care about how I feel or what I need? My father won't back off, my wife is a needy bitch, and my son, well, sometimes let's just say that he does not really feel like he is my son. You are the only thing in my life that is right, and now you're getting ready to marry this joker. I hope he loves you, Brianna, because I damn sure do! But at this moment, I got to leave. I need to take a break from everyone and everything!"

He moved her aside and left. She stood there motionless. Brianna wanted to tell him about his father, Melissa, and the little boy. She wanted to be sensitive to his feelings and thought that if she told him what she knew, the information that Phoebe shared would crush him. His father seemed like a cold-hearted irrational man; he was less than a good father to Maxwell. He thought nothing about pimping his own son out while he was reaping the benefits. Brianna wanted to fix things for him, but when and how?

Later that day, she decided to check her voice mail. She had at least ten messages. All of the messages were from Peter, confirming that things were being handled in her absence. Brianna got dressed and went into the office. It was hard, but she managed to get a lot done. She gave Peter and the other two associates, Stephanie and Amy, off on Monday. They had been really going beyond and above the call of duty, so she wanted to reward them with a three-day weekend. Moving through the day, the work was almost therapeutic. She was distracted from thinking about Maxwell and managed not to dwell on Phoebe's death. Friday night, Allan gave her a call.

"Hey, sweetie, what's the date?"

"Huh?" Brianna had no idea what he was referring to.

"Babe, we need to set a date. Since the death of Phoebe, I have realized that time is of the essence. We don't need to prolong this engagement, so what do you think about getting married in January?"

This is not what I want to deal with right now! Is he kidding me?
"Allan, let's slow down. We just got engaged, and besides, wouldn't you like it if we both got to know each other's families first? Not to mention, I haven't had the pleasure of meeting your lovely daughter." She was desperately trying to make her case.

"Brie, you are acting like we are just getting to know each other. Hon, we have known each other for at least four years. Your parents seem like my kind of peeps, and my parents are laid-back, so don't sweat that. I agree with you about my daughter. I will be back in the states early tomorrow morning. I will pick up my daughter, and we will be at your house around tomorrow afternoon. She's a handful, but this will get you ready for our children," he said while trying to contain his laughter.

"Allan, can we talk about this a little more when you get here?" She was pissed that he would be that inconsiderate to believe that she would plan a wedding this soon after a friend's death. *Damn him! Damn him!*

While driving, Brianna noticed she hadn't driven far, only through two lights, to be exact. She was at Creek's Edge Apartments, where Alice stayed when she's in town. She dialed Alice's number.

"Hello, Ms. Brianna!"

"Hi, Alice."

"You don't sound so happy. What's wrong?" Alice was very concerned.

"Alice, are you busy? I am sitting outside of your apartment," Brianna said, feeling slightly embarrassed at being so intrusive.

"Come on up."

When Brianna arrived at her door, Alice was standing there waiting to greet her. "Here, have a seat. I have already taken the liberty to pour you a little tea. Put your sugar in it. I didn't do that." Brianna spooned in a couple of teaspoons of sugar. She took a sip and smiled at her.

"Umm…Alice, this isn't just tea."

"No, darling, it isn't. I poured in a little dark rum. It will help you to relax." They both started to giggle like two little high school girls. "Brianna, you aren't happy about your engagement, are you?"

"No, I'm not. What gave it away?"

"When you looked at your girlfriends and did not instantly respond with a yes." Alice reached for Brianna's hand. She felt bad for her when she saw a tear about to surface. "Who is he, dear?"

"What…what do you mean? I'm just not ready that's all." Brianna wasn't ready to completely confide in her.

"Brianna, did you make that decision after that gentleman kissed you at the gala or before?"

"Oh my god. Alice, I don't know what to say. I'm sorry. I know you think very highly of Allan. I will make this work with him. It's not what you think. Please don't think any less of me."

"Calm down, Brianna. How easily do you forget about my situation with Mr. Conti? Do you love Allan?"

"Yes. Yes, I do."

"Do you love that gentleman that kissed you?"

"Yes, Alice, I do. I am in love with him." At that point, she filled Alice in on the whole story.

"Brianna, your heart and your mind are warring against each other. You have a lot of decisions ahead of you. Either way, it will not put you in a good place. This may be your opportunity to fix what happened eleven years ago. It's strange that all of this has resurfaced. Think things out first and follow your heart. Just know that if you decide to marry Allan, I will be there to cheer you on. If you decide that you can work things out with Maxwell, I will be there to cheer you on. If you lose both of them, I will still be there for you."

Brianna's liking for Alice really had grown that night. She knew that even though she had a natural mother that loved her, Alice was also like a second mother. So much so that Brianna wanted to please her as well. On her drive home, she conference called both Tamika and Angel.

"Girls, I think that I should tell Maxwell."

"Uh, I think that you should stay out of it. Brie, you have no proof. How do we know if Phoebe wasn't trying to get back at Melissa for something?" Tamika answered.

"While she was in that much pain like Brie said that she was? I don't think I could stay that focus to form a lie just to get back at someone," Angel rebutted.

"Let's think. We need to find out some blood types, not to mention monitor Melissa's time that she disappears to spend with Maxwell's father."

"Tamika, what are we going to do with that information?" Brianna asked.

"We can figure all that out when we get that information collected. Then we can analyze it." There was a loud sound from Tamika's background. *Baaammmm!*

"What was that?" both Angel and Brianna asked.

"That was my literature book. I have to go, ladies!" Tamika hung up.

"Her literature book? When did she become a heavy reader?" Brianna chuckled.

"I know right. Did you hear her switch up on her vocabulary again? '*Collecting* information and *analyzing.*'" Angel laughed out.

CHAPTER TWENTY-TWO

The Instant Family

It was now Saturday morning, and she was hoping that Allan would call her to inform her that he couldn't make it. She was also hoping that Maxwell would call her too. Brianna wanted to see how he was doing since the whole engagement thing. He never made an attempt to call her. Melissa was so unstable that she probably had his phone tapped.

Later on, around 2:00 PM, Allan and his little girl arrived. She was a beautiful three-year-old by the name of Jasmine Nicole Jones. Like the typical little girl, she was dressed in all pink. She clung to her daddy very tightly. After about an hour, she began to warm up to Brianna. She fed her lunch and was even able to rock her to sleep. She placed her in the Pack 'N Play and covered her with her little blanket.

"Baby, motherhood agrees with you." Allan kissed Brianna and gave her a big hug. "Okay, let's talk about our wedding date. I know I was rambling on the other day, but is January okay?" Allan asked with much optimism in his voice.

"Well, actually, baby, can we do it in the spring?" Unbeknownst to him, Brianna was really trying to compromise. If she has her way, she would have the wedding two years from now.

"What? Hell no! Are you changing your mind? I wanted to do this like yesterday to be honest. Are you changing your mind, Brie?" Allan was trying to read the look on her face.

"Allan, I just don't want us to rush it."

"We're not rushing anything. If not January, can we do it in February?"

"That is only giving us five months to plan it!" Brianna was growing very irritated with the whole discussion. "Allan, let's plan for July. Baby, I am just starting my business, and I am still dealing with Phoebe's death. It's just too much, too fast."

"Okay, Okay. July, it is," Allan said while forcing a smile. He reluctantly compromised with her. "You weren't the only one who lost something."

"What do you mean by that?" Brianna gave him a complete look of confusion. He barely knew Phoebe.

"Never mind, Brie."

She wanted to experience the married life and to one day have kids, but she knew that now she had to face the reality that it would not involve Maxwell. In her heart, she needed Maxwell's blessing to move on.

CHAPTER TWENTY-THREE

Ms. Sunshine

Monday morning, she went into the office. The phones were busy, but it was nothing that Brianna couldn't handle. Still with her staffs' absence, she was able to work on a lot the upcoming events, and once done, it allowed her to call some of her vendors to now book them for her own wedding. They were all happy for her and promised her that would be more than happy to be at her service. As she was wrapping up her day, Tamika walked in the office.

"Hey, Tamika! What a surprise!" she joyfully shouted.

"Hi, Brie! I was over at the mall, so I couldn't resist dropping by to see your new office. It's tight, girl."

"Thanks. Tamika, it still hasn't hit me that I am running my own agency. It's like a wonderful dream. The downside is that I think that Allan sees it as a hobby."

"Seriously, I thought that this is what men wanted. An independent woman, at least that's what all the rappers are spelling out in their raps nowadays." Both of them started laughing. "I see the bridal magazines in front of you. Have you guys set a date?"

"Oh, yeah, I haven't had a chance to tell you about his assertiveness in that matter. He called the other day to inform me that he wanted to plan the wedding in January. I had to do some fast-talking, so we agreed on July."

"What's the rush? You had to wait how long for him to get his act together? Wait one minute, should I ask you why you are procrastinating?"

Brianna started to laugh. "Procrastinating?" The old Tamika would have simply asked, "Bitch, why all of a sudden you startin' to trip?" She decided not to bring it to her attention. "Okay, real talk, I am in love with whom? Girl, after the funeral, Maxwell spent the night with me. He wasn't trying to sex me up. He just wanted to hold me. My significant other, so to speak, wanted to treat me like shit. Allan could care less. He wanted me to fuck him. Where is the sensitivity in that? Can someone please explain that? Again, with Maxwell, I am dealing with him walking out on me. He saw that damn engagement ring on my hand and left!"

Tamika was staring at Brianna in complete awe. From this conversation, she could sense that her friend was hurting and thought it would be a good idea to try and distract her. "Come on, Ms. Sunshine, let's go over to PF Changs and get a bite to eat."

"Ms. Sunshine?" Brianna asked.

"Yeah girl, like in that movie when he told that chick she had *sunshine* between her legs. That character that was married left his wife over that stuff." They began to laugh uncontrollably but were abruptly interrupted; both girls were shocked to see a very unpleasant and unexpected guest.

"Ladies." Melissa stood there practically demanding both of their attention.

"So look what wandered off the street. What the hell do you want, *Mrs. King*?" Tamika asked, hoping that Melissa wanted to be smacked around a little.

"Ms. Whoever You Are, I have no beef with you. I would appreciate it if you would listen quietly or leave." Melissa really did not remember who Tamika was, nor did she care.

"You must be out your rabbit-ass mind if you think that I am going to bow down to your pathetic ass. Whatever you think that you need to say, just remember to choose your *loving* words carefully. Whatever you say just may be your last words!" Tamika said with a stern glare.

Melissa turned to completely face Tamika, but as she was getting ready to fix her mouth to say something that she should not, Tamika walked from behind the desk to stand beside Brianna who was seated. Tamika reached in her purse and placed a .38 on the desk to send her a little message. Brianna did a quick glance at the gun, then immediately fell into position.

"Melissa, what is so important that you had to come in here and disrupt me planning my wedding?"

Melissa, who was not ready for the gun, pretended that she was not fazed by it. "Brianna, I'm glad to hear that you have found your own man. Now you can leave mine alone."

"Ain't nobody messin' with your man!" Tamika yelled at her.

"You know what? I got this, Tamika. Melissa, I am so tired of your petty ass! You couldn't measure up to me the night you met him and your dumb ass came back for more. If you know like I know, you should pack up your house of lies and leave!"

"You have something to say, Brianna, then say it! Otherwise, stay away from my husband. Does your fiancé know that you are still in love with another man? It would be awful if he found out."

With quickness that shocked Tamika and Melissa, Brianna sprinted around the desk and with great force to shove Melissa. Tamika heard Melissa's head thump against the wall. Tamika covered her mouth, trying to conceal her smirk—she loved this. However, when she thought that Melissa was going to get into a shoving match with Brianna, she walked over with her .38 in hand and cocked the trigger.

"No, no, no, sugar, if you want to roll up on big girls like you are a heavyweight champion and shit, then let me show you how the big girls in the 804 get down."

"Before you get hurt, Melissa, you need to leave." Brie looked at her with a face that was almost as deadly as the gun that Tamika had drawn.

She got her composure and was trying to say something again, but Brianna wasn't having it. "Are you that stupid? Shut up and go home, but know this, sweetness, you are on my turf. If I were you, I would be looking over my shoulder!" Brianna said sternly.

Tamika held open the door to let her out. When Tamika watched her get on the elevator, she came back and locked the door to slow down a possible reappearance. "Do you believe her?"

"No, Tamika, I can't believe you! Girl, give me that damn gun!"

Tamika willingly handed the gun over. Brianna, who was standing at that time, fell back in the chair, laughing. "You are so my girl!"

"What? What?" Tamika asked while laughing at her. "So! I know it's not loaded. I didn't have time this morning. The clip is in my purse. I wasn't going to use it on the trick anyway. I just wanted to scare her," she said as if she was a little kid.

"Help me cut these lights off so we can go get something to drink. I was going to buy but girl you stressed me out worse than she did, so it's your treat." She chuckled.

"B, we are going to get to the next step and get rid of that girl for good, right? You know I have people."

"Tamika? Hush, girl, and slow your roll."

CHAPTER TWENTY-FOUR

The Proof Is in the Pudding

It was another day, and she had a lot on her plate. "Peter, can you come in my office please?" When he came in, he was looking like a sophisticated younger version of Tim Gunn from the show *Project Runway*. "As always, Peter, you are looking quite fierce."

"Thanks, Brianna." Then he began whispering to her, "Your Manolo Blahniks and leather bag that you are sporting today would look even better with my outfit." Both were very tickled at that quiet confession.

"Peter, as you already know, Melissa is not my biggest fan, and this all stemmed from a man that we met while we were in college." Peter covered his mouth while placing his other hand on his chest and let out a gasp. "What? Is the guy hot or rich?"

"Yes and yes, he is hot and his pocket just happens to be full-grown. However, technically, he should have been my husband. She did her dirt and twisted his arm to marry her. Now she wants to rub it in my face. I have reason to believe that I can rock her world and make her disappear by exposing her, but I need some proof. Peter, in my absence from the agency, did you ever overhear her talking to any doctor's offices here in Richmond?"

"Mmmm...let me think. Yes, she did. Matter of fact, I had to make an appointment for her son. He has allergies and had to get some lab work done."

"Really, Peter?" Brianna was getting excited. "Do you remember the doctor's office?" She practically was crossing her toes and fingers at this point.

"Sure do. My cousin, Rita, works there."

"Okay, Peter, here is the kicker. Can I get a copy of his records? I can promise you that no one will get in trouble."

"Let me contact her. I'm sure that I can get it."

Brianna was relieved to hear that. She immediately got up and gave him a big hug and closed-mouth kiss on his lips. He looked at her with one eyebrow arched and started to laugh.

"Brianna, you know I think you're sexy and a fabulous dresser, but you know that I like men, right?" They both began to giggle.

CHAPTER TWENTY-FIVE

What a Turkey!

For the next couple of weeks, the girls were determined to work on their little vendetta. Brianna and Peter went after and successfully obtained 80 percent of Melissa and Natalie's clientele.

A month had managed to slip by and still no word from Maxwell. It felt like she was having déjà vu with the disappearing act all over again. She was sad, but she was tired of going through the same stuff with him. Brianna kept reassuring herself that eventually he would show up. When she would get out her car, Brianna would look over her shoulder. She even hoped that while meeting with a client in DC, he would somehow track her down. Another month had come and gone, and nothing had change—no Maxwell. Since Thanksgiving was approaching. She and the girls decided that they would head to Atlanta to have dinner with Brianna's parents, a little shopping, and hit the clubs.

"I don't believe you, Brianna. This would be our first Thanksgiving together as a couple and you have decided to go to your parents!" Allan was yelling at the top of his lungs. "You didn't even think that we should be together? Damn!"

"Allan, I really don't want to argue. I must finish packing and be at the airport in one hour to meet the girls. Baby, just let me do this without you throwing a fit. Do I piss and moan when you're flying out two to three times a month? I bet you that I will spend more time alone when we are married." With this argument, Brianna was not about to give in. She noticed that Allan had to always manipulate the situation, always wanting people to do things on his terms. This time it was not about to happen. She was putting her foot down.

"I guess you are going, huh?" he sarcastically asked her again.

"Yes, baby, I am. I just want to get away." While still on the phone, she finished packing and was walking to the door with one of her bags.

"Fine, Brie, do you and I will definitely do me!" Brianna went to ask him what he meant by that, but he hung up on her.

Okay, that was a real bitch-ass move. Whatever!

When she arrived at the airport with the girls, they were off to Atlanta. The good thing about having the girls with her was that she didn't have to stay at her mom's house. The next day was Thanksgiving, and her mother outdid herself with all the food she had prepared. The house was packed with her mother's family and a few new friends that just joined her church. Before going out that night, they headed back to the hotel to take a nap, shower, and change. When Brianna had gotten up from her sleep, she wanted to call Allan, making sure that they were okay. He picked up the phone promptly when she called. She heard Jasmine laughing and playing with someone in the background.

"Hi, baby," Brianna said, being full of life.

"Hey," Allan replied coldly.

"Sounds like you are having fun."

"I am. My parents are here, Jasmine, and Stephanie."

"Stephanie? As in your ex-wife Stephanie?"

"You got it. She helped me cook for Thanksgiving. Look, I would like to keep chatting with you right now, but we are about to take the dessert and coffee into the living room. Love ya!'" Again, he hung up the phone before she could respond. Brianna shook her head and began to laugh at his childishness.

"Ladies, let's have fun tonight!"

"Is everything okay?" Angel asked while pulling her outfit out of her bag.

"Why is he at his house, having a big family function with his ex-wife cooking?" Brianna was pissed just mentioning it.

"Shut up, girl!" Tamika couldn't believe what she was hearing. "Why would he invite his ex-wife to come to the house and cook for his parents? See, there he goes trippin' again!"

"Yeah, but you know what. I am quite sure that he thinks that I am going to let that ruin my trip. How do you say 'that is not going to happen'?"

"Hell nah!" the girls both answered together.

"That's right," Brianna said. Tamika pulled out a bottle of Patron, and they started getting ready.

It was eleven thirty at night, and the girls were ready to get their party on. Since it was Thanksgiving, there was a lot of in-town and out-of-town people looking to dance their turkey dinners off. Brianna and the girls had rented a black fully loaded Escalade. Guys were trying to get a good look, but because the windows were tinted, they were unsuccessful. However, the girls could peep them out. Based upon seeing a few well-known rappers going in, they appeared to have found *the* spot. As they parked and walked up to the line, they caught a glimpse of more celebrities going in.

"Damn, I don't feel like standing in this line," Brianna said with a playful pout.

"Oh, we're not, hold on." Tamika was looking like a tall model out of a magazine. She had on a sexy form-fitting dress with her back out and a black long weave that she pulled and gathered over one shoulder. She was looking like a darker version of Beyoncé. When she walked up to the front of the line, one of the bouncers could not take his eyes off her.

"Miss, you are coming in, right?" She pretended that she was busy looking for someone across the street, pretending that she did not hear him. "Miss?" This guy was sexy—six feet and seven inches, dark skinned, with curly hair.

"Oh yeah, I met some guy earlier today that said he could get me and my girls in without waiting. I don't see him. I should have known, huh?"

"Baby girl, I'll let you in, but do you think you can slide me your number?"

"Sure, baby. I would love to give you my number." Tamika summoned for her girls to come up so they could all go in. The bouncer was impressed with her entourage. When the girls got inside, they knew that they were in the place to be. The dance floor was packed; people were doing their thing to one of Fetty Wap's song. Brianna and the girls were dancing where they stood when three drinks were sent over.

"Here, ladies, these came straight from the bar by Antonio, who is our charming bouncer working the door." Tamika began to smile and decided to go back to tell him thank you. Angel, all of sudden, let out a scream. Her boo-thang, Craig, came out of the blue walking toward her.

"Girl, is your boy missing you that much?" Brianna laughed.

Brianna spoke to him, and he gave her a hug. He really was good for her. Angel never talked about him too much, but they knew that she was really feeling him. Since he was five years her junior, she sometimes felt like he would wake up one day and realize that he was trying to get with an old lady.

"Okay, lovebirds, go hit the floor." The song changed to one of Big Sean's latest songs. A fine brother came over to scoop Brianna up and take her on the floor. Brianna had her hair down with a tight red sleeveless dress. Her four inches Jimmy Choo black boots gave her a model look; her curvaceous build made guys do a double stare at her that night. The girls were having a ball. Angel disappeared with her beau. Tamika and Brianna were going to do breakfast with Antonio before they headed back to the hotel. When the crowd was thinning out, Brianna looked with nervousness and disbelief.

"Tamika, pull out your camera phone."

"Why? What's wrong?" Tamika asked while trying to get her phone.

"I'm going outside by the truck. Tell Antonio to take a picture of that little waitress. But make sure she's standing right in front of the VIP section right there. Don't look now, but Melissa is behind you in the VIP section, sitting with Maxwell's father."

"You have got to be kidding me! Okay. I got it." Tamika willingly accepted her task. Brianna went outside, and Tamika got Antonio to take a picture of the waitress, saying that she wanted some snapshots so she can prove back home she was here. She then pretended that she had to run to the bathroom while he took the picture. She was sure that the flash would make them look over, and she didn't want to be spotted by Melissa. When he came outside to give her the phone, they all left for breakfast. The girls could not wait to get to the room and talk about seeing Melissa. Brianna ran up to the room and left Antonio and Tamika pulling up the rear. She rode with him and allowed him to drop her off at the lobby. Tamika finally got in the room.

"Tamika, let's look at the photo," Brianna said like an excited little kid.

"Girl, why he said that he took two pictures because he wasn't sure if the first one was clear enough."

"Good!" Brianna was glad to hear that. Tamika began to review the pictures with Brianna. The first picture was of Maxwell's father holding Melissa's face in his hands. "Wow, they look comfortable." Tamika chuckled as she scrolled to the next picture. Tamika hit Brianna's arm so hard that she screamed. It was a picture of them kissing.

"Tamika, send those pictures to my phone and you a keep a copy too."

Sunday, on the flight back home, the girls were exhausted from shopping and partying. When Brianna got home, it was six o'clock that evening. She unpacked, took a shower, and relaxed. The relaxation came to halt when a call came in from Allan. Her first thoughts were to ignore him, but now she was ready to show him who was running things. With a very upbeat, carefree tone, she answered the phone.

"Hello, Allan."

"So how was your trip?" Brianna could clearly hear the annoyance in his voice.

"Thanksgiving was good, and the girls and I had a lot of fun. How was Thanksgiving with your family?"

"Brie, cut the crap. You know you want to say something about Stephanie being with us." Allan was ready to push Brianna's buttons.

"Allan, why would I care that the mother of your child was with you and your parents? Baby, if you need someone to step into my place and stroke your ego, then by all means, let her do the work. We're both attractive and intelligent people, so surely, we should never take for granted that we could never find someone that would like to keep company with us." Brianna smirked because she knew that had to sting.

"Brianna, I thought it would be nice to invite her over to help me prepare dinner. I couldn't be rude and ask her to leave. Not to mention, Brie, you chose to be with your girls over me, your man. Don't think for one minute that I am going to stand by while you continue to put me on the back burner. When we are married and you move up here, let's see if your girls can make it without you then."

Brianna hadn't thought about relocating anywhere. "You think that I am going to ditch my friends? I figured that you would be relocating at least halfway. We could find a home maybe in Fredericksburg."

"Okay, Brianna. I don't think so." He smugly chuckled.

"You know what, Allan? I was really trying to keep my cool. Tell you what, Mr. President, call Stephanie and see if she would like to reconsider." Brianna hung up before he could respond. He called back at least twice, but she wasn't going to give him the satisfaction of replying. It also appeared that he did not leave a message either. For that, she was glad. She went in the room that was set up like an office and began transferring the photos of Maxwell's father onto her computer. She was also able to enlarge them and print them both out. She retrieved the folder that contained Maxwell Jr.'s medical information, which indicated that he was O negative, and placed it all in there for safe keeping. She wasn't sure how she was going to find out both Max's and Melissa's blood type, but she was sure there would be a way. However, the pictures alone would be enough to expose her.

CHAPTER TWENTY-SIX

Wanted but Still All Alone

December was now here, and she began to settle down a little bit with her company; she now had one benefit and three corporate holiday functions to execute. Brianna and Allan obviously had the physical distance to contend with, but now they were dealing with mental issues. In addition to that, she still had not heard one word from Maxwell. More importantly, she was glad that she had not received any surprise visits from Melissa. Brianna purposely did not accept any events one week prior and one week after Christmas. She wanted to enjoy the holiday and for the staff to do the same. This Friday, two weeks prior to Christmas, Brianna was still in the office after letting her staff go home.

"Hello? Is anyone here?"

When Brianna looked up, Natalie was standing in the doorway of her office. Brianna was shocked.

"Hi, Brianna. I am sorry to interrupt you. Do you have a few minutes?"

"Sure," Brianna said suspiciously. "Have a seat."

"Thanks, Brianna. First, I would like to apologize for the way things happened. I had no idea that I was going to be a part of a personal attack on you. I was really excited when I received the invitation to buy the company. However, one of the owners said that they also had another buyer in mind. They felt that it was only fair to present me with the opportunity, but at the end of day, I am left to believe that their sense of obligation was motivated by money alone. However, seeing now firsthand how Melissa operates, I am quite sure there was some sort of hidden agenda." Natalie was staring Brianna directly in the eye. Not one sign of arrogance that she was known for was on display.

"Natalie, in retrospect, I do remember you referring to her as an associate. At that very time, I did not know that you were referring to her. As you can imagine that at some point, I would be left to believe that you are a part of this mess." Brianna was anxiously awaiting her response.

"No, you are mistaken. Brianna, think about it. Do I talk about my personal life? Have you walked in my office and heard me on the phone, laughing it up with any friends, male or female? Being in a strained marriage and no one to vent to, here came Melissa. Not only was she a potential business partner but also a potential friend. One night, I had her over for dinner. She asked me to give her the names of all the employees. I was asked to tell her about each employee and what I thought of them. When it got to you, she became very excited as if she could not wait to see you. She went on and on about how you girls were best friends from college, but because one of your boyfriends left you for her, unfortunately, you both lost touch. Over time, you guys managed to work things and rekindled your relationship. I had no idea that this information was not true. She asked that I not mention anything to you because she wanted to pleasantly surprise you. Brianna, I did I know the so-called boyfriend is her now husband."

"Well, Natalie, what about seeing you at the club that night?" Brianna asked.

Natalie took a big sigh. She was sincerely hoping that Brianna believed what she was telling her, because it really was the truth. "I was scheduled to do dinner with her and her husband. We didn't do dinner because she called me, saying that she was at a pharmacy. Her son had taken ill. She insisted that Max and I go out anyway. She told me that he likes to dance and to see if the girls in the office had mentioned any particular club. If so, that was the best one to take him to. Fortunately for me, you had mentioned that club before. Otherwise, I wouldn't have known where to go." Suddenly, Natalie started laughing while shaking her head in disbelief. "Wow! What a conniving bitch!"

"What?" Brie asked, knowing the answer.

"Ta-daah! And there I was, dancing with Maxwell. Letting you know, in an unannounced way, *she's baaaaacck*. Brianna, she kept telling me that she wanted to surprise you. When I saw your friend Phoebe hanging around, and I am sorry for your lost, I was told that they were planning your surprise. As you can see, just from that, I bought in to the whole hush-hush thing. Brianna, can you forgive me?"

"Now that it makes sense to me, yes, I can absolutely forgive you! You have done nothing, and I thank you for not participating in her craziness. So how is business?"

Natalie laughed before answering. "I think that you already know the answer to that. Brianna, we have lost over half our clientele to you and not to mention some of our best employees. Melissa has bought me out, and I am glad. I am relocating to Boston to see if I can salvage my marriage, and I hear that congratulation is in order for your engagement."

Brianna got up to walk Natalie to the door. "Well, thank you and thank you for coming by to clear things up. You did not have to do this, but you taking the time out to clear things up between you and I, speak volumes of your character."

Natalie gave Brianna a hug. "Brianna, for all it's worth, from the arguments that I would hear resonating from Melissa's office, I think he must still love you and she knows it."

Brianna drove all the way home thinking about what Natalie told her. She could feel her anger grow more and more for Melissa.

How dare she just walk around like a spoiled brat and just mess up people's lives and dreams. Count your days of false entitlement, baby. I'm getting ready to put an end to that.

CHAPTER TWENTY-SEVEN

Happy Holidays

It was Christmas Eve, and Brianna was wrapping her remaining gifts. The girls would be coming over to do brunch and exchange gifts; she had agreed with Allan that she would be spending Christmas at his house. Tamika and Angel was at the house by 1:00 PM. Brianna had a rotation of Christmas music playing in her six-CD changer. She had everything from Destiny Child, Toni Braxton to Brian McKnight. After taking time out to remember Phoebe, they change the mood by cracking jokes and carrying on like they usually do.

"Brianna, are you looking forward to spending your Christmas with Allan and his daughter?" Angel asked.

"Girl, I don't know. Allan is a good guy, and I know that he will take care of me but he wants to do everything *Allan's* way. We can go from laughing to giving each other the silent treatment in about two seconds."

"And still no sound from Maxwell, Brianna?" Tamika asked.

"Nope, not one peep. You know what? Screw this! Let's exchange gifts," she said like a little kid. Brianna just wanted to change the conversation. Tamika did a little hooch dance because she received a pair of leather boots from Brianna and Angel gave her a one-hundred-dollar gift card to her favorite store. Angel gave Brianna a pair of Gucci sunglasses, and Brianna gave Angel the Coach Portfolio since she attended so many meetings at work. Tamika gave Angel a pair of black UGG boots, and Brianna, the Marc Jacobs bag she had been eyeing. Then Tamika gave both girls a flat small gift box.

"What is this? We said one gift a piece," Angel scolded Tamika.

"Okay, but open it." Tamika nervously smiled. Angel opened the box while Brianna stood over her shoulder to read the small card that was inside Tamika's box. They both screamed and hug her, knocking Tamika over on the sofa.

"When was all this going on?" Brianna asked.

"Well, that's just an impromptu invite that I made up from my computer. I will be receiving my bachelor's degree from VUU in the spring."

"I am so proud of you. So that explains the slight change in your vocabulary and the book that fell off your table that we could hear over the phone. Not to mention that you would be missing for hours in a day! Why didn't you tell us? We would have supported you!" Brianna sincerely asked her.

"I just wanted to make sure that I could go through with it. I'm getting older and I can't keep doing my thing in the streets. You guys thought I was being cheap, but I was paying for my classes and banking the rest." Tamika had the most self-pleased smile ever. The girls couldn't have been any happier than a parent. They kicked the celebrating up another notch when Brianna pulled out a bottle of champagne.

When the girls left, she began straightening up when she heard a light knock at the door.

One of those crazy girls must have realized they had to pee from all that drinking they were doing. Brianna was laughing as she was trotting to the door. "Oh my god! Come in!" It was Rico holding up Maxwell.

"Maxwell, what happened to you?" He didn't answer. Seeing that he would or maybe could not answer her, she questioned Rico. "What happened? Who did this to him?"

"Ma, do you have to ask? His papi! That man is crazy," Rico mumbled to her. Maxwell's face was swollen on one side as well as his lip. She covered her mouth in disbelief as she watched Maxwell grip his side from the pain. It was obvious that he had been punched. According to Rico, thankfully, his ribs had not been broken.

"Brianna, let me leave him here until tomorrow morning. I need to take care of something for Maxwell."

"Okay, but can you help me take him upstairs to my room?" Rico helped Maxwell upstairs and then Brianna walked him back to the door.

"It's good seeing you again, Brianna," Rico said while giving her a hug. "Brie, don't give up on him. That man loves you. Since he found out about your engagement, he has been fucking up left and right. He needs you. Take care of him. I should be back around 9:00 AM to get him."

"Okay," Brianna responded.

"Hey, how is my girl, Tamika?" Rico asked.

"She's good. She's about to graduate from college."

"That's what's up. Tell her that I asked about her."

When she went upstairs, Maxwell was asleep. She went to retrieve a glass of water and to also call Allan to inform him that she would not be coming up until tomorrow, mid-morning. Of course, he was pissed, but Brianna really didn't care. She placed the bottle of water on the nightstand, and he grabbed her wrist.

"Can you help me remove these clothes?"

"Sure, baby." She slowly removed his shoes and pants and eased his Armani knit shirt off. "Baby, do you need anything?"

"Come lay with me," he whispered. "Remove your clothes so I can feel you against me."

Brianna, without asking any questions, honored his request. She left on her bra and panty set and let down her hair. She crawled in and placed her arm lightly over the lower half of his stomach. She was trying to avoid touching his rib cage. He reached down and removed her engagement ring and asked her to put it way; she did exactly that. They laid there for what seemed like two hours, but it had only been one hour. He had awakened and was getting up.

"Baby, where are you going?" she asked. She jumped up to give him a helping hand.

"To the bathroom, I got it." She walked behind him anyway. She stood outside the door as he was peeing. He started yelling her name. She came and started shaking the pee off his penis. With great pain, he was trying to hold back his laughter. "Bae, why are you doing that?" he asked her.

"I thought that was what you needed me to do?" She had the cutest naive look on her face.

"No, baby. I was going to ask you to turn the water on in the shower."

"Oh." She laughed. "Sure." She cut the shower on while he leaned against the wall and slowly took his boxers off. "Are you getting in with me?"

"If that's what you want." She removed her remaining items, pulled her hair up, and went in after him. Brianna looked at him while he was letting the hot water run over his shoulders. Even the water looked like it was enjoying gliding over his beautiful body. She soaped up a loofa and began gently bathing him. He opened his eyes and began to stare at her. Brianna was being so gentle. She asked him to turn around so she could bathe the back of him; he obliged. Not like most black woman, Brianna could care less about getting her hair wet; she just wanted to take care of the man she loved. He turned around to look at her. He kissed her and held her close. She could see the hurt from what had happened to him in his eyes; she wanted to make that pain go away. Brianna kneeled and lovingly gave oral pleasure. He looked down at her and saw how beautiful her heart was. With every moan and groan he uttered, she took him further in her mouth. Brianna looked so sexy to him as the water was running over her and down her face. It was like the water was not an inconvenience to her at all. Before he could release, she stood up and held him, just in case he needed a little physical support.

"I love you, Ms. Godfrey. I really love you."

Brianna knew that he did. She could feel it. They got out of the shower, and she dried him down so he could get back in the bed. "Let me make you something to eat." She blew out her hair, threw on a T-shirt, and went to the kitchen. It was now 10:00 PM, and she had three texts from Allan saying that he missed her, he wanted to make love to her, and please don't renege. She sent him a text saying that she missed him too and she would be at his house not later than 1:00 PM tomorrow.

She returned with a small plate of food and something to drink. "Thanks, baby, but you don't have anything stronger than that to drink?"

"Yep. Since I gave you that medicine, I don't think that is what you need right now." Watching him, her curiosity was getting the best of her. "Baby, may I ask what happened?"

"I feel like I have no control over my life. Over the Thanksgiving holiday, don't you know that my wife decided that she had to meet a client in Atlanta? My father decided that he had to handle a small business deal. Max Jr. and I were left in Miami to do our own thing. Those two have been a pain in my ass to deal with lately. She finds more reasons for me to stay from home but says I don't make her happy. I must get damn near drunk to have sex with her. Sometimes I even wonder how my son got here. I'm a grown-ass man that cannot stand up to his father, who also just happens to be a heartless gangsta. What you see tonight is the result of his undying love for me. It was my fault. I didn't catch something while making a deal. It caused my father to lose a hundred thousand dollars."

"So what, Max, your father is loaded."

"That man does not care about that at all. He is greedy. Look at me, Brie, I can defend myself against any man, but against him, I just take the hits. I'm a man who is thirty years old and will be turning thirty-one shortly, and I am like this kid who still seeks his father's approval. I can't take this anymore, Brie."

Maxwell closed his eyes for a second and then stared at her. She thought that the eye that was slightly swollen was beginning to hurt him a little more, but he continued to speak.

"Have you set a wedding date yet?"

Maxwell, who Brianna had seen fight and totally mess guys up, walk into a room with guys gritting on him, acting like straight-up little bitches, was now so vulnerable, unbelievably exposed.

"Baby, let's not talk about me right now. I am worried about you. Come on, let me take that plate. Here, take this Xanax and lay back."

"Baby, you know I don't like taking pills, and why you look like you don't want to answer me?" he said with a frown.

"That's not it, Maxwell. I'm just really worried about you." She so desperately wanted to change the conversation.

"Brianna, is there something that you want to tell me? Go ahead and tell me. Things could not possibly get any worse, but if it does, I'm prepared to just leave! Maybe just flee this freaking country."

"What do you mean you are prepared to leave if it gets any worse?" Brianna just got him back and she didn't want to lose him again. "Look, Maxwell, I am tired of you coming and disappearing when you want!"

"Brianna Monique! You are the one that is getting married and obviously soon because you can't even tell me the date!"

"Oh, really? Yes, you are right! I am getting married in July if you must know! But let us not forget that you are the one who is already married, and I have never been the one you thought that you should fight for! So what? You want to use me when you are not getting any from your wife, or you want me to comfort you because you can't stand up to your father?" Brianna knew that she went entirely too far with that comment. "Maxwell, I didn't mean to say that. I'm sorry."

"You meant it, Brianna. Come here." She walked over to the side of the bed where he was sitting; she sat down beside him. They started to passionately kiss when they were interrupted by his phone. You could hear someone on the other end yelling and screaming profanities to the top of their lungs. Whoever it was on the other end, Maxwell was giving it right back. Maxwell disconnected the call, and his phone started to ring immediately after that call.

"Buenos, Rico." He spoke to Rico for about fifteen minutes in Spanish. Brianna interpreted a few of the words she could hear. What she could hear was something about a trip to pick up a lot of money. "Brianna, help me get dressed. My plans have changed. Rico will be here in twenty minutes instead of in the morning."

Brianna helped Maxwell get dressed. She didn't want him to go anywhere, but she knew that Maxwell didn't make a move unless it was important. "Brianna, I will try to give you a call in a couple of days or so. At some point, I will make arrangements to see you. I would like to spend more time with you." Maxwell felt like he was going to lose her to Allan. "Brianna, I have this feeling that you have something you want to tell me. What is it?"

Brianna wanted to run up to her office and get the information so he could see it for himself. With all that he had been through today, she would wait until they meet again. "Maxwell, I just worry about you. What is your blood type?"

"What? My blood type? Why?" He was puzzled with her odd question.

"Max, don't you think that I should know? You scare me. I should know important information like that." She was hoping that he would buy her explanation.

"Aren't you sweet? I am B positive. Any more questions, Doctor?" He managed to chuckle.

"What is Melissa's and your father's?" She was hoping that she wasn't pushing it.

"Girl, I don't know. Melissa's is AB positive, and that man that calls himself my father is O negative. Sad thing is, I bet if you ask them what is my blood type? They wouldn't even know."

"That's okay, baby. I am B positive too. If it's ever needed, I can donate to you. Which there won't be a chance for that, right? Because whatever you are about to get into, you will be careful!"

"Listen to you." His phone began to ring. "Hold on, Ms. Butterfly... Okay, Rico, I'll be right out."

They kissed and he left. By this time, it was 10:15 PM. Brianna thought about getting on the highway, but she wasn't ready to deal with Allan. She called Alice to wish her a merry Christmas. Alice was already in DC. They decided that they would meet up after Christmas to get caught up.

CHAPTER TWENTY-EIGHT

Is This Merry or What?

Upon arriving at Allan's house, there was another vehicle in the driveway; it was a big burgundy Yukon Denali. She parked to the side of the SUV and got her suitcase and the oversized bag of gifts. When she walked in, the house was quiet. She put the gifts around the tree and went upstairs. As she walked toward Allan's room, she heard voices. When she walked in Allan's bedroom, she saw him lying in bed with his daughter jumping around and a petite woman sitting on the edge of the bed laughing. When they saw Brianna standing there, he lost his laughter, and the unknown woman lost her smile. However, Jasmine waved at her.

"Good morning, Jasmine. Allan, when you get yourself together, why don't you meet me downstairs?" Brianna turned to exit the room.

"Brianna, hold on." Allan couldn't get out of the bed fast enough. However, she did hear Stephanie tell Allan that she didn't want a rude person around her daughter. If it weren't for the little girl in the room, she would have gladly shown her what's *rude*. Brianna went in the kitchen and looked in the sink; there were three of everything—three drinking glasses, three forks, and three plates.

This is bullshit, she thought. Finally, she heard a quick run down the stairs.

"Brie!" Allan yelled in panic.

"I'm here." Brianna was still standing by the sink. "How long have she been here?"

"What? How long has she been here? She came yesterday around 8:00 PM. Brie since you called me last night and told me that you wouldn't be here until 11:00 AM, I thought it would be okay if they both stayed."

"Let me get this straight. When I can't comply with your schedule, she is my fill-in. Now that's interesting." Brie walked to the living-room closet and retrieved her mink vest and suitcase, leaving the gifts.

"Where are you going, Brianna?" Allan followed her outside.

"Your house is full. I am going home. Your daughter, I can accept all day long. However, I am not sharing the spotlight with your ex. Since the divorce, you guys have been up under each other every time I turn around!" Brianna was throwing her overnight bag in the car and obviously forgetting about Maxwell, Allan's fill-in.

"Brie, okay, I have asked her to leave! I didn't think it was a big deal."

"The first time you did it, okay. You were trying to get me back for going out of town, whatever! I didn't drive up last night, but I got here earlier then what I said I would. Only to get here and see her in your bedroom!"

"Calm down, Brie." He came close so that he could hold her around her waist. "Baby, it's not like we were in there sleeping together. Don't leave. I didn't have you for Thanksgiving. Let's enjoy this holiday. I'm sorry, baby. She's in there packing right now." As he kissed her, it dawned on him that is was freezing outside. "Can we go back in the house?" He only had on his pajama pants, no shirt and no shoes. He grabbed her bag and walked back inside. She saw Stephanie putting on her coat as the little girl was crying for her to stay.

"Stephanie, don't leave yet. I am quite sure that your daughter would like it if you stayed while she was opening her gifts," Brianna said to her.

"Sure, I would love to spend time with my child. Are we sure there will not be another issue?" Stephanie asked with sarcasm in her voice.

Okay, this bitch is being a little slick in the mouth. This is going to be entertaining. "No, there shouldn't be any other issues if everyone plays their position. There should not be any issues at all," Brianna said with a "Don't play with me" smile.

Allan could feel the tension mounting up, so he tried to change the mood. "Okay, cupcake, let's open some gifts!" He picked up his little three-year-old and took her over by the ginormous tree.

"The tree is pretty, baby," Brianna said sincerely. However, she quickly lost her smile when Stephanie replied.

"Thanks, we went and picked it out the day after Thanksgiving. I'm sorry you could not make it. Where were you? Atlanta?" Stephanie was letting Brianna know that this was what she would be in for as long as he was dating him. She would be the one that Allan would come back to stroke his ego.

"Yes, girlie, I was in Hotlanta. I'm glad he has you here to do those things. He'll probably need your help taking it down too. Girl, what you want to do next year is check out the ornaments at Neiman Marcus. The ornaments there are quite costly, but they are not common. A tree like this would have gone from pretty and predictable to stunning." The little girl let out a big scream, which defused the cattiness.

"Thanks, Brie-Brie."

Brianna had given her a large box that contained a lot of little gifts. She had given Jasmine a Hello Kitty outfit, a pair of UGG boots, two educational toys, and one age-approved fun child toy. She ran over and gave Brianna a big hug and a kiss. Stephanie was too annoyed to watch. She went in the kitchen. Allan looked over and whispered, "You are bad but thanks, baby. She loves all her gifts."

Stephanie returned from the kitchen. "Allan, we have to go. My parents are ahead of schedule, so they will be at my house in about thirty minutes. Jazzy, put your shoes on."

"I don't want to wear my shoes. Brie-Brie, can you help me with my boots?"

"Stephanie, is that all right?" Brianna was pretending that she didn't notice that Stephanie was throwing a silent grown-up tantrum.

"Sure."

"Stephanie, let her stay here and I will bring her later," Allan said.

"No, I want to take her home now to get her ready. Plus, *my* friend is on the way over too." It was obvious that Stephanie said this only to get a rise out of him.

"*Your* friend, okay! Then go," Allan said as he walked away.

I'm a little confused. Brother man looks like he was a little hurt by that news. I am going to sit here and watch this shit play out, Brianna was quietly thinking as she was pulling up Jasmine's boot.

"I can put everything in a bag so she can open the rest of her gifts at home," Stephanie said while retrieving an oversized bag out the closet. Brianna noticed how well she maneuvered around his house. For a house that she did not share with him, that was pretty interesting.

"Like hell you will, Stephanie. Let Jazzy open homeboy's gifts at your house. He ain't taking credit for mine."

"Whatever, Allan! Are you ready, Jazzy? Later, Brianna!"

Stephanie was on her way out the door and Allan went out there with her, but this time, he had sense to put on a jacket and shoes. Brianna, while watching through the window, remembered what he had said earlier that she was packing. Yet she went to the car only with her purse, a baby bag, and the child, no overnight bag. Brianna ran upstairs into Jasmine's room. She had a full-size bed with rails. She looked in the closet, all little pretty pink outfits, but what caught her eye was a pair of adult slippers, female adult sneakers, and pumps shoved in the corner. When she looked up from the floor, there was about a week's worth of outfits for an adult female.

Well, look what I have found. How interesting.

She went to the dresser and there were all of Jasmines things. She went to the armoire and noticed in the last two drawers, panties, bras, and two Victoria Secret negligees.

What the hell?

She could hear Allan saying goodbye as he was opening his front door, so she ran in his room and turned on his shower and removed her hoodie and shoes.

"Brie!" Allan was calling her as he was coming up the stairs; she pretended as though she did not hear him. She continued to remove her sweats. "Now that's what I am talking about. That's what I have been missing!" He started kissing her down her neck and over her breasts, down to her stomach. What Allan didn't pay attention to was that she was forcing herself to respond. Brianna wanted to know what was going on with him and Stephanie. She also wanted to know why Stephanie had some of her clothes here.

"Baby, I miss you," Allan muttered.

"You do? Why don't you show me?" Brianna said, baiting him to take on the small challenge. In response, he smiled, indicating that he was about to please her. The foreplay lasted for five minutes and then, bam! It was over in less than ten minutes. He, like always, was very satisfied, and she had nothing. "See, I told you that I missed you."

"I see. Allan, I forgot the water was still running. I'm getting in. Would you like to join me?" She was hoping that he would say no.

"Yes, ma' am," Allan gladly replied.

After the shower, they decided to exchange gifts. He gave her a David Yurman bangle, a chocolate diamond three-karat bracelet, and a pair of Manolo Blahnik shoes.

"Thanks, baby. All of my gifts are beautiful. Open your gifts, Allan." Brianna had given him an Armani Jacket, Tag Heur watch, and a pair of very expensive Italian boots.

"You are so good for me. Thanks, baby."

"Wait one more thing." She pulled out one more gift box.

"Baby, you have done enough," Allan said with all sincerity.

"No, I actually picked this up in Atlanta. Think of it as an 'I'm sorry for not being here during Thanksgiving.'" When he opened it up, it was a classy platinum signet ring with a small diamond accent.

"Aww, baby, is this my engagement ring?" He chuckled and leaned over to give her a big sloppy kiss.

"You are so silly, Allan." The rest of the day they spent talking, getting ready to go to his parents. Brianna's parents called to thank her for the gift. She had sent them tickets to go on a cruise to the Caribbean.

CHAPTER TWENTY-NINE

Showtime

The dinner at Allan's parents was pretty awkward. His mother pretty much thought that the sun rose and set around her son. His sister, Alana, was a character. She was abrupt but real, and Brianna could appreciate that.

"Well, nice to meet you again, Ms. Brianna. I heard all about you. Let me see your ring." Brianna gladly extended her hand. "Now that's interesting. Hey, Allan, this look exactly like—" At that very moment, Allan's mother called everyone into the dining room. Once Mr. Jones blessed the table, they took a seat. Alana was sure to take a seat by Brianna.

"Mom, everything looks good. This is one thing that I hate doing, cooking." Alana chuckled.

"Is that right?" Brianna asked. "Your schedule keeps you busy too?"

"I guess you can say that. I work with the BET location here in DC. Since it is just me, by the time I get home, there is no need for me to cook a lavish meal."

"I can understand that," Brianna said in agreement.

When Allan finished drinking the last of his iced tea, he could not wait to join in the conversation. "What you mean you can understand that? Baby, you can cook."

"Thank you. I know I can cook, but like your sister, with the hours I keep, there are days when I don't get to prepare any meals. So that's going to leave you in the kitchen."

"Oh, is that right? Well, all that is going to change after we walked down the aisle, right?" He was smiling. The smile that once melted her heart, now made her question any and all of his motives. She thought they were having a lighthearted discussion, but she could tell that he was serious. Finally, Mrs. Jones interrupted.

"Brianna, do you think that you would like to have kids?"

"Yes, ma' am, probably in two or three years."

"Is that right? I thought that you would want to start having kids as soon as possible. Especially since you are about to turn thirty." Instead of Mrs. Jones being amazed that she did not have a gold-digging daughter in-law to-be, Mrs. Jones sounded as if she was a little disgusted.

"Ma, we know you love Daddy, but women these days are pretty ambitious. Women don't have to sit still and wait for a man to be their hero. Not to mention, I personally think that it beats sitting around, pumping out babies one after the other anyway." Alana was laughing while tapping Brianna's knee under the table. It was one of those "I got your back, girl" moments. Brianna looked over at Alana and gave her a thank-you smile.

Mrs. Jones was slightly annoyed with Alana's logic. "Oh, okay. What's that child's name? Beyoncé! Even with all her fame, she must have realized she was ready to take care of a man at some point. You girls better get your priorities straight."

Mr. Jones, who had been silent and taking the conversations in, began shaking his head. He placed his focus on Brianna. "Baby, enjoy your food. Don't let my wife and son worry you about kids and cooking." He turned to look at Mrs. Jones to give a glare of disapproval, in hopes of getting her to stop with the unneeded attitude.

"Brianna, enjoy life, health, and happiness whenever and wherever you can find it. Shucks! Enjoy a little quietness. That's always good too." The family must have known that this was his way of saying shut up or change their conversation. As quietly instructed, they began to talk about family members, potential vacationing spots, and the joys of having Barack Obama to take office. They were interrupted by the doorbell. Allan hurried to stand.

"I'll get it."

They could hear voices in the living room when, suddenly, Jasmine appeared.

"Grandpa!" Little Ms. Jasmine, who was still wearing her black UGG boots, ran to hop on her grandfather's lap.

"Well, what a surprise. Merry Christmas, pumpkin!" Mrs. Jones reached over to pick her up. Without Brianna taking her eyes off Jasmine, she heard the voice of the insecure woman from earlier that morning. Stephanie said as if she was going to break out in a freaking song, "Merry Christmas, everyone!"

What kind of fuckery is this? Allan wants me to share my holidays with her? Again, this brotha is out of his rabbit-ass mind! While being in her deep thoughts, Brianna was trying not to shake her head.

"Allan is tripping hard, huh?" Alana said to Brianna under her breath. After sitting for forty minutes trying to pretend that Stephanie's being there did not faze her, Brianna decided to excuse herself to the bathroom. As Brianna began washing her hands, she started staring at her engagement ring and instantly began to tear up.

Pull yourself together!

Brianna wanted so desperately to get in her truck and head back to Richmond. When she was approaching the living room, she couldn't help but notice Allan sitting beside Stephanie. Allan saw Brianna staring, so he immediately got up, walked over, kissed Brianna on the cheek, and whispered in her ear, "I love you, baby. I can't wait to get you home." Brianna knew he did that to save face once more. She didn't respond. However, she quickly took his seat beside Stephanie. Everyone could clearly see the annoyance on Stephanie's face.

"Stephanie, where is your friend? I thought you were leaving earlier to get home to see him?"

"Yeah, we exchanged gifts, and now he is with his family and friends." For some reason, you could see that she was not trying to talk about it. Brianna wanted to have a little fun.

"Really, I would think that he would want to be with you and Jazzy. He is really a good man to let you hang out with your former in-laws. Who knew a man like that existed? I will be here for the week. Why don't you have him to come over, and we can all have dinner together?"

Alana was looking on like it was a television show. All eyes and ears were focused on Stephanie. "That sounds great. Yes, let's all do that. I have taken a couple of days off too." Alana and Mrs. Jones could see the anger in Allan's face. Was Allan mad at Brianna for stirring things up, or was he upset with having dinner with Stephanie's new lover?

"I'll have to get back with you. I am not sure about his schedule." At this moment, Allan was about to go in the kitchen with his mother. "Allan, I think I need to run. We have some other people to see."

"Are you sure? You haven't been here long." Allan seemed as though he was a little sad. Brianna's blood began to boil. Everyone, but Alana, scattered around to help them get ready to walk out. Mrs. Jones came from the kitchen with a fresh cake that she had baked along with two gifts. One of the gifts was for Stephanie. The cake was prepared for her because it was her favorite.

Ain't this some bull! The momma can't let Stephanie go either. Allan walked Stephanie out with Jasmine. Mrs. Jones couldn't look Brianna in her face. *How funny! Mrs. Thing had so much to say when I was sitting at the table.*

"Brianna, I am heading back to the den to put my feet up. Feel free to join me." Brianna could tell that Mr. Jones was the peacemaker. It was a shame that Allan did not take on that trait. "Thank you, Mr. Jones, but I think I will be leaving as well. Alana, can you show me where my coat is located?"

"Sure, girl, follow me."

They walked down the hall to what looked like a spare bedroom. She retrieved the mink vest as well as took out Allan's leather jacket. "It was nice meeting you, Brianna. You are definitely the woman!" Alana said while smiling at her.

"It was nice meeting you too, and why am I the woman?" Brianna asked while smirking.

"Well, you handled the little questioning session from my mother very well, and let's face it, my brother is a man from the dark ages. He loves his ego stroked, and I really think you are one that might teach him a lesson."

Brianna didn't want to elaborate on Alana's truthful comments; she just laughed and told her to keep in touch. As they were walking back into the living room, Allan was sitting by his mother, eating sweet potato pie with a big scoop of vanilla ice cream.

"Baby, why do you have on your vest? Come have some dessert with me." Brianna looked around and didn't see an extra serving. Again, thank goodness for Alana.

"So where are our plates? Did you think to fix ours, Momma Jones?" she playfully asked while scolding her.

"Lana, you and Brianna can go in the kitchen and fix you both a plate," Mrs. Jones snapped. Brianna's nerves were shot. She knew that she could not keep this little visit going. She was absolutely done. Mrs. Jones was getting on her last nerve. *Mrs. Thing needs to relax. That son that she thinks so highly of is far from being an angel.*

"Allan, I'm ready to go. I am going to head out to the car. Mrs. Jones, Merry Christmas and take care."

"Brianna, you don't have to rush, but I understand, take care." Mrs. Jones didn't even bother to get up. Mr. Jones came back into the living room to say goodbye and to give Brianna a big hug. Alana gave her a big warm hug as well. When Allan finally stood up, you could see that he was annoyed that Brianna wanted to leave.

"Mr. Jones, you and Alana have been a complete delight to dine with this evening." Brianna hoped that Mrs. Jones felt that indirect punch to the gut in her praise to Mr. Jones and Alana; she had enough of her nonsense.

"Allan, you don't have to leave. Lana can run you home." Mrs. Jones obviously wanted to show Brianna this was what she would be putting up with if she was going to be a part of that family. Brianna threw Allan a look that would have made a grown man cry.

"She's right, Allan. You do not have to leave now. If it gets any later, just stay with your mom tonight."

"Ma, no, I think I'm going to head on back to the house. I'll give you a call tomorrow."

When Allan and Brianna got in the car, the tension could have been cut with a knife. She immediately located her earplugs and played music. If Allan liked it when people—namely, his mother—disrespected her, then she was going to show him how it felt. She wanted to send a message to Allan; he did pick up on the message and was annoyed with her as well. When they got in the house, she went directly to the bar and fixed herself a strong drink. Allan was already in the room, undressing. She sat the glass down and began removing her clothes. He walked over and began drinking her drink.

"Damn, Allan, I made that one for myself. There is more downstairs!"

"I know there is more downstairs—I bought it," he sarcastically mumbled.

"Well, you looked good buying it. Now all you have to do is call your mama or Stephanie to ask one of them to pour it for you!"

"What does that mean? Better yet, you can leave my momma out your mouth, and Stephanie doesn't have anything to do with this!" Allan was really pissed; he didn't mind that they were about to go at it. "Brianna, I have been dealing with your snobby ass all day. You didn't have enough respect to introduce yourself to Stephanie. You didn't even try to bond with my mother, and furthermore, it was bad enough that you wanted to abruptly leave. You didn't even tell her good bye correctly or tell her thank you for the invitation to dinner!"

"Negro, please! How would you feel if you found out that your fiancé's ex is always around? Not just dropping off the child but staying for the holidays. Who knows, maybe she is staying here off and on! Is she?"

"Brianna, you are just trying to find stuff to bitch about! She doesn't stay here!"

"That's interesting. Well, if you say so. Let's get this straight! You are lucky I didn't go off on your ex-wife this morning or this evening. Hell no, I wasn't trying to introduce myself to her. That was your damn job. Your mother, she hasn't gotten over Stephanie. Ms. Stephanie must enjoy kissing her ass, but guess what, I am not kissing yours or theirs either for that fact!" By now Brianna had changed out of her savvy little outfit and replaced it with a sweatsuit. She started throwing her clothes in the suitcase.

"Brie, what are you doing now? It's eleven o'clock. Where are you going?" Allan asked her. Brianna was not answering but was putting on her jacket and heading to the front door. "I know you hear me talking to you! I am not chasing your ass to your truck this time."

Brianna smirked at him. "Yes, I hear you talking to me, and trust, I'm not worried about you chasing me. No, let me start that sentence again. You don't have to worry about chasing my snobby ass anywhere. I'm good. I am leaving so I can enjoy the rest of my holiday." Brianna grabbed her stuff and went out to her truck. She drove back to Richmond. That two-hour drive flew by. Before she knew it, she was in her garage.

This is too much. Why is my life feeling like it is out of order? Why?

CHAPTER THIRTY

What a New Year

Brianna decided that going into the New Year, she would rest and take it easy. She decided to do lunch with Alice and exchange gifts. Brie also went out with the girls one night for dinner and visited Phoebe's grave. Allan called once or twice, but Brianna was not having it. One of the messages left by Allan even ended in him saying that if she did not call him back immediately, he was going to call off the engagement. *Go ahead with your punk ass,* she thought. Brianna began to seriously doubt that she knew Allan.

Here it was, New Year's Eve, and Tamika insisted on partying in DC; Brianna wasn't feeling this little spontaneous trip at all. Angel was with her boo, loving on him in New York, but here she was still, ignoring Allan. She didn't ask Tamika for any details. She just knew that Tamika was excited about tonight. She kept trying to reassure Brianna that tonight was going to be her night. Brianna really missed Maxwell but was too tired to keep putting a lot of thought into him. His continuous disappearing games were beginning to wear her down.

"Tamika, this is a nice hotel." They pulled up in front of the Westin Grand. When they checked in, they were escorted to a suite; the suite was stunning. "You are really trying to celebrate, huh, Tamika?"

Tamika chuckled before answering, "I guess you can say that. I'm really surprised that your cell was not ringing every five seconds. I can really tell that Allan is officially pissed off."

"Yep, not one peep out of him, so maybe it's *officially* over." There was a little remorse in her voice.

"Well, baby girl, let's do our thing tonight! I ordered a bottle of Dom and a couple of appetizers. It should be arriving shortly. We can nibble and drink while getting ready." The girls proceeded to do just that. They giggled and reminisced about some of the crazy things that they used to say and do; they were laughing so hard that their stomach began to ache. Finally, they decided to make moves and get dressed.

"Brie, are you ready?"

When Brianna came out of the room, she was sexy and sophisticated. Her dress was by Hervé Leger, strapless soft gold foiled-looking dress with a pair of her favorite Brian Atwood pumps.

"Work it, girl!" Tamika yelled, giving her an approval.

"Well, look at you, Ms. Tamika. You're doing the damn thing too!" Brianna threw a compliment right back. Tamika had on a sleek black body-con dress that was sleeveless, baring a long keyhole in the front that tastefully, and playfully exposed, a little of her breasts. The dress showed off her shapely long legs with insane five-inch heels. Both girls completed their stunning looks with their full-length black mink coats. Upon reaching the lobby, a chauffeur was waiting for them and took them to the New Year's Eve party. It was a private gala about two hundred people tops. Brianna, being an event planner, began inspecting everything. This party was top-notch. No plastic but crystal glasses, sterling silver flatware, and the finest of linens. There were ice sculptors flowing with premium vodka. In every corner, there were champagne and action stations in place. No celebrities were spotted, but the service and food was on that level.

"Tamika, who do you know here?"

"You'll see." Tamika started moving to the music.

"I'll see? I'll see who?" She was too puzzled.

"Brianna, here take this cold shot of vodka. If you knock this back and let all your worries go, you won't need me to keep telling you to have a good time." Brianna did as she was instructed.

It was now about 11:45 PM, and they had been dancing and mingling with just about everyone. Tamika kept a close eye on

Brianna because she polished off about four or five shots. Brianna would never let herself get sloppy, but she would allow herself to get a little tipsy. Especially if something was bothering her, and obviously, there was something bothering her. The girls were standing with their backs to the doors when Tamika turned and let out a small scream. She was hugging some man. After she and the gentleman let go of each other, Brianna recognized who it was that was hugging Tamika tightly—it was Rico. He reached around and gave Brianna a hug as well.

Rico was a fine man that was from Miami; he was 100 percent Columbian. His golden complexion was a perfect match with his big beautiful silky locks of curls. Usually, he kept it pulled back in a ponytail, but tonight, he was sporting a low Caesar haircut. With Tamika and Rico standing side by side, if pursued, they would make an attractive couple.

"Rico! What a surprise? I haven't seen or heard from you since Christmas Eve. How is Maxwell?" she asked with great concern.

"Why don't you turn around and ask him yourself?" he said with a big smile.

"What do you mean ask him?"

Tamika spun her around and there he was. She was so happy to see him. While Maxwell was giving her a hug, Tamika and Rico walked away.

"Maxwell, what are you doing here?"

As he was about to answer, a server came by with champagne for the midnight toast that was about to happen in exactly two minutes. When they began to do the countdown, he held her tightly around her waist. As the crowd yelled "Happy New Year," he passionately started kissing Brianna.

I want this man until its beginning to hurt, she was saying to herself while passionately kissing him back.

"Happy New Year, Ms. Godfrey. Let's go back to the hotel."

"Okay, let me tell Tamika."

"No, you don't have to do that. They are going to meet us back at the hotel."

When they arrived back at the Westin, they found Rico and Tamika cuddled up on the sofa, laughing. "Now wait a minute. Call me slow but was all of this planned or what?" Brianna laughed.

"Yes, girl, you are slow! It was so hard trying to keep this from you. I got a surprise call from Rico. Rico asked if I would lure you here because Max wanted to see you. Since you had an awful Christmas and you are not with you know who, here you are." They all smiled at her and chuckled.

"You guys think that you are so smart." Brianna could not help but laugh too. The rest of the night was wonderful. They did a little reminiscing and sharing catch-up stories. They were having the best time ever, drinking, eating, and laughing. Brianna could not have planned a better New Year's. It was now 3:00 AM, and they were getting a little tired. Tamika didn't play games. She pulled Rico by his hand and led him into her bedroom. Maxwell followed suit; he led Brianna into the other room.

"Brianna, I never got to thank you for taking care of me that night when Rico needed to drop me off. I have never loved a woman as much as I love you. With you, I know there are no secrets, and you are not trying to hustle me. There is something that I would like to give you." While he looked in his bag, Brianna began to shed a tear. She, indeed, was keeping a major secret from him; she would tell him, but when?

"Here, baby." He handed her a small gift box.

Brianna opened the box; it was a beautiful 6.5-karat platinum diamond ring from Harry Winston.

"Oh my god!" she yelled as he put the ring on her right hand. It had a large clear 4.5-karat solitaire in the middle with two clear diamonds on each side. The clarity of each stone was unbelievable. "Max, this looks like an engagement ring."

"I guess you can call it a *soul mate* ring, because that is what you are, my soul mate. I love you, Brianna Godfrey, and don't you ever forget it." She could see it in his eyes and she could feel it. The words made her hair stand up on the back of her neck. She wanted him—she wanted him right then, and she wanted him for forever. They began to kiss as if they were trying to devour each other. While kissing, she finished removing his bow tie and unbuttoned his shirt. He unzipped her dress and watched her step out of it. There she stood, completely uncovered. He picked her up and held her against the wall. Every muscle that he had was flexed. This man was sexy as hell, and tonight, he was hers. He entered her as he was still holding her up.

"Tell me you love me," he whispered. He felt so good. As he was hitting every spot, she couldn't formulate a sentence. "I guess you want me to stop because you don't love me, huh?"

"No, no, don't stop. I love you, Maxwell," she whispered back.

"I don't think you do. If I am asking you to say it, then maybe you don't. Here, let me go deeper." Amazingly, that's what he did. He went deeper, and his thrusts were earth-shattering. She began to moan loudly and began to cry and tremble.

"I love you, Max. I love you, Maxwell! I want you and only you!"

Both came together. When they got in the bed, he wrapped his arm around her. Their love for each other was so deep-rooted that it was unexplainable to both. It was a strong love.

CHAPTER THIRTY-ONE

The Bold and the Truthful

Both couples slept late. They got up around 2:00 PM and ordered up room service. They were enjoying their lunch when the suite door came open. While Brianna and Maxwell thought they were staring at a ghost, Tamika and Rico jumped up immediately.

"I thought your ass was here with that bitch!" Melissa yelled.

"It's not going to be too many more bitches in here!" Tamika yelled at her. Rico went to the door and put the bolt on. Surely, he did this based on his last couple of run-ins with Maxwell's father and his goons. Melissa remembered Tamika's fascination with guns, so she didn't address Tamika's comment.

"Maxwell and Brianna, if you think that I am going to let you both do this one more time, you are sadly mistaken. Max, maybe our fathers would like to know that I am not happy with your actions." Melissa was grinning from ear to ear.

"Look, Melissa, your ass never stays at home. You are always running down to Miami anyway. Do I fucking ask you what you are doing? Weren't you spending New Year's in Miami?"

"Don't you worry about me. You need to start worrying about yourself. And if you don't want anything to happen to this trick-ass bitch, you better put her in her place before—"

Bam! Boom!

No one saw it coming. Brianna got up quickly and punched Melissa in her stomach and the side of her head; she doubled over. It caught Melissa off guard so much that she fell back, and she slid down the wall. When she went down, it appeared that it was not enough

176

for Brianna; she kicked Melissa in her side. Tamika was cracking up, and Rico covered his mouth in disbelief.

"Oh shit!" he mumbled.

"You can call me a bitch, but this will be the last time that you will call me a trick, you dumb-ass bitch!" Brianna was ready to spit fire. Maxwell ran over.

"Brie, chill baby. I can't send her back home to our son looking like someone beat the shit out of her."

"You heard that, Ms. Brianna, *our son!*" She was trying to get up, but had to do it slowly because she was in pain from the multiple blows. "You didn't give him that, huh?"

"Shut the fuck up, Melissa! You didn't either!" Brianna couldn't believe that she just said that. Maxwell was now looking at her. "Why don't you tell him the truth?"

"What truth? What are you talking about, Brianna? What is she talking about, Melissa?" Melissa was silent, and Brianna could not stop the confrontation now that Maxwell was witnessing.

"Before Phoebe passed away, she said that she overheard Melissa talking to your father on the phone. He was saying that he missed her and wanted to see his son. Her response was that she couldn't keep bringing *him* down to Miami."

"She is lying, Maxwell. Don't listen to her!"

"Bitch, shut up and let Brianna get rid of you for once and all," Tamika yelled.

"Maxwell, when we were in Atlanta, Melissa was hugged up with your father at a club. I have a copy of Max Jr.'s blood work, and if you remember, I asked you about your blood type. You are not an exact match. He is your father's son."

"She doesn't know what she is saying! You have no proof."

"Proof, Melissa? Are you saying that this is true if she can produce it?" Maxwell asked.

"I have proof of what I am saying, Maxwell. Of course, it's not with me, but I have it. I'm so sorry, Maxwell."

"Melissa, take your ass back to Richmond and pack your shit!" Maxwell yelled at her. "Brianna, how could you keep this information to yourself and not tell me? When did you change? You didn't want to tell me that you were engaged, and now, you have been looking me in my face and keeping this shit to yourself? For what, Brianna? For what! Who can I trust? Rico, I'm going to the car. Bring my bags, man. I can't stay in here another fucking minute." He began speaking in Spanish and proceeded to walk out the room.

Before Melissa could get out of the door, she turned to Brianna. "If I can't have him, it should be obvious now, you won't have him either!"

Rico went into the room that Brianna and Maxwell shared and retrieved his bag. Tamika came out with Rico's bag. Rico gave Brianna a hug. "Ma, give him time. You should have told him as soon as you found that out."

Brianna was crying uncontrollably, but she managed to respond. "Rico, I was going to tell him. He just kept disappearing, or it was never the right time." She continued to sob but harder. Rico looked over at Tamika. Tamika came over to hold her. Rico kissed Tamika on the cheek and left.

"Brie, it will be all right. Like Rico said, give him some time." She led Brianna over to the sofa and gave her a glass of water. "I wish I knew what he said in Spanish. Whatever he said, he had a lot of hurt in his eyes," Tamika said with a very concerned look.

"It wasn't good, Tamika. He said that he had been betrayed, and he can't love anyone anymore." Though Brianna got herself together, the tears were still trickling down her face.

CHAPTER THIRTY-TWO

The Devil Appears

Three weeks had gone by, and no word from Maxwell. Tamika said that Rico had called her one day to check on her and Brianna. This pain was not foreign for her. The loneliness was all too familiar.

Left in the office alone, she decided to stay a little longer to get some extra work done. Her quietness and focus was disrupted when in walked the devil himself.

"Well, hello, Ms. Godfrey! Long time no see, darling." Her uninvited guest was of a very dark complexion and stood six feet tall; he looked to be about in his mid-fifties. His hair was shaven very low and sported a well-groomed beard. He was dressed in a two-piece black Armani suit, dress shirt slightly unbuttoned with a small gold chain. At first glance, she didn't remember him from the encounter or the picture. However, his Haitian accent and his two cronies that walked in jilted her memory.

"Mr. King, I am closed, but if this is for a very important event in which you are planning, perhaps I can refer you to your daughter-in-law, or is it your mistress?"

"You are a beautiful girl. Nice, curvy body, just how I like my women. I see why my boy cannot focus. You know, Brianna, he doesn't want to bother with me or his wife now. He doesn't want to be bothered with *his* little boy either." He had a fixed glare on Brianna that was slightly frightening.

"Mr. King, we both know that child is your son. You should have told Maxwell that he has a brother. If you are here to try and scare me, it won't work. So again, how can I help you?"

"Brianna, I am here to help you or your parents. They are in Atlanta, right? You know Atlanta is not that far from Richmond or even Miami. How about I will fly them up first-class for your wedding?"

"What the fuck! My parents?" Brianna was fuming.

"I think when you get back home to that cozy little condo that my son has paid for, you should call Allan. It is Allan, right? Call him and tell him that you are ready to tie the knot. I will give you at least two to three weeks to do so. We can't wait for July. If this is a problem for you, then Allan may find it difficult to raise his beautiful little girl. I know you would feel guilty if something should happen to him. Or, maybe me talking to your parents, they may volunteer to be the sacrificial lambs? Have a good night, and should my son contact you, feel free to invite him to the wedding."

"Fuck you, Mr. King. It's a shame that you would pimp out your own son. He really loves you. You ain't shit!" At that moment, she must have struck a nerve. He leaned across the desk and grabbed her face.

"Mind your tongue, woman, or I'll have it removed! It's your tongue that got you into this mess! You and Melissa can fight in a ring, but you are messing with my money. I love *both* of my sons. Don't you question how I love! Now, do as you are told!" He turned and walked out, and his thugs followed.

Brianna could not believe what just happened. She wasn't afraid for herself, but she was afraid for Allan and her parents. She locked up the office and started driving home. She dialed Allan's number. It was 8:00 PM, and she knew that Allan was at home, probably working in his office.

This is stupid. Just a few days after New Year's Eve, I had a big argument with Allan. How am I going to pull this off! He was mad at me for leaving Christmas night and not returning his phone calls. To put the icing on the cake, I refused to spend New Year's with him. How am I going to get this man to forgive and forget? She impatiently waited for an answer.

He sarcastically answered the phone, "What, Brianna?"

She wanted to snap back, but since this was a matter of *his* life or death, she had to eat this one. "Allan, can we talk?"

"Now you want to talk, Brianna? Who are you playing with? I was trying to get a hold of you for almost two weeks!"

"Are we truly over, Allan? I know you still want me and I know you still remember how I make you feel." There was silence on the phone for about ten seconds. "Allan, are we over, baby?" She was trying to sound as innocent and hurt as possible. A week ago, she was planning to drive back, to Northern Virginia to give his key back along with the ring. Now the tables had turned.

"What do you want, Brianna? You told me in the beginning, if you thought that I wasn't trying, you were going to walk away. You lied. I was trying and you walked away. Brianna, you have—"

"Baby, I love you. Let's push the wedding date up," Brianna abruptly interrupted and tried to cry. However, it was at that very moment she knew she couldn't even stand the sound of his voice.

"Brianna, are you crying? I tell you what, I must go out of the country for about eight days. Actually, I leave tomorrow, but when I get back in the states, I'll fly back into Richmond. We can talk more then or run to the justice of peace. You know what? I'm going to miss your birthday. I'll have something nice for you when I see you. I love you, baby!"

Well, damn, that was easy, she thought to herself. *Is this man bipolar or what?* "I love you and I am sorry. See you when you get back."

Brianna began to cry like the day when Maxwell walked out of the hotel room. She really felt as if she was betraying Maxwell even more, but she had no other choice. *Who can I tell? If I tell Angel, she would tell Tamika. Damn! If Tamika finds out, Rico and Maxwell would know. Allan would be good as dead. I am on my own with this decision.*

CHAPTER THIRTY-THREE

The Misery Begins

Seven days had now gone by, and Brianna trusted Peter to oversee a large function for Saturday. Saturday, she was turning the big 3-0. Brianna felt raw; she felt like she had nothing to lose yet everything to lose. She didn't want to think about the well-known business-woman that she had become in such a short time. She didn't want to think about the man that she had finally lost for good, and she definitely did not want to think about marrying a man that she wasn't in love with. Tonight, she wanted to be numb to all the bullshit she had been dealing with and could not express it. Tonight, she was going to go and celebrate her birthday the best way she could, with her girls, fashionable, and with drinks.

With her makeup looking flawless, she was fabulous. She pulled her hair up in a stylish hair bun, exposing her diamond hoop ear-rings. She put on her diamond butterfly necklace, with her beautiful engagement ring on her left hand and the breathtaking ring that Maxwell gave her on the right hand. Tonight, she was rocking a pair of skinny jeans, Louboutin boots, and a sexy Versace top. With her Louis Vuitton bag and her full-length black mink coat, she left the condo; Her look was complete. Brianna was looking like she should had a top single on the music charts; the look was that of a fierce hip-hop queen.

She picked up Angel and scooped up Tamika. When they got to the club, it was packed. The owner of the club escorted them to a table that was reserved for the girls. Females were gritting on them, but the guys couldn't stop staring. The waitress brought over a bottle of their finest champagne and three shot glasses of Patron.

"Happy birthday, Brianna!" both girls yelled.

"Thanks, girls. I love you both." They leaned over the table to embrace.

"You must be the birthday girl. Can I take you out on the floor?"

He was sexy. This man was about six feet, eight inches with a muscular body. His clothes hung on him perfectly. The dark man-candy looked like he was straight from Africa. Surely, he was a king of something. He had an accent, but she could not make out the origin over the music. They walked out on the dance floor, his moves were just as sexy as he looked.

"My name is Olu. What is your name, sweetheart?"

"Wait, are you Haitian?"

"No." He laughed. "I am from Nigeria."

She was relieved. She didn't want this fine specimen of a man to be someone that Mr. King could have sent. "My name is Brianna and nice to meet you."

They danced the night away, and Brianna was doing her thing with Mr. Olu. After what seemed like six songs later, she went back to the table, and Brianna polished off two glasses of champagne and two more shots of Patron.

"Damn, Brie, slow your roll!" Tamika scolded.

"Yeah, girl. Let's order something to eat," Angel said. She wanted Brianna to enjoy her birthday but not be a sloppy drunk; they ordered fries and wings. That still did not slow Brianna down. She ate, but she kept on drinking. Men were sending over drinks, and the women were still giving their table the evil eye. Olu was Brianna's dance partner for much of the night. That was partly because most of the men in the club were intimidated by him and his boys. It was getting late, and the girls were getting nervous watching her. She was loud, she was getting mean, and she was still hurting.

"Let's go, Brie," Angel said with a smile.

"Okay. I love you, Angel." Angel thought that she would not want to leave, but was happy to hear her agree so quickly. She could sense that something wasn't right with her, but it was not the time to address it.

"I love you too, girl." Angel was helping her with her coat. Brianna was not necessarily unbearable, but she was a little faded; they followed Tamika out. Tamika could clearly tell that Brianna could not drive everyone home.

"Brianna, give me your keys. I'm going to drive. Okay?" Tamika was prepared to take the keys even if Brianna said no, but to her amazement, she handed the keys right over. As they were going to the truck, Olu and his two boys were behind them. Tamika made sure that Brianna kept one step ahead of her. She knew that the guys were going to continue to follow them. She hit the remote to the Range Rover; Angel was trying to quickly open the door so Brianna could get in.

"Ladies, why don't you join us back at our hotel for a little after-party?" Olu insisted.

"Thanks, but we are good," Tamika said with a stern voice. She was irritated by the men's presence.

"No, you're not good yet. Come, we have a place to party more." Olu started to walk toward Brianna. Tamika stepped in front of him. Angel told Brianna to get in the truck. However, Brianna wasn't trying to hear it. Olu's eyes were fixed on Brianna as if he was going to take her. "Bitch, move. I don't need you to have a good time. It's Brianna that I want."

"Why does everyone like to refer to me as a bitch? Damn. You know what, Mr. Oooh-chew or whatever your name is? Here let me get something for you. This is where you can find us tonight." Tamika started rummaging through her purse. Angel looked over and smirked because the purse was only so big. Brianna was staring and suddenly let out a laugh that made her fall back on the truck.

"Here, love, take this bullet first, and should you wake up, I will be in hell with you. Come, we party, yes?" The guys' eyes could not believe that she had a silver .357 pointed right at them.

"Fuck you, Americans!" Olu yelled as he walked away.

"Bye, bitches!" Brianna yelled. Tamika and Angel both looked at her and started to laugh.

"Girl, get your drunk ass in the back seat!" Tamika chuckled. When they all got in, Brianna started to joke about how she did not know that her own SUV had so much space in the back seat. Something silver caught Tamika's eye from the passenger side. "What was that, Angel?"

"Oh, this?" Angel responded innocently. She was taking a gun from her coat pocket and placing it in her purse; it was a small handgun. Brianna plunged forward to see it and could not believe what she had just seen. Tamika was speechless.

"What! Don't let us find out you are an undercover gangsta!" Brianna laughed from the back seat.

"Damn, Angel, we didn't know you got down like that! We always thought we had to protect you! Go ahead, a professional gangsta. Now that's what I'm talking about!" They laughed on the drive back, so much so until it seemed like Brianna sobered up. Tamika allowed her to drive herself back home only if she agreed to talk to her on the cell until she arrived home.

That night, or morning rather, Brianna cried herself to sleep.

CHAPTER THIRTY-FOUR

Lights, Camera, Action

Sunday morning, Brianna jumped out of bed and flew in to the bathroom. She was vomiting. *Whoa, I guess I had way too much to drink.* She took a shower and did the usual morning routine. *It's one o'clock. I slept that long?*

She checked her phone. Allan left a message stating that he would be at her house around 7:00 PM. She was relieved because she was not ready to act like all was forgiven. She spoke to the girls and chatted with Alice too. It was so good to hear her parents' voice also. To keep herself from thinking about the ultimatum that she was given, she began working. The events were pouring in, and Brianna had to decline a few of them. Some clients were planning events around Brianna's schedule. She was looking over the calendar. There were two events that were coming up that had her flying out to New York and to Miami. She considered getting out of the Miami one, but that event was worth forty-five thousand dollars in sheer profit. Before she knew it, the day had gone by; she dolled up just a little and prepared dinner. She looked down at the ring that Maxwell gave her and refused to remove it. Finally, there was a knock at the door.

"Hi, Allan."

"Hey, baby." Allan kissed her on the cheek and went directly to the bathroom. She went ahead and poured him a drink and placed it on the bar. He walked right past it and sat down on the sofa and removed his shoes. "Babe, can you be a sweetheart and fix me a drink? Girl, I am exhausted."

Same old Allan! Give me strength, please! "Here you go, baby. I cooked. Would you like to eat now?"

"Sure." He followed her in the kitchen and took a seat at the table. She fixed him a plate with baked tilapia, broccoli, and yellow rice.

"Brianna, this looks good." He began to dig in before she could even sit down with her plate. *How rude!* she thought. During dinner, they did not talk about the wedding or what happened at Christmas. Once he was finished, he kissed her on the forehead and placed his plate in the sink and paid her a nice compliment on her cooking. When she finished straightening up the kitchen, she sat with him on the sofa.

"Brianna, how about you become Mrs. Brianna Jones in two weeks?"

"How about I will become Mrs. Brianna Godfrey-Jones in Miami in two weeks? I have an event down there. Why don't you come and join me after the event? We can invite a couple of our closest friends and get married on the beach."

"Okay, baby, that sounds like a plan. Brianna, do you love me?"

"What? You know I do?" She cringed a little inside.

"Show me." He laid back. She began to kiss him as if she was feeling the passion. She kissed him around his neck while he began to unbutton his own shirt. "Lick my nipples, Brie!"

What? She did it and he was getting turned on. She stood up and was about to remove her leggings.

"No, baby, you don't need to do that. You are on punishment, so you don't get a treat tonight—just me. Come here, baby." He began to pull her back down so they could finish the kissing. He unfastened his belt and unzipped his pants. He laid back as an indication for her to render services with her mouth only. Her blood was boiling.

I should let Mr. Haiti just go ahead and kill this bastard!

She began to perform her duty on him. Because she was angry, she was a little more aggressive. He began to moan and groan, twist and jerk. She could feel that he was about to release, so she jumped up. He didn't even care. He stroked it for a quick second and released.

"Damn, baby. I believe you. You are definitely sorry."

"Yeah, you are right. You just don't know how much." She went upstairs, brushed her teeth, threw on a T-shirt, and crawled into bed. He came up behind her.

"Baby, I am going to crash here with you and leave out around 5:00 AM." He got in the bed and put his hand on top of hers. He noticed the ring that he wasn't responsible for buying. "Damn, when did you get this?"

"I bought it for myself as a birthday gift."

"That's huge. I bet you that it came with a huge price tag too. Well, there is no need to get you anything. Once we get married, we are going to chill with all this extra spending." He laughed. "Oh, happy belated birthday."

She closed her eyes and became very quiet so that he would not keep talking to her. *What have I gotten myself into? Damn you, Maxwell!* She could have sworn that she had only closed her eyes for a moment when she was awakened to hearing Allan in the shower. Her head was hurting, and she felt a little queasy. She went downstairs and got a glass of ginger ale and an ibuprofen. *It's only freaking 4:00 AM. I should be still sleep.* When she went upstairs, he was still in the shower. Allan's phone was vibrating. She looked at the bathroom door and decided to hurry up and look at his phone. Stephanie's name was displaying. *Why is she calling him so early in the morning?* Brianna heard the shower stop. She quickly placed his phone back on the nightstand and got back in the bed. He came out buffed and dripping wet, but it was not enough to turn Brianna on. She really wanted him to hurry up and leave. After checking his messages, he quickly threw on his clothes. Brianna noticed that his pace was picking up; he was clearly on a mission. He walked around to her side, leaned down, and gave her a soft kiss on her lips.

"Bye, baby, I will give you a call later on today."

Brianna made her voice a little extra groggy. "Okay, Allan. Be safe driving home. Let me walk you to the door."

"That's okay. I'll lock the door behind me. Plus, you look a little drained. Love you, Mrs. Jones." He kissed her one more time before standing up to leave. Brianna tried to go back to sleep for a little bit, but her mind was in overdrive. She got up. Trying to distract herself from her own drowning thoughts; she went into her office to see if she could throw herself back into her work. While sitting at her desk, her eyes were drawn to the envelope that was marked "Special Client." It was the envelope that had the pictures of Melissa with Maxwell's father and the lab work from the little boy's doctor visits. She shook her head and began to put her heart, mind, and soul back into her work.

Later on that morning, as she was about to walk out her door to go to work, Rico was standing right there. She jumped back.

"Whoa! I'm sorry if I scared you, Ma. Can I talk to you for a minute?"

"Sure, come inside."

"Brianna, that man loves you. You know that, right?"

"Does he, Rico? Why does he always leave me? It's always me that he disappears on. I am always left dealing and fighting on my own. But you know what? I'm a woman with mine. I *handle* my shit! I don't run from the people I love. I run to them!" The tears she was shedding for the last couple of days had now turned into anger.

Rico reached over to grab her hand. "I hear you, ma. I was worried about you. Look, Maxwell is my best friend. That man has helped me and my family in so many ways. It would take my life to repay him. You are good for him and you are good to him. You feel me? Brianna, please don't give up on him?" Brianna could see it in his eyes that Rico was a sincere friend.

Maxwell became his friend in the hardest way. Maxwell was walking back to his car when Rico came around the back of him and pulled a knife on him; Rico was trying to rob him. He was in his teens, rebellious and being raised by the streets of Miami. Maxwell didn't live in the streets but was being raised by the meanest thug ever. Unannounced to Rico, Maxwell was a very good fighter. That night in Miami, with a sharp knife pointed at Maxwell's rib cage, Rico was demanding his cash. Maxwell wasn't giving it up without a fight. They both managed to give each other a fight that neither one would ever forget. The fight almost seemed to go on for about an hour. For every blow, one would be given with the same equal amount of force. The battle soon began to draw a crowd. A man standing against the building came by to see the quality of the fight. For fun and to earn some cash on betting, he sent in two other guys to fight against them. When Maxwell and Rico noticed blows were coming from other fists, they instantly joined forces against the strange men. Like a skillful team, Rico and Maxwell was faring quite well against them; they received cheers of victory! Suddenly, someone fired warning shots, signaling that the cops were coming; Maxwell and Rico began running to the car. They both got in the white Mercedes SLK. After driving three blocks, Maxwell looked over at Rico strangely. Rico, who had taken the bottom of his T-shirt to dab the blood from his lip, noticed him staring.

"What? Keep driving mofo. It's the least you could do since I didn't get shit from you." They laughed and introduced themselves. Since that day, they were inseparable.

Maxwell one day visited where Rico lived. His family was dirt poor. His family's lights were disconnected, and his family could barely afford groceries. The following week, Rico's mom got a wad of cash that afforded Rico's family to move and get on their feet. To this day, Maxwell has never owned up to having anything to do with the cash that was given to Rico's mom, but he knew that it was Maxwell who looked out for him. For that, he would always have Maxwell's back.

"'Don't give up on him'? Rico, I am tired. Now I am involved in shit that I can't get myself out of. I am done and Melissa has won!"

"What do you mean? You can't get yourself out of what?" Rico was really perplexed.

"Hold on, Rico." Brianna walked away and returned with the envelope that was marked *Special Client*. She handed it to Rico.

"What's this?" Rico asked while examining the outside of the envelope.

"It's the proof that I was talking about. It's all there. It's the photos and lab work. I am done. I will be marrying Allan in two weeks."

"Don't do it, Brianna." Rico even looked crushed at that moment.

"I have to. I have no choice. Do I love Allan? No. I can't change things, not even if I wanted to." Brianna was cold.

"He got to you, didn't he? Maxwell's father got to you."

CHAPTER THIRTY-FIVE

Emotional Roller Coaster

Brianna was exhausted from her trip to New York; however, the event she planned was spectacular. On the plane ride home, Brianna slept all the way back; she was really feeling dizzy and drained. She wrote in her planner that she really needed to make a doctor's appointment. Something had to be done about the extreme exhaustion. Once the plane landed in Richmond, it was 4:00 PM. She called the girls to make sure they were going to meet her at the condo this evening. Brianna also called Alice to make sure she was on her way too. When she arrived home, she fixed herself a glass of wine and jumped in the shower. Due to her not feeling up to par, she had to lean back on the shower wall. *Damn! That's it for the drinking.* The wine was not agreeing with her. Then she suddenly remembered that she hadn't eaten since last night.

Alice was the first to arrive; she gave Alice a big tight hug. "Wow, well, it's good to see you too!" Alice let out with a warm smile. This was actually Alice's first visit to Brianna's home. She looked around and gave honest compliments. Brianna's artwork on the walls was impeccable. The muted color tones on the walls were tastefully impactful with her accent wall. The cranberry-colored sectional sofa, the rich mahogany floors, the well-thought-out selection of furniture screamed volumes about Brianna's naturally expensive yet not over-the-top taste.

"Brianna, are you all right?" Alice could sense that Brianna was not herself. "Are you taking care of yourself? You look a little weak, and not to mention, you look like you have dropped a few pounds."

"I'm stressed out. I have been working so hard that I have neglected to plan anything related to this wedding. You know it's in a few days?"

"I know but why, Brianna? I thought you were going to do this in July? Why are you rushing this? Are you pregnant?"

"No. Alice, our sex life is almost like nonexistent. Alice, things aren't going well. I don't love Allan."

"Then, Brianna, you can't marry him. I can hear something else in your voice. What is it? What aren't you telling me?"

"I have to save—" The doorbell interrupted her sentence. "Alice, we will finish this conversation at another time, just not to night, okay?" Alice nodded and Brianna answered the door. That evening, they spent two hours planning Brianna's wedding. With Brianna's body reacting to all the tension, at the end of the night, she could only manage to hold down one slice of pizza. After which, she went straight to bed. It was 3:00 AM when Brianna's much-needed rest was broken by her phone. She cleared her throat and answered the phone.

"Hello?"

"Is he there with you?" the screaming voice questioned.

"What? Is who here with me, and who the hell is this?" Brianna began to sit up in her bed.

"I haven't seen nor heard from Maxwell since DC! If he is there with you, let me say this, Ms. B, you will be sorry if he is!"

"Melissa, he is not here with me. It is so funny how you are so stupid. Think about it, your daddy had to blackmail someone to stay with your pathetic ass. All you people are sad. Don't ever contact me again. Don't you have what you want? Trust and believe, if you ever come across me again, you may not get up!" Brianna disconnected the call. *Why won't these people leave me alone? Damn the day that I let Maxwell come into my life. Maybe I should pack up and move to Atlanta. I bet that still would not be good enough for these crazy people!* Brianna found herself looking through her purse, hoping to find any type of medication. Her head was pounding yet again, and she was feeling sick to her stomach. Unfortunately, her Xanax were all gone. *Oh, you have got to be kidding me!* She threw the prescription bottle

192

against the wall. She went to her bar and got the bottle of Grey Goose and poured a little in some ginger ale she had in the fridge. Brianna drank half of the beverage, praying that it would take the edge off. She got back in the bed, but was only able to toss and turned. Giving up, she went in her office and began working on her next major event. She went to the actual office around 10:00 AM. "Good morning, everyone," Brianna said with a "sorry that I am late" smile. Her staff loved her dearly. They felt as though they couldn't have asked for a better boss. Brianna knew how to build a strong loyal staff. She made them empowered and appreciated. That, in return, made them want to come to work, please the clients, and help their boss stay focused. Now they were becoming really worried about her. She was becoming less passionate about her work, even her appearance looking quite awful this morning. Peter followed her into her office with a steaming cup of coffee and a bagel.

"Oh, thank you so much, Peter. I really need this." She blew him an air-kiss and began sipping the coffee immediately.

"You're welcome, Brianna."

"Peter, are we all set with everyone's travel arrangements down to Miami?"

"Yes. All of the arrangements have been made. Brianna, if I may ask, are you okay?" He was hoping that he was not crossing their professional line.

"Why do you ask?" Brianna became instantly nervous.

"Brianna, you have become like a workaholic but on automatic pilot or something. I have been noticing the actual times of the e-mails you are sending out. Some of them are being sent at three and four in the morning. Not to mention that you are dealing with your own wedding." In Peter's questioning, he broke out in Spanish, "Chica has estado bebiendo?"

"No, Mr. Peter, I have not been drinking," Brianna quickly replied with a smile. Peter's eyes widen for two reasons: One, because he had forgotten that Brianna was fluent in Spanish. Two, because he still could not believe she still felt the need to rush the wedding.

"I mean, have you found the time to plan out your special day. Vendors? Decorators?" Peter was still asking with great concern.

"Not really. I gave Alice, Tamika, and Angel the same answer the other night. They tried to pull thoughts out of me, but honestly, I do not have any cool thoughts."

"Okay, well, if it is all right with you, I will speak with Alice. I am thinking simple, quaint, and chic. Can I trust you to find a dress, or would you like for us to handle that? I really do not mind. How many people will be there?"

Brianna was quite amused with his slew of questions. "Peter, let's go with your thought. For the ceremony and reception, I'm thinking approximately twenty to twenty-five people."

"Easy enough, Brianna. Please go back home and get some rest." He stood there holding her coat, assisting her with putting it on. As she was leaving, he caught her by her hand. "Brie, if you want to change your mind and not do this at all, your friends would definitely understand." Brianna gave him a big tight hug; she could feel his sincerity. They stood there looking at each other as he wiped her tear away. She assured him that she was fine and briskly walked away. Instead of her going to Saks or Nordstrom to find something for her wedding, she went home. As she reached for the phone to call the girls about making their travel arrangements for Miami, her father called.

"Hey, baby girl! I'm glad I got you on the line. I wanted to give you a call before your mom and I left for our cruise. Baby girl, we never would want to ask you for anything, but that's the best gift you could have ever given us. We are both tired, and your mom has been a fussy little thing. I think it those changes you ladies go through. Thing is, I could have sworn that your mama went through that years ago!" He was cracking himself up with that one. Brianna began to chuckle as well until she started feeling lightheaded and couldn't catch her breath.

"Well, Dad, you and Mom have lots of fun and call me when you get back. I'll try to get out there to visit you soon. Hey, someone is at my front door. I'll talk to you soon. I love you both!" Brianna got off the phone quickly. No one was really at the door, but she knew that she was experiencing a panic attack. The anxiety was coming from not being able to tell her parents about the impromptu wedding, Maxwell, Melissa, and Mr. King was starting to take a toll on her. After lying on the sofa for a while, she was able to take a much-needed three-hour nap. What served as an alarm was Allan giving her a call. He was the last person that she wanted to speak to.

"Hey, Allan."

"Hey, baby, you sound like you were asleep?" Allan said as if he was concerned.

"I guess so. I came home to get a little work done, but I must have fallen asleep." Brianna really didn't want to explain herself or mention the fact that she just experienced a panic attack. She whole-heartedly could give Allan a lot of the credit for her anxiety that she had been experiencing.

"Well, baby, that is what I was calling you about. I love the fact that you are not a lazy woman. I also respect the fact that you are so damn ambitious!"

Brianna put her hand to her forehead while rolling her eyes; she knew that they were about to have a conversation that she did not want to have, so she began bracing herself.

"But, baby, we need to make arrangements to get you up here."

Brianna wanted to scream but managed to keep her composure. "Allan, what do you recommend that I do about my company? This company was a blessing, and I just don't want to throw it away."

"Brianna, I am not asking that you just throw it away!" You could hear the agitation in Allan's voice and Brianna did not feel like arguing. "This is what I will let you do. After we are married, we can figure how we can make your company run with you living here. Then figure out when we can place your condo on the market as well as what to do with your furniture."

Oh, this is some real bullshit! Pass me the freaking gun; I can save Mr. Haiti the trouble. "Baby, that sounds like a plan. Look someone is at my door. I'll call you later tonight." Brianna lied again but just wanted off the phone. She had no plans on making any of those things happen, so why discuss it?"

"Okay, baby, love you!" Allan could care less that he wasn't putting Brianna's thought first.

CHAPTER THIRTY-SIX

Miami

With days coming and going, before she knew it, they were on a plane heading to Miami. Once they arrived at the Ritz-Carlton in South Beach, Peter, Amy, and Stacey went to the restaurant to grab drinks and a quick bite to eat. Brianna, who was about to embark on her life-altering weekend, just wanted to be in her room. After changing in more comfortable clothing, she went to the outdoor elevated pool that overlooked the ocean. It was beautiful. She sat out there for about forty minutes. Once the air began to get a little nippy, she headed back into the room to check her cell phone. She noted that she missed four calls; she recognized the numbers of Tamika, Angel, and Allan, but not the fourth call, which was the unidentified number. That number started ringing again. The repeated call, who had a Miami area code, was now on its third ring.

She answered, "Brianna Godfrey speaking."

"Bonjour, Madame Godfrey, I am so glad to know that you are finally in Miami. Are you set for the wedding? I will be more than happy to offer any assistance."

Brianna was furious, "Mr. King, I do not need you checking on me. You gave me an ultimatum and I will do it! After that, do not call me for a damn thing." Maxwell's father was not that surprised by her anger; for some sick twisted reason, he laughed. He was honestly entertained by her feistiness. Being that she was tired of his interference, she thought that she would have a little fun with him too.

"You think that you are so tough? You're not! You have threatened people's lives to get what you want? You're so disgusting because not only did you sleep with your son's wife but got her pregnant and is now trying to pass the child off as your son's. You are grimy! You are basically pimping out your own child to earn your money. What kind of human being would beat on their grown son, when all he wants to do is earn your freaking love? You are a fucking monster! Maybe you need to watch your mothafuckin' back! Be careful you low-life punk because one day someone will make that dark decision to end yours!"

She hung up the phone and powered it off. She then called the front desk immediately to tell them not to transfer any calls to her room for the rest of the night. Brianna placed the bolt on the doors, even making sure all doors leading to the balcony were locked as well. All that night, Brianna felt like she slept in increments of thirty minutes at a time. She would look around the room to make sure everything was still locked. She knew she had pissed him off and didn't know what to expect.

It was 9:00 AM and Brianna was exhausted. She took a hot shower and finally powered her phone back on; there were no messages. She called the front desk to let them know that it was okay to send calls to her room. When she walked past the full-length mirror in the room, she walked back to get a good look at herself.

I look terrible and I have lost weight! Brianna knew that she had not been taking care of herself. From eating poorly, to not resting adequately, it was taking a toll on her physically. She called the spa and pleaded with them to fit her in; she needed to be pampered desperately. When she got to the spa, she immersed herself in what was called the juniper muscle-soothing treatment; her eyes closed, and she drifted away. After her pedicure and manicure, she met with the master hairstylist. Brianna handed him the reigns to do whatever he saw fit with her hair and looks. While he was styling her hair, she was enjoying their conversation; she instantly thought Peter would find him extremely gorgeous. She told him about Peter and invited him to her wedding on Saturday. After fifty minutes of chatting and twirling the chair, Ricardo handed her a mirror. He was thrown by her tears.

"Ms. Godfrey, I am so sorry." Ricardo covered his mouth. He felt so badly about her not liking his work with her hair.

Brianna got herself together. "Sorry? Are you kidding me? This is beautiful! This is a change that was needed." He gave her a stunning bob. It was long in the front and flawlessly layered in the back. The swoop of her hair over one eye was her signature look; she was fabulous. Her hair was full of body and moved with her every step. Brianna, being very impressed, gave him a huge tip with a tight hug.

Noticing the time, she had ten minutes to meet with Peter and the clients for lunch. She quickly changed, ran to the restaurant, and greeted Peter and the clients with a smile. Peter did a double take and gave her a nod of approval; he loved her new look! Fortunately, the clients knew exactly what they wanted, which left Peter and Brianna just going over the plans of execution. Brianna noted that the nicely spoken client of the two was beautiful; her smile was warm and inviting. Her name was Maria Perez; they had spoken many times over the phone but had never met. The other point of contact was an older gentleman, a rich businessman who obviously had no interest in making small talk. The event was for some of the most elite people in Miami, most being of Colombian and Puerto Rican decent. It was after the older gentleman devoured his steak that he handed what looked like a list of questions to Ms. Perez.

"Thank you, sir and beautiful lady. I will leave you in the hands of my daughter, Maria." He nodded and left.

"Brianna, I was telling Peter that I know that this must have presented a challenge, always working with me via phone and e-mail. I sincerely thank you for your dedication and patience. As you know, I have a lot of special guests coming to this event tonight, one of which is a family member that I have not seen in a while. I won't bore you with the details. I'm just hoping that I will be able to find him among the five hundred guests that will be attending." After Brianna was able to address all the last-minute changes, Ms. Perez stood up to leave. "I'll leave you two to your work. Brianna, please keep that glow that you are wearing for the rest of the night. It becomes you." Instead of a handshake, she gave Brianna a tight hug. Once Ms. Perez left, Peter smiled at Brianna.

"There goes one classy lady, huh?"

Brianna adoringly agreed, "She sure is, Peter." Brianna held a meeting with her staff and vendors before heading to her room. Upon arriving in her room, she was exhausted. The four bites of her salad were no longer evident in her stomach. She called room service to have mini crab cakes and two bottles of water delivered. With no strength, suddenly, she could only eat one of the three mini crab cakes, but managed to guzzle both bottles of water. Into her much-needed twenty-minute nap, Allan called.

"Hey, Mr. Jones," she dryly answered, secretly hoping that he was not calling to cause any drama.

"Hi, sweetheart! I was just calling to tell you that I will be down in the morning. Alana will be with me. Mom and Dad cannot make the trip."

"Wow, she really does not like me, huh?" She sounded as if she was hurt, but inside, she was rejoicing that the mean hag wasn't coming.

"Don't say that! Dad isn't up for the traveling, so Mom is going to stay at home with him."

"That's fine. My parents are on their cruise."

"What? You mean that they would rather take a cruise than be at our wedding?"

"Calm down. I didn't tell them." Brianna was tickled that she managed to hit a major nerve in Allan.

"Unfucking-believeable! What do you mean that you didn't tell them? What's that about?"

"Allan, please stop yelling. They had the trip already planned, and I didn't want to stop them! Look, it will be okay. We can plan a big reception and have both of our parents there when we get back home."

After hearing her alternative solution, he calmed down just a little bit. "We'll have to talk about this when I get there. I'll see you tomorrow." He hung up the phone abruptly.

Whatever, Allan! I am so over his freaking tantrums! Then it hits her, *Oh damn, I have no stupid ring for him.* She called Alice at the store; thank goodness, she was still at work.

"Alice McNeil speaking"

"Alice, this is Brianna. I am so glad that you are still at work."

"What's the matter, dear? Are you all right?"

"I forgot his ring. I didn't think to get a ring!" Suddenly Brianna began to cry.

"Brianna, sweetheart, it's okay. I will pick one up before I leave out for the airport. Is a platinum band okay?" Alice was worried. She could hear in her voice that Brianna was breaking down. "Brianna?"

"I'm here. I don't care if it is sterling silver, anything is fine Alice; he wears a size 8. Thank you, Alice, I will write you a check when you get here."

"Brianna, I am not worried about that. Please take it easy until I get there. You have a big day ahead of you tomorrow."

"Okay, I will Alice." Brianna always felt so comforted whenever she spoke with her. Alice had qualities that Brianna wanted to adopt. She was sophisticated, smart and something about her demeanor commanded respect. You could feel that anyone would be foolish to cross her.

Brianna had forty-five minutes to get ready. She wore a beautiful royal blue midi dress with long sleeves that were embellished with rhinestones around the cuffs. This was complemented with a pair of Kristali laser-cut metallic leather pumps by Christian Louboutin. Brianna was five feet and five inches, but with her heels and this length of this dress, it looked like she had legs for miles. Her bob hairstyle was still perfectly bouncy; the blue eye shadow with her long lashes and shiny nude lips were more than enough—she perfectly applied everything. The men in the lobby loved her long confident strides; when walking to the ballroom, she looked as though she was on a runway. She was not from South Beach, but tonight, she blended in very well. Her staff looked wonderful too. Peter looked very dapper as usual while the girls sophisticatedly wore white line trousers and crisped button-down blouses. They pinned on their royal blue corsages and placed in their earpieces right before showtime. Once the music, food, and drinks were in full effect, it was great to see everything move so smoothly. In doing these parties, you could see clearly who had never experienced a recession or hard times. Brianna could faintly hear her name being called. When she turned around, it was Maria Perez. She was standing there with her brown wavy hair going down her back. Her skin had an amazing bronze tone that required next to no makeup. She was dressed in Robert Cavalli, a long white sleeveless dress with blue designs. Ms. Perez was stunning.

"Brianna, you and your staff are doing an excellent job!"

"Thank you, Ms. Perez. I am glad that you are pleased. Have all of your family members arrived?" Before she could answer, a photographer came to take their picture. After the picture, Brianna's knees buckled, and Maria caught her arm.

"Here, Brianna, let's go through this door to get some fresh air. Are you okay?"

"I am. I've been working and trying to get ready for my wedding tomorrow. I guess it is all catching up with me."

"Brianna, congratulations! Dear, I insist that you turn in for the night. There is only two and a half hours left, and I am quite sure your staff can oversee the rest of the party, yes?"

Brianna felt embarrassed; she did not feel comfortable with not seeing the event all the way through. "No, Ms. Perez. That is not how I do business. I will be absolutely fine." She sounded as if she was pleading for her job.

"Brianna, I am not having it. Thank you for all that you have done!" She gave Brianna an endearing hug. "Again, please call it a night."

Brianna knew that there was no way she could win this battle. She humbly surrendered. "Ms. Perez, thank you, and if you are not too tired, please drop by the wedding tomorrow. Also, please bring a guest."

"I will. I must say that I did notice your engagement ring. The wedding seems to be happening soon. Brianna, you had a special glow today, but as you speak of your wedding, I see no twinkle in your eyes. Forgive me for speaking out of turn. If this marriage is something that you do not want, please do not do it." Maria had the look of a loving mother.

"I am just nervous and tired. I am ready." They both smiled and said good night. Brianna could not believe that a stranger could see her pain so clearly.

When Brianna got back in her room, she felt overwhelmed again and exhausted. She immediately changed into something comfortable. When hearing the doorbell to her suite, she became nervous. *Please no drama and no surprises!* In looking through the peephole, she let out a scream and opened her door. There stood her partners in crime bearing gifts, gelato, and champagne. A few hours later came Peter and the two assistants with two bronzed male strippers; they partied to 3:00 AM.

At eight o'clock the next morning, the girls woke to hearing Brianna throwing up in the bathroom.

CHAPTER THIRTY-SEVEN

Dreaded Wedding Day

Tamika and Angel rushed in the bathroom to check on her. Brianna was waving them back. "I'm okay. It's the ice cream and champagne! I guess it's not mixing well."

Angel made her some hot tea and grabbed the crackers left on the room service tray. Hearing the doorbell, Tamika rushed to let Alice in. Brianna's face lit up like a Christmas tree, but Alice was not buying it. She saw Brianna's distress.

"Brianna, what's wrong? You look weak and tired," Alice said while giving her a kiss on her forehead. Tamika interrupted them, "Brie, we are going to start getting ready. Let us know if you need anything."

"Okay, Tee, thanks, girl." Once Tamika left out her room, she shifted her attention back to Alice. "I'm just tired. I've been working hard, and I just need to slow down, that's all. Do you like my haircut?" Like a little girl, she was trying her best to change the conversation.

"Yes, I do, Brianna, and the attempt to deflect was lousy!" They both laughed. "Let's get you ready for your big day, love! And, Brianna, at any point you would like to change your mind, no questions asked, we can board the plane and leave."

She did not wait for a response. She got up and laid out a wedding dress for Brianna, Allan's wedding band, and Brianna's pumps. Brianna could not believe how close they had gotten. The only blessed thing that came out of being associated with Allan was Alice. Just before hopping in the shower, she called him.

"Hey, Allan! Where are you?"

"Hey, baby!" he responded cheerfully. "Alana and I just checked in. You want to meet up so you can show me how excited you are to be Mrs. Brianna Jones?"

"Mr. Jones, that would be bad luck. I will see you in five hours." She was dreading it, but it had to be done.

"Girl, I know. I was just kidding but you know we haven't worked out our plans for when you are moving after our wedding."

Brianna began to do instant eye rolls, but he had a point. "Babe, you are right. It will be fine, trust me. Allan, I have to go. Alice needs me," she lied.

Finally, she was ready! Tamika and Angel took pictures with her. Not trusting Brianna's lack of good judgment later, she knew that's why Alice brought her wedding dress. Alice made an excellent selection; the dress made Brianna look quite angelic.

Peter kissed her cheek and began escorting her down stairs to the garden. Once there, he allowed the wedding coordinator from the hotel to take over. Before Alice could go take a seat, she grabbed Alice's hand.

"Alice, thank you for everything. I know that I have a mother, but I really do respect you just as such. You are my friend, my confidant, and more importantly, my second mother. I love you, Alice."

That melted Alice's heart. She always wanted a daughter, and she found that in Brianna. She cupped Brianna's face with her hands and looked directly in her eyes. "I love you too, my little butterfly."

Brianna's heart dropped. Alice went in the garden to take her seat beside her husband. The music began to play, and at the queuing of the coordinator, Brianna began her entrance. As she started to take a small step down the aisle, she smiled nervously and viewed her attendees. The twenty people there seemed like a hundred to her. There stood Allan in his all-white linen suit. If you could overlook him being cocky, he made a handsome groom. The girls had a weird smile plastered on their face. What caught her attention was to the far right, there he was, Maxwell's father. The way that he was positioned, no one could really see him.

You have got to kidding me! He is here!

Despite the weird smiles and Mr. Haiti hiding himself, she still managed to keep in line with her steps to the altar. What caught her off guard next was so unbelievable. Ms. Perez, who was invited to the wedding, was waving and mouthing something to her. Ms. Perez was waving, mouthing the words, "This is my son." Brianna turned her focus to the gentleman, who turned around at his mother's nudging. It was Maxwell. Instantly, it was like Brianna could not breathe, and everything went black.

CHAPTER THIRTY-EIGHT

Surprise Package

"Brianna! Brianna! Mom, I am taking her to the hospital now!" Maxwell yelled. He was beside himself. The blood all over his shirt was scaring everyone.

"What the hell are you doing? Wait, don't I know you?" Allan jumped in front of him and yelled up close and personal.

Maxwell, carrying Brianna, walked around him. "Yeah, man, you do. Look, I can get her to the hospital before the ambulance can get here!" Maxwell, carrying her, picked up his pace, with Allan trotting closely behind.

"Look, man, I will go with you!"

Not breaking his stride, he replied to Allan, "No, I have a two-seater. My mother, Maria, will take you!"

Maria, was a little thrown at the amount of passion that she saw her son display for Brianna but managed to grab Allan's hand, ensuring him that she was going to do just that. I'll have the driver rush us all over."

Alice, Allan, and Alana jumped in the car with Ms. Perez. Tamika, Angel, Peter, and even Roberto had the hotel's shuttle take them over as well. While everyone was making way to the hospital, Maxwell was able to make that thirty-minute commute in traffic in ten minutes. Upon arriving, he jumped out and took her inside. When the nurses saw the blood all over her dress and his suit. They took over immediately. Twenty minutes later, everyone started to arrive at the hospital. Alice, Allan, Tamika, and Angel walked over to the admittance station immediately; the nurse informed them that the attending doctor would be out shortly with an update. Maria, who was in a deep conversation with Maxwell, stopped when the girls walked over. Tamika gave Maxwell a hug.

"It's good to see you, Max. I know that Brie would be happy to see you as well."

"Thank you. Tamika, how has she been doing since—?"

"Since New Year's Eve? Honestly, not well at all," Tamika replied. "She's been working herself to death. Haven't been eating and losing weight. Maxwell, she was devastated when you walked out on her."

Angel, who had now been standing by listening, turned to face him. She did not know Maxwell well enough to comfort him, but she loved Brianna enough let him know how she felt. "So if you feel the need to disappear, do it now!" Before Maxwell could respond, the doctor came out. Allan, Alana, and Alice jumped up immediately to greet him.

"Doctor, how is she doing?" Allan asked.

"Who are you, sir?"

"Allan Jones, her fiancé. We were in the middle of our wedding when she passed out and bumped her head. This is my sister, Alana Jones, and a dear friend, Alice McNeil." By now, Tamika, Angel, Ms. Perez, and Maxwell were standing nearby.

"As you all know, in passing out from exhaustion and dehydration, she hit her head on a planter of some kind. She required twenty stitches and suffered a small concussion. In looking at her lab work, we had some questions and felt a need to follow up with an ultrasound. The baby is doing just fine. Dad, if you give her a few days, perhaps you can pick up with your wedding. You can go back and see her for a few minutes. She is groggy. We will keep her overnight for rest and observation."

Allan turned to Alice in disbelief. "What? A baby?"

Tamika and Angel grabbed each other's hands. Allan and Alana went back to see Brianna. Alice, who was shocked, turned to the girls. "Well, judging by your reaction and faces, you two didn't have clue about the baby either."

Simultaneously, they answered, "No, we didn't."

"Well, I wonder what else she is not telling us," Alice said with great concern. "The man that brought her here, is that the man she is in love with?"

"You got it," Tamika answered.

"Ladies, once Allan and Alana leave, let's stay behind and speak with her." Alice wanted answers. Most of all, she wanted to protect and help Brianna.

Angel tapped Tamika's hand and nodded toward the door. Maxwell was leaving with his mother.

"Damn," Angel sighed. "And there goes the infamous disappearing act."

CHAPTER THIRTY-NINE

What Baby?

There Brianna was lying in bed with an IV and monitor hooked to her. Allan lovingly bent down to kiss her gently on her lips while Alana rubbed her hand. Brianna began to slowly open her eyes.

"Hi, sweetheart, you gave us a big scare. I know that you are a drama queen but damn! Did you have to steal the entire show?" He smiled when she smiled back. "Brianna, when were you going to tell me that we were expecting?"

"What are you talking about? Expecting?" Brianna was ignoring the pounding headache due to the numbing information that she had just received. She noticed that Alana had a look of concern on her face.

"Wait, Allan. Brianna, you didn't know, did you?" Alana was concerned.

"No, I didn't know." Brianna was devastated. Allan was excited and was going on and on. Brianna didn't hear a word he was saying when she cut him off.

"Allan, who is here with you guys?"

"Alice and the girls are here of course. Oh, a guy insisted on driving you here. He and his mother, Maria, just left. I feel like I have met that guy somewhere, but I can't seem to place him."

"Baby, can you and Alana head back to the hotel and apologize to the remaining guests? On the way out, please send in Alice and the girls. I just want to say hi to them and get some rest."

"Baby, I was going to stay with you tonight."

He was not picking up her nonexcitement for the baby, but Alana did. "Brianna, we would be happy to do that. Feel better."

CHAPTER FORTY

The "King" Is Out the Bag

When Tamika, Alice, and Angel came into the room, Brianna began crying uncontrollably.

"Brianna, you have to stop crying. We don't know what you need or what you are going through until you tell us. Look, we love you and want to help you, but you have got to pull it together," Alice demanded.

Tamika held her hand. "Brianna, you didn't know that you were pregnant, did you?"

"No, I didn't. I thought that suddenly, my body couldn't handle the alcohol. This…this is all wrong! I can't be pregnant!" Brianna began to sob again.

Angel rub her leg through the layer of sheets, trying desperately to comfort her. "Brianna, if this helps, Allan seemed very happy with the news. Maybe he won't push the wedding right now, but just want to focus on his baby."

Almost as if someone had turned off the kitchen's faucet, Brianna's tears stopped immediately. "The baby may not be his. After Allan left out of here and just before you girls came back, the doctor told me that the ultrasound revealed that I was approaching five months."

"Brie, okay. You were with Allan on Christmas," Tamika said.

"Tamika, I was with Maxwell in December as well. Not to mention on New Year's Eve."

"Well, damn, Brie!" Tamika couldn't help to stay true to who was, Ms. Straight Shooter. "Brie, I would have given you a condom or two!"

"I know, guys. I don't know what to do?" Brianna said while closing her eyes and shaking her head.

"There is nothing to do. You will not marry Allan. If Maxwell can't get his act together, you will end that craziness too!" Alice's motherly statue had now turned cold. Tamika's and Angel's eyes had widened. Alice was no joke!

"Wait, it's not easy," Brianna said reluctantly. "I have to marry him or—" Brianna froze.

"Or what, Brianna?" Alice asked.

"With the whole blowup from Melissa's visit on New Year's Day, Maxwell's father decided that he needed to pay me a visit at my office. To sum it up, he ordered me to marry Allan or else!"

Tamika could not believe what she was hearing. In her world, there were no polite threats. "Or else what, Brie?"

"Or else, something would happen to Allan. He said that his daughter, Jasmine, would not have a father to raise her. I am not in love with Allan, but I feel so badly that I got him, unknowingly, involved."

"Are you fucking kidding me?" Angel asked in disbelief.

"Brianna, what is this man involved in that he feels he can fulfill threats like ones he's imposing on you?" Alice, who did not blink an eye, was standing there with her arms folded. She was not impressed, nor intimidated.

"Alice, this man is heartless. He has always used his son to get what he wanted. Maxwell was used to find people who were hungry for money opportunities. While he dabbles in drug trafficking, he flips the money by luring or pressuring people in making real estate investments. Mr. King comes equipped with power, money, and thugs. Melissa is the daughter of a high-paid lawyer that works for Mr. King. He makes sure that the IRS and Feds stays off his tracks. I have exposed that Mr. King and Melissa is having an affair behind Maxwell's back. The result of the affair is that Maxwell Junior is the brother of Maxwell, not the son."

"I had no idea that this mofo was threatening someone! How do we get rid of this trash?" Tamika was furious.

"Ladies, go back to the hotel and pack Brianna's things. I will be back with her in the morning. We will all fly out on my plane tomorrow. I am going to ask John to give Allan an emergency assignment that will take him out of the country for a few weeks immediately.

"Are you sure, Alice? Allan is not going to want to leave Miami without marrying her," Angel said with great concern.

"Alice, please do not tell your husband the details about my dilemma. I wouldn't want Allan to find out that there is a possibil- ity-" Brianna couldn't finish her plea without tears and her voice giving away. Like a true mother, Alice was quick to comfort her.

"My only goal at this very moment is to keep Allan very busy. My husband does not need any extra details. Everything will be okay."

The girls gave Brianna a kiss and left for the hotel. Alice pulled her chair close to bed and smiled at her.

"Alice, thank you for everything. You have got to be saying to yourself that these black people are crazy and full of drama," Brianna said laughingly.

Alice chuckled. "Brianna everyone has a little craziness in their lives. Whether they want to admit it or not, sweetheart, it's there. Brianna, my child would have been your age."

"Your child? I didn't know that you were pregnant at one time."

"Yes, we were expecting at one time. I was all set to tell him that I was pregnant with our first child. When I left from my doctor's visit, I purchased a lot of books on pregnancy. I placed them all on the coffee table, hoping that when he got home, he would put two and two together and become equally excited. But there it was, the fatal knock at the door. It was a woman who was ten years my junior. She was stunning. A beautiful woman from Argentina named Ariella. Ariella was five months pregnant and currently had a little boy who was two years old."

"Wait, are you saying that not only was he having one with this woman but already had one? Alice, was he living a double life?"

"Yes, Brianna, he did just that. He knew that I desperately wanted to start a family, but he kept telling me that it wasn't the right time because he was continuously traveling. He was right—he traveled all the time! However, it all made sense when I met Ariella. Ariella came to ambush him into giving me a divorce. Of course, I had pumped her for all the information that I could stomach."

Brianna was I speechless. With her eyes still widen, she managed to speak, "How did you handle that, Alice? You are a strong woman. You are still with him!"

"Am I, Brianna? Am I really with him? When he came home, he found Ariella and I having tea. At first, he was trying to deny everything that she had shared with me. Then it shifted to a desperate attempt to get me to believe that she did not mean anything to him. Those two began to bicker back and forth so much so that they did not see me leave the room. When I sat back down, placing my .357 on the table, both shut up instantly."

"What?" Brianna's laughter only lasted a brief second, as the pain from head got her attention. "Alice, what were you going to do with that?"

"I just wanted to make both, shut up and listen. I told her to never show up on my doorstep unannounced again. I also informed her that I would end this marriage when I felt like it, not because she wanted to pressure him. Then shifting my attention to him, I told him to keep this situation out of my sight! If I see or hear of anything relating to his estranged family, he would regret it. I called her a cab and have not heard a peep out of her in years. The next day, I made him drive me to my impromptu doctor's appointment."

"What appointment, Alice?"

"The appointment in which I foolishly terminated my pregnancy. He cried, and I did not shed one tear. I came out of the room cold, angry, and damned. Now as it stands, I regret that I did that. If I could go back in time, I would have had my baby and left him. Now my days are filled with many tears. Tears I should have shed then are occasionally flooding my eyes now. Today, Brianna, when you called me your second mother, it was like I was being forgiven for the darkest decisions I could have ever made."

When Brianna looked into her eyes, she saw the flood of tears and motioned for her hand.

"Alice, I am so sorry that you had to go through that."

"Brianna, no need for that, dear. Just allow me to help you fix this."

CHAPTER FORTY-ONE

And Life Goes On

"John, you have got to be kidding me. Are you sure you can't send someone else to take care of this?" Allan was furious. He had been dealing with Mr. McNeil all morning, trying to desperately convince him to let another coworker from the office handle this one assignment. However, once Mr. McNeil concocted a story of how this would push him up the ladder, Allan soon changed his tune. "Okay, I'll go. Will Alice watch over Brianna until I get back?"

"She sure will. You know, she really cares about Brianna." John patted Allan on his back as they were both about to hop in the cab. Mr. McNeil knew that Allan didn't know the real deal, and honestly, he didn't either. However, his wife called the shots. He wasn't going to take no for an answer anyway.

After hearing the conversation between Allan and Mr. McNeil, Alana wanted to call her brother out on his selfishness. This was what she witnessed all her life with her brother. For one moment, she thought he was changing, but no, his constant need to elevate his career was still there. His ego was not going to be pushed to the side for his future wife at all; Alana was majorly annoyed.

Due to Brianna just speaking with Allan over the phone, she was relieved that he would be out the way for a while. He kept apologizing, and Brianna kept insisting that everything would be fine. Alice escorted Brianna to her suite to meet the girls; she went to her room to make a few calls. Brianna and the girls were so happy to see each other; Peter was gushing all over her because of the pregnancy. He hugged Brianna tightly and whispered in her ear, "I took care of everything from your wedding. Me and the girls are headed back to Richmond. Please get some rest."

Without a pause, she whispered back, "Thank you. I don't know what I would do without you, Peter."

As he began walking to the door, he smiled. "Honey, you will never find out. Oh, and here, Maria Perez left this for you. Okay, ladies, we see you back at home!"

While the girls were sipping on coffee, waiting on Alice, Brianna took a seat to open the envelope.

Brianna,

Many thanks to you and your staff. You executed a flawless and stunning event. I have been receiving an abundance of compliments. My father, who does not impress easily, was quite smitten with you.

I am sorry for your mishap at the wedding. I was glad that Maxwell was there for you. It seems that you and I will need to speak soon.

Warm wishes,
Maria

PS: El verdadero amor nunca puede ser destuida.

She was right, true love can never be destroyed. She folded the note, along with her check for the final payment of fifty thousand, and placed it her purse.

"Why do you have that look on your face?" Angel asked. "Are you feeling all right?"

"Guys, I thought I was dreaming. Was Maxwell really at the ceremony?"

"Girl, he was the one who picked you up and drove you to the hospital," Tamika said matter-of-factly.

"Ladies, when my client Maria mouthed to me that Maxwell was her son and then seeing Mr. King standing from far away, I couldn't handle it anymore. Everything went dark. Ladies, we have got to go. He is here!"

Angel could see that Brianna was getting upset. "Brie, go take a shower. I will call Alice to see what time we're going to be leaving."

Two hours later, they were on a chartered flight back to Richmond; once they had arrived, they began to gather their things. Alice grabbed Brianna by the hand before departing the plane.

"Wait, would you like to stay with me at my condo? You will have plenty privacy, and not to mention, I will feel better if you stayed with me until we can figure this out."

"Alice, I could not bring myself to impose on you any longer. You have done more than enough. I probably can stay with one of the girls, or have one of them to stay with me."

"Brianna, stay with me this week. I want to make sure you're eating and resting properly. After that, we will see if you are able to go home, okay?"

She knew that Alice wanted the best for her. She decided to give in. "Okay, Mom Number 2! At least let me go home to pick up my mail and pack a fresh duffle bag of clothing." Alice's heart melted from the sound of her new title.

"Go straight home, Brianna. I will have a warm meal waiting on you when you get to my home. Tamika, I know that you are worn out, but do you think that you could make sure she's okay while doing that? You and Angel are welcome to come over for a bite as well."

"I can definitely go home with her. I may need to take a raincheck on dinner. I'm pretty exhausted. Thank you so much for the offer," Tamika said with a kind smile. Angel did the same.

Upon arriving at Brianna's condo, she parked in her garage. Tamika parked her car and walked with Brianna inside. A powerful stench almost knocked them back through the door.

"What the hell is that smell?" Tamika yelled while covering her nose and mouth. They began to search around the kitchen. There was no trash that needed to be taken out, and nothing left in the stove. They walked down in the living room, and there it was—dead rotting fish was sprawled across her coffee table.

"Seriously, what the hell!" Brianna's confusion began to evolve into anger. Tamika ran back to the kitchen and retrieved a dish towel to tie around her nose. She also got a garbage bag and rubber gloves to clean up the mess. After the contents were placed in the outside garbage, the girls opened all the windows. Finally, Brianna noticed that the heat was turned on and set at eighty-five degrees.

"Tamika, who came in here without setting the alarm off?"

"Your guess is good as mine, Brianna. We better do a little more looking around," Tamika suggested. Brianna started to go up the stairs until Tamika discovered a small problem. "Wait, girl, are you slipping? I thought I taught you better than that. You know that I don't have mine. Where is yours?"

"My what, Tamika?" Then it hit Brianna. "Oh! She came back down the stairs, knelt, and ran her hand under the sofa. She pulled out a handgun, a .22.

"What the! Uumm, Brie! You might as well just take the bullets out and throw them at the person." Tamika was frustrated with her like a mother would be with a child. Luckily, no one was upstairs. The spare room was trashed a little. Her bedroom had things knocked off her dresser and night stands, but her office was gone through with a fine-tooth comb. Clearly, someone had a purpose in that room. They were looking for the evidence. The files were searched and dropped on the floor.

"Brie, this wasn't done by a man. A man would have torn this room to pieces. This person needed order and could physically only do so much. A man would have flipped furniture over. Things would have been ripped open and torn. What man is petty enough to take time out to place fish on a table?"

"Another dead smelly fish—Melissa King," Brianna said while shaking her head.

"You got it. Plus, Brie, you haven't been feeling well, so it's probably a good chance that you forgot to program it before you left."

"How could I have been so careless!" When Tamika asked if she wanted to call the police and file a report, Brianna was shocked. Since Tamika was associated with some of the shadiest people, she was never a big fan of the police.

"Tamika, call your connection over at the crab shack. Ask if they can deliver one bag of fish guts over the Mrs. Melissa King's office. If they can throw in a good Go-Go CD, that would be beautiful."

Tamika started laughing. "Brie, are you serious?"

"And you know it, ma!" Brianna quickly replied.

"What about Allan? Are you scared that he may get caught in the middle of back-and-forth war that is about to start?"

"Nope. Remember, he will be out of the country for a while. I must resolve this before he gets back. Not to mention, I got this baby to worry about now. I have decided to move on with my life, even if it means that I must do it without Allan or Maxwell. Enough is enough!"

Tamika made the call while Brianna packed a week's worth of clothes. Before leaving the condo, they both made sure every window and door was locked. Brianna even called the security company from the car, making sure that they were reading the alarm was on and activated.

When Brianna finally arrived and parked at Alice's home, Maxwell's father gave her a call.

"You didn't tie the knot? I saw your little spill, but you need to do what I say!"

Brianna was beyond annoyed, as her tone reflected. "Mr. King, just what are you afraid of? Surely, you have heard the news. As you have seen, I have met Maria. Wow! She is really an intelligent, beautiful, and sweet woman. How did she end up with a low-life monster like you?"

Mr. King totally ignored her sarcasm. "Have I heard what news?" he snapped.

"I'm pregnant. Allan and I are expecting a baby. Maxwell heard the news and left immediately. He is done with me, and guess what! I am done with you, and I am done with your son! But who I am not done with is *Melissa*!"

"Stay away from her, Brianna. I will see to it that she never bothers you again."

"WELL, START DOING IT NOW!" she yelled and ended the call.

CHAPTER FORTY-TWO

The New Family

When Brianna knocked at the door, Alice greeted her with a big smile. "Come in, sweetheart!" Brianna, with an overnight bag in tow, stepped inside and could smell the yummy food cooking.

"Alice, that smells delicious!"

"Yes, it does. Let me get the chef."

A familiar voice came around the wall. "No need to yell for me. I am right here." In walked Mr. Conti with a warm smile and a big hug for her; he planted a fatherly kiss in her cheek. Mr. Conti had swagger that you would not believe. You could tell that he was 100 percent Italian. His dark complexion, shiny black hair, which was thinning probably due to age, was always combed neatly back. Mr. Conti stood about five feet and ten inches, with a healthy nice slim build. He had on tan trousers with a small cuff at the bottom, complemented with a cream knitted fit shirt and a thin eighteen-karat gold chain.

"Mr. Conti, it's so good seeing you!"

"Brianna, you call me Edmundo and likewise, my dear!"

They ushered her directly in the kitchen. Alice and Brianna sat at the table while Edmundo was putting the finishing touches on dinner. In ten minutes, he plated chicken piccata for them that was upscale restaurant worthy. After fifteen minutes of small talk, Edmundo took over the conversation.

"Brianna, tell me about this man who thinks he is a god of some sort? I'm told that he dictates if someone should live or die?" Edmundo had a look on his face of disgust and sheer annoyance.

"He is the father of my ex-boyfriend. This ex had been out of my life for about seven years until, I guess, his wife became bored and wanted to taunt me."

Having a concerned look on his face, Edmundo shifted his weight in his chair. "And the father is involved because…?"

"Maxwell, his son, my ex, was to keep her happy in exchange for her father keeping the feds off him. He is a cross between Madoff, the shady investor and a major kingpin."

"Interesting." Edmundo leaned back and begin sipping from his glass of Merlot. "Since Miami, who has contacted you?"

Brianna started to chuckle. "Funny you should ask that. Well, when I went home to get my clothes, Tamika and I found dead fish on my coffee table. Nothing was taken, but you could tell that some-one was looking through a few of my things. Tamika said that it was a woman who had done it because of how things were out of place but not necessarily destroyed. Also, Mr. Haiti, himself, called me when I pulled to your home."

"Really, Brianna! What did he want?" Alice asked.

"He wanted to confirm that he indeed was at the wedding and he saw me fall."

"What a bastard!" Alice blurted out.

"Oh, it gets even better, Alice. He wanted to know if I was going to follow through with the ultimatum. I told him that there was no need for me to adhere to his ultimatum since I am pregnant with Allan's child."

Alice reached for Brianna's hand. "But you're not pregnant with Allan's child."

"But, Alice, there is a slight chance that it is Allan's child. However, Mr. King and Melissa don't know this. I'm praying that this information will make Mr. King and Melissa go away."

"Is that his name, Mr. King? You called him Mr. Haiti earlier. I am guessing that Mr. King is from Haiti?" Edmundo asked.

"Yes, you are exactly right." Brianna took the last bite of her chicken piccata. Alice immediately removed her plate and brought over a tall glass of milk and a slice of tiramisu to her. "As much as

I detest Mr. King, I can't stomach Melissa. She is becoming a real thorn in my side."

"And what are your true feelings for Maxwell since you are carrying his child?" Edmundo asked. Brianna, who was devouring her dessert, paused for about fifteen seconds. Brianna looked at both Alice and Edmundo.

"I love him but I can't keep letting him come and go as he pleases. Plus, to have him in my life is to allow his father and Melissa in my life. I can't! I just can't! Our child—I mean my child deserves better than that! He accused me of betraying him, then he walks out on me." Brianna's voice begins to weaken. "Guys, I'm really tired. Do you mind if I shower and turn in?" Alice showed her to her room. Upon Alice's return to the kitchen, she found Edmundo staring into the air.

"What is it, Eddy? Alice asked.

"Say nothing to her just yet, but I know of this Mr. King. Let her stay with you until I can find out somethings for myself."

CHAPTER FORTY-THREE

You Are Not the Daddy

Three weeks had gone by, and she knew that she had to deal with her parents and Allan sooner or later. Alice and Edmundo did not want her going back to her condo. They had pretty much had forbidden her. Alice had even joined her on her trip to visit her parents.

It was a bittersweet visit; Brianna had to tell her parents that they were going to be grandparents. They were happy to see her, but being devout Christians, they were not happy about her being pregnant out of wedlock. The visit got worse when she informed them that she and Allan would be going their separate ways. Her mother was furious, and her father was saddened deeply. It crushed her when her father gave her a hug while saying she had let him down by this bit of news. It was then that Brianna immediately knew that if they couldn't handle this little information, then surely, the baby possibly not being Allan's would place then under cardiac arrest. When Brianna went back to her hotel, Alice was there waiting for her; she knew to have a box of tissues waiting for her.

Now back in Richmond, it was time to speak with Allan. In trying to avoid a hostile argument, she decided to meet him at PF Changs; he was delighted to see her.

"Baby, I miss you so much! Look at you—you're glowing. What are you officially? Two months or so? It's hard to tell. You really aren't showing." He was grinning from ear to ear. The amount of tension she was feeling at that very moment made her want to throw up. "Brie, so what's going on with us officially tying the knot and selling your condo?"

"What do mean, Allan?"

"Remember, we had the talk about selling it, as well as relocating your business to Northern Virginia." Allan was back to be condescending. This time she welcomed it because she needed all the ammunition she could in helping her execute her next move.

"What, Allan? I was thinking, you should put your house on the market and commute from Richmond. How about that?" Brianna knew she was being unreasonable, but it felt good.

"Brianna, we have already discussed this. There is no need to bring up other silly options."

Brianna was annoyed and was trying her best not to blurt out that the baby, possibly, was not his. She wanted to keep pushing his button. Now it was time to address the Stephanie thing. "Allan, you are never home anyway. So why would I want to be stuck up there when I would be leaving my friends here in Richmond?"

"Oh, grow the hell up, Brianna! You will be a full-time mother. You won't have time to hang around your little ghetto friends anyway!"

"You know what? You are one arrogant fool! Let me tell you something. I was a woman before I met you, so I am thinking that I can make my own decisions as to who I should have as friends. Those ghetto friends, as you have rudely called them, has always been there for me! If you think that you can control me like that airhead Stephanie, you will be highly disappointed. That might work with Stephanie, but you can forget that with me!"

"Lower your voice, Brianna, and learn to leave Stephanie out of our arguments."

"Well, you learn to leave her out your bed!" Brianna got up and walked out. When she made it to her Range, she could hear him yelling her name. It was when she was in her driver's seat when he caught up with her.

"What the hell are you talking about, Brianna? How are you going to say some mess like that and just walk out?"

Brianna just wanted to get away from him. Thank goodness, she was staying with Alice. A bad rainstorm came out of nowhere.

She knew that if she did not make it back to the Alice's home quickly, Mr. Conti and Alice would have helicopters out looking for her.

"You know what I am talking about! Stephanie keeps clothes at your house. I saw them in Jasmine's room. We are talking work clothes, sweatpants, lingerie, and thongs—come on, bruh!" By the look on his face, Brianna knew that she hit a nerve.

Not paying attention to the rain, he still wanted to argue, "What? Did you go through the house? Look, I wouldn't have given you a key if I had something to hide."

Brianna began to laugh. "Remember, I went to college too. I believe that both of us have taken at least psych 101. Allan, I am cold and tired. I'm going to leave now." She began to let up her window he began yelling at her.

"Don't forget that's my child you are carrying!"

Brianna went back to Alice's condo, only to find her sleeping on the sofa. She woke up wanting to hear about her encounter.

The next day was Brianna's doctor appointment. Angel, who wanted to attend, could not be there due to a large project she was overseeing. Tamika, who typically runs late for everything, was already seated and waiting to be a part of her prenatal visit. Alice came strolling in with a big smile. Brianna was in being examined.

"Yes, Ms. Godfrey, you are most definitely pregnant. You are in your second trimester. If all goes well, and I am sure that it will, you should be delivering this bundle of joy on September 13. Due to that being the case, I can see the sex of your child. You, my dear, are having a girl!" The nurse, who had quietly left, returned with Tamika and Alice. "Ladies, would like to hear something special?" They both smiled and nodded. Suddenly, they were able hear the baby's heart-beat. The girls were giggling with excitement.

After the appointment, Alice went to work, and Tamika had some things that she had to take care of, which left Brianna going into her office. When she walked in, her staff ran to her, giving her gentle but loving squeezes.

"I miss you guys too! As you know, I am a preggo, but I can still pull my weight."

"Brianna, we need for you to take it easy. You gave us a big scare in South Beach!" Peter said while adoringly holding her hand. The girls totally agreed.

"I know, thanks for everything. I have something that I want to give you guys." She reached in her purse and pulled out three envelopes; she gave them each one. Stacy and Amy, who opened theirs first, gasped. Both of them, grinning from ear to ear, received unexpected bonus checks of $1,500 apiece; they hugged her one more time.

"Thank you, Brianna. This was so unexpected!" Stacy said with a big smile.

"You ladies deserve it, and you are very welcome. Peter, let me see you in my office." Peter followed Brianna in her office and closed the door. She nodded for him to open his envelope. He clutched his imaginary pearls and began to tear up.

"Brianna, if I wasn't gay and wanted to wear your pumps, I would marry you!" They both started laughing.

"Peter, I don't want you to ever think that I take you for granted. You have gone above the call of duty for me and this company. I sincerely thank you."

"You are welcome, but $5,000, Brianna?"

"Don't say that too loudly! Your bonus is three times larger than theirs. If you continue to look in the envelope, you will find your new business cards and a letter. Your new title is director of events, and the letter is informing you of your pay increase."

His mouth was wide open. "I don't know what to say!"

"Say thank you for the bonus and say that you will accept the position. With my pregnancy, I will work from home a lot more, and not to mention, I will be traveling a lot less. I will rely on you being my eyes and ears for me. Go ahead and hire one more person. I want you to supervise more than trying to do it all. Are you up for it?"

"Thank you, Brianna, and yes! So I have to ask, no further wedding plans, huh?"

"Nope. I'm not feeling him." She began to laugh at her own cavalier answer. Peter thought it was funny too.

"Well, I hope you are still feeling that ring he gave you? If not, maybe my boo can buy it from you and propose to me?"

"Your Boo? Who is your boo-boo?"

"Ricardo," he smirked.

"From the hotel? The cutie that did my hair? Shut up!"

"Okay, I'll shut up. However, if I shut up that means that I cannot tell you that he is visiting me this weekend and is thinking about relocating here to start his own salon."

CHAPTER FORTY-FOUR

The Truth Shall Set You Free

Another week had gone by and Alice had finally convinced Brianna to meet with Allan once again to tell him the truth about the baby. She recommended that she says nothing about the death threats. In reaching for the phone, Allan called her and it freaked her out.

"Hey, Allan?" she curiously answered.

"Brianna, I don't know what's going on with you, but you are changing on me. You called and wanted to get married. Now you are acting like you are having second thoughts.

Brianna was so tired of hearing his voice; she was ready to end the chaos. "Allan, is she still sharing a bed with you? If I were to ask Jasmine if mommy and daddy sleeps in the same bed, what would she say to me, Mr. Allan Cordell Jones? Don't lie to me. Give me some credit. Apparently, I was creeping with you when you were creeping on her. That being said, this is who you are! Allan, we can still be friends, just stop lying, please."

"Brianna, I love you, but to answer your question, yes, Stephanie has been in my bed!" Allan had absolutely no remorse in his voice.

Brianna was pissed but relieved. There were times when she truly had wondered what it would be like to be his wife. He had the right friends, the right job, and drove the right cars, but he always seemed as though he had something to prove. His ego was thirsty. Pouring out compliments only made him want more; his silent cockiness was deafening.

"Okay. Let's end this now, Allan," she said very calmly.

"No, Brianna! This is your fault! You never made any time for me!" he yelled. Brianna instantly became lost in her thoughts. *See, this is the stuff that makes a person snap! Someone always want to push a button that makes people label us the angry black woman. I just want to end this, but did he just say that this was my fault?*

"What did you just say, Allan?"

"Brianna, instead of you making me your main focus, you did your own thing. Stephanie had to find out the hard way about not having her priorities in place. She had a problem with me working, she had a problem with me networking, she had a problem with everything. All she had to do is stay home and let me take care of her. This is who I am! Take it or leave it!"

"You know what, Allan, let me show you what real women do. I really don't care about you hanging out with your frat. I could care less about your opportunistic networking, which ironically led you to me. Please make no apologies for being *who you are*. However, what I won't let you do is blame me for your lack of self-esteem or your inability to be a *man*. Let me spare you the added aggravation. This child that I am carrying is not yours." She sat quietly for what seemed like thirty seconds before he went ballistic.

"What the hell, Brianna! When were you planning on telling me this? I guess what they say in the streets is really true. You can't make a whore into a housewife!" Those words hit Brianna in the gut hard. "Who is he and when did this happen?"

She held her composure as well as held back her tears. She was blown away by him having the nerve to call her a whore. "I just had my first appointment last week. With the calculations given, I believe that you are not the father."

"You are simply *believing* that I am not the father?"

"This happened when I realized that Stephanie was in your life to stay. My intentions were to call off the engagement. I, my darling, started seeing my first love again."

"Whatever, Brianna! So again, you cannot be absolutely sure this is not my child? You know what! You were right when you said let's end this, but I see you in a few months! You better hope you are right, or I swear I will make your life a living hell!"

He hung up the phone and Brianna fell apart. Not because of what Allan said to her, but what if, indeed, he was right? What if he was the father? What if she and the doctor was wrong? They screw up on due dates all of the time.

On her second appointment, the doctor did not go out of the way to rule out the possibility that there was a slight chance for a miscalculation. For the next couple of months, Brianna would find her doubts haunting.

CHAPTER FORTY-FIVE

The Doors of Hell Are Open

The possibility that she was not carrying Maxwell's baby was constantly weighing on her. However, things were eerily quiet. Maxwell had not been in touch with her, nor Rico. Oddly enough, Melissa had not retaliated when the girls sent her the fish guts, and Mr. King had not come up with any additional threats. Brianna was thankful, but as her grandmother would say years ago before her passing, "There is always a quiet before a storm."

On her next appointment, she spied Alice's and Angel's cars parked in the lot. She waved at the girls when going to sign in. "You guys beat me here. You must be more excited than me."

Tamika came in a little winded. "What's up, ladies. Have I missed anything?" She apparently had jogged across the parking lot.

"No, Ms. Track Star, Brianna just got here," Alice chuckled. Alice was fitting in quite nicely with the girls. She never spoke about any of her girlfriends; the girls agreed that there may be a reason for that, so they never asked. As they got to know her, they just chalked it up to being a classy white woman who just kept it real. Perhaps for the timid, that would prove to be too much. You could tell that Alice connected with all walks of life, and for that, the girls had a fondness for her.

"Brianna Godfrey!" The perky nurse was summoning for her to come back to the examining room.

"Ma'am, do you think that my mom and my sisters can come back and see the ultrasound as well?" Brianna giggled at the thought of a white mother and three black sisters.

"Ms. Godfrey, it may be a little too crowded for you and the doctor?" the nurse responded.

"I know but these ladies mean the world to me. Okay, I'll take a larger room."

The girls yelled out a joyful scream when they found out that she was having a girl. She had not told them the sex of the baby from the last appointment. After that appointment, Peter called Brianna over to the office to check out two proposals. He also informed her that a certified letter came from Florida. As requested, she went right over to the office. She caught the office up on her doctor's visit. Peter was happy to hear about her having a little girl. They went over the two lucrative events and decided to take both of them; sipping coffee, she went in her office to open the certified letter.

My dearest Brianna,

I knew when I met you that you were special. I had no idea that you and my son was connected until the incident that happened on your wedding day. My son and I became somewhat distant after his father convinced me that he wanted to step in and take care of him. It was at seventeen that he decided that he wanted to get to know his father full-time. I had no idea that he would purposely destroy my son's life. It was Rico that recommended that we contact your company. He asked that we did not mention him. It is Rico who makes sure that Maxwell calls me from time to time to say hello, making sure I hear his voice.

The night before your wedding, I saw it in your eyes that you did not want to get married. When Maxwell picked you up, after your fall, I saw the man that was madly in love with you. However, when the doctor mentioned your pregnancy, he cried uncontrollably. Brianna, he is hurting and drinking excessively. I feel that he is doing dangerous things without thinking; I need your help. I will be in Virginia next month and will contact you once I have arrived.

Sincerely,
Maria

Brianna was not sad but annoyed. *You have got to be kidding me!* Instead of giving the letter any extra thought, she went to run errands. Brianna wanted to reclaim her life. In retrospect, she has endured one crazy encounter after another. Brianna wanted to enjoy her pregnancy. To do this, she decided that moving back into her condo to fix up the baby's room would get her excited. A day of retail therapy was in order. She managed to get a lot of nice items at Short Pump Mall while grabbing a few things in Nordstrom for herself. Once Brianna placed her items in the trunk, she hopped in her truck, but when she went to close her door, her hand hit someone's midsection. Pulling her hand back immediately, she found Melissa standing there, wedged between her and the door.

"Melissa! What the fu—"

"Why isn't he talking to me, Brianna? He is not returning my calls and he has not been home!" Melissa seemed so angry that it was sad. "I know he is talking to you, trick!"

Why does this crazy woman feel the need to keep calling me out of my name? Didn't I beat the life out of this chick the last time? Brianna snapped out of her thoughts to finally answer her questions. "Melissa, please shut up and go get a life! You are like a pathetic broken record! No! Maxwell is not talking to me! I don't care if he is not returning your calls. And, you don't know jack! Get the hell up out of here, Melissa!" Brianna immediately started her car. "Melissa, move!"

She continued to stand there, yelling obscenities. Brianna put her SUV in reverse and began moving. "Wait, are you trying to roll me over? I wish you would!"

"Oh? Okay!" Brianna said with a devilish grin. She gave her vehicle a little more gas, which caused Melissa to lose her footing and stumble, her eyes widen. Appearing not to get the message, Brianna hit the gas more, and she stumbled quicker. She finally began to fear for her life and ran out the way.

"I hate you, Brianna Godfrey. *I hate you!*"

At the moment, Brianna seized the opportunity to shut her door. When completely out the parking spot, she rolled down the window to give her some truthful words. "Yeah, you hate me, Melissa, but your man doesn't!" Brianna laughed and sped off.

CHAPTER FORTY-SIX

Six Degrees of Separation

Brianna had reach her sixth month of pregnancy and was quickly approaching her seventh month. Maria had never made it to Richmond as her father had grown ill. This evening, Alice and Conti were coming over for dinner; she wanted to show them the baby's room. As always, they were punctual; it was seven on the nose.

"Brianna, the food was delicious, and the baby's room is lovely. I can't wait to see our little angel." Alice had gladly taken on the role of a doting grandmother.

"Yes, Brianna, I can't wait to meet her either." Mr. Conti handed Brianna her hot chocolate, then went back to retrieve a cup of coffee for the both of them. Brianna was tickled. With all the visits that she had enjoyed with the both of them, Mr. Conti made his way around her condo comfortably.

"Edmundo, I can't shake this feeling that you know Mr. King. Do you?"

Brianna noticed the quick stare that Alice gave him with the placement of her hand on his knee.

"Yes, Brianna, unfortunately, I do. It was when I lived in Miami. A group of us businessmen had various types on business. For me, it wasn't so easy. I was sacrificing a lot in order to get the money that was needed. My wife's medical costs were overwhelmingly expensive. Finally, I got fifty thousand dollars together to buy into a lucrative car dealership. Mr. King was the partner. In being greedy, he took my money and drove up the buy-in price. When I told him that my wife was having more health issues, he laughed. He pushed me out of the deal and kept my money. He promised me that if I came after him for money, I could kiss my wife goodbye before God was planning on making room for her. He swindled me out of money that would have benefited my wife's health and our future."

Brianna could not believe this awful story. At this point, she was a firm believer in the meaning of six degrees of separation. "Edmundo, I am sorry you had such crazy dealings with this man! Can anyone escape this devil?"

"Brianna, Edmundo and I really want you to watch yourself. Steer clear of him and his family. Your health and that of your baby depends on this." Alice's face was covered in worry.

CHAPTER FORTY-SEVEN

Nothing Good Ever Happens After Midnight

Brianna's business was still doing very well without her physical presence there every day; business was being booked well into in the summer of next year. Her belly was nice and round, and her hair was growing like weeds. Her beautiful glow was an indication that her pregnancy was agreeing with her. Approaching the very end of her eighth month, she appreciated no craziness was happening. There were no calls from Allan, Maxwell, Mr. King, or Melissa. For that, she was grateful.

This day, Brianna was extremely tired; her belly was not allowing her to get comfortable. After a midnight snack, she warmed up a cup of milk and honey; this aided in her finally drifting off to sleep. Unfortunately, her sleeping suddenly came to an end when she was awakened by a stinging pain in her thigh. She grabbed her leg when she felt the pain yet again. When she opened her eyes, she could not believe what she was seeing.

"Melissa?"

"Yeah, it's me! Where is my husband?"

Melissa looked like a mad woman. Her hair was all over the place. Her clothes were soaked with something, perhaps drenched in cognac because the smell was overpowering. "Melissa, you are a stupid fool! Get out of my house! I don't know where your husband is, nor do I care!" Brianna yelled angrily.

"Lies! Lies, Brianna! I have never hated someone as much as I have ever hated you! He is so in love with you!" She began to weep. Brianna began to reach for her cell phone when she heard a clicking sound. "Don't play yourself, Brianna!"

Melissa had pulled a .45-caliber gun out of her pocket. "One more move and I will shoot you!

"Are you serious? You are going to kill me and my baby, for a man? Melissa, what has happened to you? You have him! You are married to Maxwell! Just get out of my damn life! You are one petty and sick female!"

"Brianna, he doesn't want me, and I be damned if I let him have you!" she screamed. She began to lunge for Brianna but tripped on a pair of boots on the floor. Brianna saw an opportunity to try and run around Melissa, who was struggling to get up. In her frantic desperation of seeing Brianna quickly move for a pregnant woman, she caught Brianna by her ankle, causing her to fall into the wall. In this moment, Brianna knew that this was not going to end well. Whatever common sense that Melissa may have had was now visibly gone. She knew that she had to fight not only for her life, but that of her unborn child. Whatever disappearing act that Maxwell was pulling, it now would cost her dearly.

"Listen! Melissa. What do you want? I will give it to you. If you want me to leave the country, I will do it! Just let me and Allan's baby go safely. You have your son. Let me start my family and move on. I promise, you and Maxwell will never see my face again!" Brianna pleaded with her. The anger had subsided and frustration had finally set in; the tears began to stream down her face. The look on Melissa's face began to soften. "Here, just let me get up." Brianna began to get up off the floor but could feel a sharp pain in her stomach. Her heart began to race with fear. In moving to her chase, she let out a scream that startled Melissa. Melissa was thrown off guard when she saw Brianna grab her stomach.

"What!" Melissa yelled. "What's wrong with you now, princess?"

She came closer to Brianna. Without blinking, Brianna surprisingly grabbed the decorative glass vase and hit her across her face. Melissa, holding her face, stumbled backward. Brianna scrambled desperately to get the gun from her. They both began to put up a great fight. The gun went off! Both looking down, they saw blood pouring out everywhere.

She whispered, "Die! I hope you die!"

CHAPTER FORTY-EIGHT

The Struggle Was Real

"No this cannot be happening to me! How is my baby?" Brianna was coming out of her heavy sedation. She was reaching for the tubes in her nose and smacking her arms as if she was trying to remove her IV.

"Ms. Godfrey, I am Dr. Sullivan. You are in St. Mary's Hospital. You were shot. The gunshot wound was right above your heart, nearly missing it. Unfortunately, you lost a tremendous amount of blood, causing your blood pressure to drop. Due to that reason, your baby's heartbeat grew weak."

Brianna began crying hysterically. "No, no, no, no! I lost my baby!" Alice seemed to have appeared out of the thin air. She quickly stood by Brianna, holding her hand.

"Brianna, sweetheart, please calm down and let the doctor explain. It is going to be okay."

Brianna instantly began to do just that, seeing and hearing Alice worked for her. The doctor resumed speaking, "Ms. Godfrey, we were able to deliver your beautiful daughter. She is five pounds and ten ounces. She had difficulty breathing, so we are watching her. Give us another hour of monitoring her closely, then we will bring her in to meet her mom." He gave her a smile in hopes that would give her a little more comfort. When he left out the room, Mr. Conti and the girls came in; Tamika and Angel eased close to give her kisses. They both were teary-eyed and didn't have much to say. While looking both concerned and angry, Edmundo gave her a kiss on her forehead.

"Brianna, I have to take care of something that is pressing. Rico contacted me. He informed me that Ms. Perez will be here shortly. I love you, girl. The baby is beautiful. I see you in about two or three days." Before Brianna could respond, Tamika turned to leave, and Mr. Conti walked out with her.

Brianna managed to start asking questions as to how she ended up at the hospital. Alice began to explain, "It appears that Melissa King broke into your home. You must have had a struggle with her gun and you were shot. Before passing out, you managed to dial 911. A neighbor, who was driving at the time, accidentally struck her as she was running away from your condo. The driver was driving about twenty-five miles per hour, bumped her, only knocking her down. When he got out of his car, she was in a daze, covered in blood and holding the gun. She kept repeating that she had just killed someone. As far as we know, Melissa is being held at another hospital, with police officers surrounding the room."

Brianna's eyes rolled back, and the monitors began sounding off repeatedly. The nurses and the doctors cleared them out of the room.

CHAPTER FORTY-NINE

The Reveal

Unknown to Brianna, three days had gone by. The clearing of her throat awakened her mother and got her father's attention. Fortunately for Brianna, Alice had delicately filled in Brianna's parents. Alice said nothing of the threats that were made against them by Mr. King and Allan. She just spoke of Melissa being a former disgruntled boss who suffered from depression and schizophrenia. After they spent time with Brianna, she and Alice reluctantly got her parents to check into a hotel to get some rest. Angel and Alice were speaking with her when they were interrupted by Maria. She greeted the women and kissed Brianna on her forehead; Angel and Alice left the room to give them a little privacy.

"Brianna, I am so sorry that all of this has happened to you. What can I do to make this better?" she asked with tears in her eyes.

"There is nothing that you can do, Maria. Your son and Mr. King have put me through so much. Having them in my life has cost me my peace and my happiness. More importantly, it almost cost me my child. Speaking of which, I have not even seen her." A tear rolled down her face, and it nearly broke Maria's heart in half.

"Well, let's get her in here." Maria left the room. After what seemed like fifteen minutes, the door opened. It was the baby being brought in by a nurse and Maxwell closely behind her. Brianna began to cry.

"Brianna, I can leave." Maxwell was completely thrown by her breakdown.

"No, just look at her. She is beautiful."

"Brianna, yes, she is." They sat for ten minutes in silence while Brianna was holding her, then he spoke up again.

"Brianna, I don't care if this is Allan's baby. I want you in my life. I will raise her as my own. I cannot see my life without you."

"Maxwell, I can't trust you. When things go wrong, you disappear! I can't keep doing this with you, and I will not let you do this to my daughter. I...I can't let you do this to possibly, *our* daughter."

"What, Brianna? What are you saying?" He was confused and stood up instantly.

"The truth of the matter is, I don't know if this is your daughter or Allan's."

"You have got to be kidding me, Brianna!"

"Oh, wait one minute! I know you are not passing judgment. Did you honestly forget that I was dealing with my fiancé?"

"No, I did not forget! What do you want to do, Brianna? I want you! We can be a family." He leaned down and kissed her and the baby. She could see that he meant just what he said.

"Let's get a test done while you are here. It would just make me feel better, and we would be doing right by her. Either way, I would want her to eventually know just who her father actually is."

"Fine by me—let's do this. Promise me that whatever the results are, you will agree to be in my life permanently!" he pleaded.

"Yes, Maxwell. I promise. Go get the doctor." Once the doctor returned, they explained that they wanted a DNA test performed. Alice pulled a few strings to get the results within twenty-four hours. After another day in the hospital, it was revealed that Maxwell was indeed the father. His tears of joy made everyone in the room sob; he named her Ariana Isabella King. Brianna could not be happier. After spending seven days in the hospital, she was starting her family with the man she loved. After all the excitement, she realized that there was no Tamika, Mr. Conti, or Rico, for that matter.

CHAPTER FIFTY

The Dream

The drive from the hospital was very quiet. Her father made small talk in between listening to the GPS in his rental, which she did not understand as her father knew the way to her condo. Her mother, on the other hand, had nothing to say because she went on and on about her disappointment the night before; she felt totally excluded from her daughter's life. She was confused by the presence of Maxwell, Maria, and the never-ending visits from Alice. Finally, the car came to a stop. They pulled into a circular driveway of a beautiful two-story brick home. It was stunning.

"Whose house is this? Is that Alice's and Angel's cars?" Her dad smiled, walked around, and got the baby. Her mom assisted in helping Brianna out the car very slowly. "Mom, what's going on?"

Her mother gave her a small look of irritation before answering, "I can assure you that it is nothing that I was a part of."

Brianna's father hurled the irritation back at his wife, "With that attitude, I am sure you will not be involved in anything forthcoming. Knock it off!"

When they opened the front door, they were all standing there with big smiles. "Welcome home!" Everyone was in attendance—Maxwell, Rico, Maria, Alice, Mr. Conti, Tamika, Angel, Peter, and Ricardo. Brianna was surprised and very confused by their greeting.

"What is going on? Welcome home!"

Maxwell came over to kiss her, then escorted her to a beautiful white-and-black chair. As a matter of fact, the decor was beautiful, and she noted a few pieces from her condo.

"Maxwell, is that my stuff?"

"Well, yes, it is. This is your new home. This will be *our* new home once you have answered this question." He reached into his pocket, grabbed her left hand, and placed an oval-cut seven-karat diamond engagement ring set on a micro pave band onto her finger. The ring was beyond breathtaking, but what was about to happen would be momentous. "Brianna Monique Godfrey, will you be my wife? Will you marry me?"

Brianna wanted to jump up, but the soreness from her gunshot wound and her emergency Cesarean prevented her from doing so. He leaned over and kissed her passionately while everyone else applauded. Well, everyone except her mother.

"Yes, Maxwell, yes!" she gushed.

People were laughing and talking while enjoying eating items prepared by their new chef. Tamika finally seized the opportunity to speak with Brianna.

"Hi, boo! I am so happy for you and Maxwell!" Tamika gave her a kiss on her cheek. My goddaughter is beautiful.

"Yes, she is but don't think for one minute that I did not notice you have not been at the hospital. That is not like you. Where have you been? Are you all right?" she sighed in a frustrating manner. Before you she could answer, a warm-looking Hispanic woman held her arm out.

"Hola, Ms. Godfrey. I am Marisol, your nurse. I will be assisting you and your new bundle of joy. I have all your doctor orders. You will need to bid your guests a good evening as it is time for you to take your medicine and lie down for a while."

"Nice to meet you, Marisol. I am too weak to argue. I will gladly comply. However, Tamika, I want answers a little later."

CHAPTER FIFTY-ONE

Fairy Tale or Nightmare

A year had passed by quickly and quietly. Tamika's explanation for not being constantly at the hospital by her side was that she had one "street" dealing that she had to take care of. Now she is done and is currently focusing on law school. Alice was amazing, and she loved her for being such an instrumental part of her life. Mr. Conti had handsomely panned out to be the best fill-in father ever. Maria was a loving grandmother who simply admired Brianna's love for her son. Angel was that true ride-or-die friend, her rock. Peter was loyal, and she never forgot to reward him greatly; he meant the world to her. Rico was that brother that she always wanted. He had a heart of gold. Brianna was glad to find out that Melissa received life in jail, with no chance of parole. It was rumored that Mr. King and his two faithful goons were dead. A building belonging to him was burned to the ground with three bodies found inside. Melissa's father fled the country. Maxwell's brother, slash son, was adjusting nicely to Brianna and his new home. Instead of waiting to later in his life, they just told him that the medical records were messed up, his dad was actually his big brother. Maxwell Junior handled that, and the news of his mother being in jail because of her mental illness, just fine. Brianna had no clue that her life would be riddled with so much controversy. Here was the day she was waiting for, her wedding day. Her thoughts were interrupted by a knock on the door of her bridal suite. It was the girls and Peter.

"Okay, girl, my goddaughter is wearing me out. She just woke up from her nap and demanding her snacks and juice box. I love that little munchkin!" he said while holding his hand up to his forehead as if he was going to faint.

Brianna let out a big chuckle. "Both of you are too much! Two drama queens!"

Natalie, who donated her services as a wedding coordinator, scooted everyone out. "Ladies and gentlemen, let's go. Showtime in one hour and thirty minutes. Brianna, your glam team will be in here in fifteen minutes. Here is your mom, Maria, and Alice." They were all giddy and teary-eyed. "Give them all hugs and then, ladies, come with me." They did as they were instructed. They didn't put up a fuss because they all had time with her that morning at brunch. Once they left, there was another light knock at the door. Looking through the peephole, she jumped as though she had seen a ghost.

"Maxwell, go away! You can't see me!" she scolded.

"Butterfly, girl, stop playing. Open the door so I can give you a kiss."

"Boy, bye!" She laughed.

"All right, hey, baby, I love you! You have me for life. You know that, right?"

"I'd better! Don't get it twisted—you have us for life. I love you too! Now go away."

Before she could take a seat to finish off her glass of champagne, there was another knock at the door. She laughed. "Maxwell, stop playing! Go rehearse your vows!" When looking through the peephole, she saw no one. Once she opened the door and stepped into the hallway, she found no one lurking around. As she was stepping back across the threshold, she noticed a large yellow envelope. It was marked, "FOR MS. GODFREY ONLY."

Back in the room, she began removing the contents; there was a letter and a dead butterfly.

Ms. Godfrey,

So you finally got your day that you have been longing for. You got the man that many women wanted and you had his child. It is amazing how people would do anything and give you everything just to have you in their lives. Are you in love with your power? How is it to be so successful, beautiful, and loved? For those who could not be you, they tried to kill you. For those who are mesmerized by you, they will kill for you. Just where did the powerful man, Mr. King, go? Did he indeed burn in the building? I bet you, Tamika, Mr. Conti, and Rico knows the true answer to those two questions.

Well, it looks like you are sitting at the head of the table. A word to the wise, don't get too comfortable. I'm coming for you. Oh, and by the way, thank you for the invitation to your lovely wedding, or not. I will be at the wedding, enjoying your big day with you.

Signed,
Not signing—you figure it out!

Cam Johnson, a native from Richmond Virginia, is an author that will probably never fit into one genre.

This can be seen from her jovial delivery of realistic matters on dating, that she shares in her blogs and from the suspenseful matters of the heart that is woven into this novel with fiction and some realities. Cam Johnson strives not to be more of the same.

This author encourages her readers to let their heart, mind and imagination be interactive and enjoy!

CPSIA information can be obtained
at www.ICGtesting.com
Printed in the USA
LVHW092350130520
655552LV00002B/416

9 781684 569472